THE BLACKSMITH

There had been a forge at Anford for about a thousand years, but not until the twentieth century was the blacksmith a woman.

From a childhood and adolescence scarred by rejection and loneliness, the forge became Ann Mayall's sanctuary, and the traditions of its craft brought her success, security, and the tentative beginnings of friendship.

But the new owners of the neighbouring manor see her presence as a threat, although she doesn't know why. She rejects their increasingly large offers to purchase her inheritance. Hostility and intimidation fail to move her, so they revert to more violence; if she will not leave, she must die – but they have not reckoned on Ann's formidable physical strength.

Unfolding with brooding and devastating menace, *The Blacksmith* is a uniquely gripping novel of suspense.

Jenny Maxwell is a Scot, was born in Egypt, educated in England and now lives in Germany.

THE
BLACKSMITH

Jenny Maxwell

WARNER BOOKS

A *Warner* Book

First published in Great Britain in 1996
by Warner Books

Copyright © Jenny Maxwell 1996

The moral right of the author has been asserted.

*Over the past few years many religious sects have sprung up, and some of them
have been known as The Children of God. To the best of my knowledge, none of
them bear the slightest resemblance to the sect described in this book. It was
certainly not my intention to depict any existing organisation.*

*Nor does the charity Reconcile represent any of the excellent associations that
help refugees and asylum seekers in the United Kingdom.*

*The Blacksmith is a work of fiction; any resemblance between the characters
portrayed in it and any existing person, canine, equine or human, is purely
coincidental. J.M.*

A CIP catalogue record for this book
is available from the British Library.

ISBN 0 7515 1804 2

Typeset in Palatino by M Rules
Printed and bound in Great Britain by
Clays Ltd, St Ives plc

Warner Books
A Division of
Little, Brown and Company (UK)
Brettenham House
Lancaster Place
London WC2E 7EN

For Sylvia and Niki Liebertz,
for friendship, for love, and for fun

ACKNOWLEDGEMENTS

I pestered a great many people while I wrote this book, and they all merit my thanks. Niki and Sylvia Liebertz opened implacably locked doors in the German racing world; at the racing stables Stall Kappel in Krefeld, Herr Joseph and Frau Marie-Louise Kappel were kind and welcoming, and the gleaming aristocrats in their care bore testimony to their expertise, both in their perfect health and in their excellent manners.

To the blacksmiths who allowed me to watch them at work, particularly Michael Kappel, I offer my sincere gratitude. And to the horses who so kindly lent me their feet, may your shoes fit closely and comfortably, and lend wings to your hooves.

PREFACE

After a hot spell everything around the forge is grey. The dust comes mostly from the quarry, two miles away behind the wood, and it's heavy, not hanging in the air for long. The wind carries it over the trees and the lorries churn it into long soft ruts on the track, clouds of grey dust, stirring a little in the breeze, but then dropping again to lie in drifts on the window ledges and the roofs of the cottage and the forge, and to cover the hard packed earth in the yard. The yard seems to be made of dust. The chickens scratch in it, scraping it over their backs and shaking their feathers so that it sifts down onto their hot skin. Dogs lie in it, in whatever shade they can find, tongues hanging out, panting. I haven't got a dog now, but most people seem to bring at least one with the horses. There are flowers in a bed against the cottage wall, and under the dust their colours seem to blend, all the same tone, dust-pink, dust-yellow, dust-white. Dust covers the bushes, there are many, many shades of dust-green. The rowan tree by the forge door has its own dust colours.

Lyric likes to mouth the rowan leaves when she's tied up outside the forge. So far as I can see she never eats them, never even bites them, just lips at them so that even in the dust a few of the fronds show shiny and clean against the golden stone of the wall. When Jake sold me Lyric he warned me that a thoroughbred will starve itself almost to death rather than eat food it doesn't like, but Lyric likes to mouth the leaves of bushes she won't eat.

Uncle John advised me to buy Lyric when I first moved into the forge. I thought he was mad, but he has never, ever given me bad advice, so I did. She cost me next to nothing anyway, and it was her or a big ugly cob. Jake said a thoroughbred is the best for carrying weight, and I turn the scales at nearly fifteen stone now. Even though I am six foot six I couldn't deny it if you were to say I'm fat, but the flab doesn't go right down to the bone. I can lift that anvil. I wouldn't want to carry it far, but I don't know many men who can do much more than raise one end of it, and I bet I'm the only woman who can do it within fifty miles.

Lyric was dirt cheap because she was a failure. She'd cost nearly a hundred thousand as a yearling filly, and she'd won three races in her first season. Lord Ackland owned her, and she was trained at Lambourne in one of the big stables. Halfway through her second season he sold her, to some Dutchman who spent the next three weeks crowing about how he'd got the better of the bargain with the old man, something not many people did, Ackland being no fool and well able to tell one end of a horse from the other. She won another race, and then she broke down, some problem with her knees she'd inherited through her dam's line. The Dutchman spent a lot of money trying to put her right, and then sold her as a brood mare down in Somerset. She had two foals, both born with shortened tendons in their forelegs, which cost more than the foals were worth to put right. Then she slipped a foal, and missed twice more. So there she was, seven years old, barren, and likely to cripple herself at any time if she was ridden too hard. It was hardly surprising she was cheap.

Uncle John said it would do me no harm at all to have a good-looking horse tied up outside the forge, particularly since she was a dark bay, so people might not notice it was always the same good-looking horse. I had to have a horse anyway, to ride through the park. It's one of the assets of the place.

There's been a forge on that site probably since blacksmithing began, which is a long time before people started keeping records. It's on one of the drover roads, near the crossing with the old coach route, and there's a stream beside the forge, fed by a spring that hasn't dried up in living memory, although sometimes the water gets a bit low. Part of that stream's been dug out and the bank faced with bricks. I keep it clean, even though there's a standpipe by the forge now, and Uncle Henry put a basin with hot and cold running water in the workshop. But somebody took trouble over that pool in the stream, and you never know.

Gorsedown Manor has been around in one form or

another for over a thousand years. It's mentioned in the Domesday Book. The house that's there now is Victorian, but some time when Henry VIII was King the Lord of the Manor lost the forge, and the land it stands on, in a game of dice. At that time, the farrier was a villein of his, paying rent and giving feudal service. From then on, the poor man had two masters, de Meureville, the Lord of Gorsedown Manor, who still demanded service from the smith and was in a good position to get it, and Baron Fitzallen, who lived a few miles away. The forge was surrounded by Gorsedown land, and the right of way of the drover road was very much at the whim of de Meureville. When Fitzallen sent his agent to collect his rent and to take some horses to be shod, the way was barred. The forge might be the Baron's, but he had no way to reach it. He took his grievance to the King, who found it too good a joke to spoil, and refused to grant him a right of way to the forge, but Henry declared the farrier and his family had the right to ride over Gorsedown lands as they wished, and with that Fitzallen had to be content. The smith rode to the Baron to pay his rent, and rode the Baron's horses back to the forge to shoe them, and the title to that right bearing the King's seal is still part of the deeds to the forge, even though the original piece of parchment is in one of the libraries of the University of London. There's a stable behind the forge, old sandstone and timber, dating from that time, the last of the Tudor buildings. It's well-made, Fitzallen caring more for his horses than for the men who worked with them. At one time there must have been stabling for about a dozen horses, but most of the stables were knocked into one large workshop at some time, and now there are just three loose boxes and a tiny tack-room. The workshop has all the machinery in it, and the racks for the materials, so the flooring is modern concrete, to take the weight of the machines. I suppose it looks incongruous, racks of tools mounted on old Tudor walls. The cottage was only built just before the war, but the forge is even older than the stables.

The Gorsedown estate was broken up in Victorian times. The village of Anford stands on the southernmost part of it, and most of the rest is farms, with the quarry and the gravel beds to the east. Gorsedown Manor has just the big park now, a long, oval shaped tract of land, with the four acres that go with the forge sticking up into its southern boundary like a thumb.

The forge fell into disrepair during the war. It and the cottage stood derelict for twenty years, nobody knowing who owned it, since the blacksmith, a childless bachelor who had joined the Navy when war was declared, had been drowned on the North Atlantic convoys. Eventually, a sister was found in Canada, and she immediately put it on the market. Uncle Henry bought it.

Henry, John and Peter Mayall were brothers. The family came from Birmingham originally, and there was a family business, making spare parts for army vehicles. Old Fred Mayall, their father, had been a blacksmith, working in the same forge as his own father and grandfather before him. When Henry left school he went into the forge as an apprentice, and later, when he passed his test to become an Associate of the Farriers Company of London, Fred gave him a partnership. By then, Fred had given up the idea of having any more children; he was over fifty when John, and then Peter, were born, and Henry was nearly twenty.

Fred himself held the higher title of Fellow of the Worshipful Company of Farriers. Fred was a proud old man, and jealous of his craft, but he could see war coming and invested his money in his cousin's engineering works. By the time the Second World War broke out Fred held the majority shareholding, and he sold the forge and ran Mayall Engineering with a work-force consisting of fifty women and half a dozen men who were unfit for military service. Peter and John joined the Navy, and Henry, despite being well over the age limit, talked and lied his way into the Royal Engineers, throwing together spare parts for broken down vehicles out of whatever materials were available, often with only the tools he had managed to cram into a kitbag. Despite his experience as a farrier, he avoided the cavalry regiments. Being the eldest, and likely to inherit Mayall Engineering, he thought he'd better learn the newer skills, but when the old man dropped dead from sheer overwork the brothers decided to accept an offer from Lucas, and sold the business. It was a wise decision. The parts they were making were mostly for obsolete vehicles, and retooling would have cost a lot of money.

John came out of the Navy and studied law. He did well, and now he's a senior partner in a practice in Holborn. Henry moved to Wales, and took his engineering skills down the coal-mines. He picked up a Welsh accent, which he never lost, and he met Ruth, a dark little woman rather older than himself with a fierce scowl and a loving heart, and married her a month later. When the coal-mines began to die from mismanagement and from having all the profits bled away, Henry saw what was coming, and left the ruined valleys of Wales for the English countryside to go back to his old career as a farrier and blacksmith. Peter stayed on in the Navy waiting for the war effort to run down and employment prospects to improve, married my mother, a good-time girl he'd mistaken for a princess, and, when that failed, returned to the sea, this time in the Merchant Navy, mostly on the other side of the world. He sent money back to Uncle John for our support. My mother once said he'd taken one look at me lying in my cot, and walked out. I don't doubt it. She never forgave him.

Naturally, when Uncle Henry found the forge, it was Uncle John who handled the purchase, and who found the piece of paper which spoke of King Henry's Deed. Henry was inclined to shrug it off as being of no importance, but John was not the man to throw away an asset. The owners of Gorsedown Manor were furious when they found out, and tried to get the deed set aside in the courts, partly on the grounds that the practice of the blacksmith riding in the park had fallen into disuse, but Aunt Ruth, who had more common sense than horse sense, had seen that one coming. She and Uncle Henry bought an old pit pony, one of the quietest in the mine, and by the time the case got to court she was bumping doggedly around the park at least once a week, and almost beginning to enjoy it. The pony was not so sure. He was a stubborn little beast, known as Fag End, and he was used to constant temperatures, a warm stable, and regular meals. Also, he had never been broken for riding, and viewed the change in his circumstances with astonished disapproval. When it rained he was inclined to turn his tail to the wind and stop until the weather changed. Where other riders carried a crop, Aunt Ruth took an umbrella.

Fag End lived in the end stable where I kept Lyric when I bought her, and, if I could be said to ride, I learned on him. He never did get used to a rider, and would roll his eyes and hump his back when mounted. He had an awkward stride, and a bad-tempered way of swishing his tail after only an hour or so. If it rained, I could make him move, but then I was a lot stronger than Aunt Ruth, even when I was only seven, and I didn't share her aversion to hitting him. He still tried to turn his tail to the wind, so we would bump home half sideways, with him threatening to buck and me trying to haul his head round and thumping his flanks with my heels. But he was a gentle pony if nobody tried to ride him, nudging at pockets for titbits, and careful where he put his feet. Aunt Ruth's cat had a litter of kittens in his manger, and they grew up in the box, scampering around in the straw at his feet, and even climbing his tail. He was a pretty colour when his coat grew back, dark golden brown, like tobacco, which I suppose is how he got his name. The ponies in the mine were shaved. Nobody could groom coal dust out of a pony's coat, so at the end of the shift they were washed, and they had to be shaved so they would dry quickly. I think they had quite a good life, even though I have heard that some of them went blind. Uncle Henry said most of the miners liked the ponies, and very few were rough or cruel with them. Fag End was certainly a trusting pony, I doubt if he'd ever been badly treated. Aunt Ruth didn't like it when I hit him, but Uncle Henry told her not to worry. You have to hit a horse quite hard to hurt him, unless you use a cutting whip, or hit him under the belly or in the face. When the horses come to the forge it's the sentimental people who are the most trouble, so careful to be gentle they forget to be firm: the horses get confused, they don't know what they're supposed to do, and then they get nervous and restless, it's just as harmful as being too rough.

Lyric was a different sort altogether. She'd been a racehorse, and it wasn't making her go that was the problem, it was stopping her. I never could. She was always running away with me, and even though it didn't matter in the park, it was dangerous and downright terrifying on the roads. We've come down that hill and round that sharp bend through the gate at a flat-out gallop a few times, and I've always been sure she'd lose her footing on that slippery tarmac and break her legs and my neck. I don't know why she didn't. Jake tried to help me handle her, even gave me a few hours' teaching, but then he gave up.

'It's not that Lyric's so difficult,' he said. 'It's just that you're such a bloody awful rider.'

It was true, but it was just too bad. Jake's a good man, he sends me some of his horses. The difficult ones, that are likely to cripple you if you get careless. He was one of my first customers, he brought a big grey three-year-old that had never been shod. I fought that gelding for more than two hours, Jake having claimed he was allergic to tranquillisers, and I only got the hoof trimmed back. Even when I'd got one of his forefeet tight between my knees and he couldn't free it, he still lashed out, one of the only horses I've ever known who'd rather fall than have his feet held. Jake paid me for my time, and then admitted I was the seventh to try, and the only one who'd got a hoof-knife to him. Seven is Jake's lucky number, or so he says. But the horse was useless, the walls of his hooves were thin and likely to split, and he couldn't be shod, so Jake sent him to Tiverton auction. That incident isn't important, you can forget it if you like. I wish I could.

He promised me Lyric was easy to shoe, and she was. When he brought her over, he brought half a dozen old rugs, which was nice of him, and a good idea. As I said, people might not notice it was always the same good-looking dark bay horse, particularly if it was a good-looking dark bay horse in a grey rug, then a good-looking dark bay horse in a blue rug, then a good-looking dark bay horse in a red rug, and so on. I had to keep in practice too, and in the end Lyric got so used to having her shoes taken off and put back on again she'd automatically lift up her feet whenever I laid a hand on her, whichever foot was nearest. The village children thought I'd taught her to shake hands, and some of them asked me to teach their ponies.

It seems that most of the time the weather around the forge is hot and dry, but it can't be so. Perhaps it's the dust, when I walk across the yard there's so often dust lifting around my feet it's the picture I have in my mind. But it rains here as often as it does anywhere else, I suppose. I love the rain. There may be blacksmiths who like hot weather, but I don't know them. For as far back as the craft has existed it's been the same, a fire, a piece of red hot iron, and a hammer to hit it with. That is hot, thirsty work. When you lay down your work for a minute and step outside, you may like to lift your face to the sun. I like to lift mine to the rain. I like a steady, heavy rain, I like it to wash the dust and the sweat off my face, I like it to run through my hair, I even like it running down the back of my neck. And this place is pretty in the rain.

The cottage is built of glazed red bricks and it and the forge are roofed with Welsh slate which Uncle Henry brought with him, most of the tiles having fallen off and broken while the place stood empty. All the woodwork is painted white, except the big doors to the forge, which are very, very old, six inches thick, solid planks of black oak with big, diamond-shaped iron studs holding them together. I was told they might be from the ninth century, maybe even older. I don't know what they weigh, but Uncle Henry made the hinges, and they are massive, and mounted on a big iron frame, I think he made that, too. You can swing those doors by pushing them with one finger, the balance is so sweet and true. Bad workmanship could cost lives in Uncle Henry's work before he came to the forge, and since in some cases, and I never knew him make anything that wasn't strong and reliable. He made the iron bench under the tree, and when you sit on it, it curves gently against you, supporting your back and your neck, and it's hard to sit on it without closing your eyes and sighing with pure pleasure. The tree is, of course, a chestnut: the old cliché amused both Henry and Ruth.

When it rains, everything sparkles. It seems to come alive in the rain, the dark red bricks, the golden sandstone, the black slate that isn't black at all when you look but a sort of green, and the flowers and trees and bushes, all dancing as the water flicks at them. Everything starts to shine, the horses' coats gleam under the rain and they step quickly to turn their tails to the wind if the rain has come suddenly. The people who come with the horses nearly always run into the forge, into the dry heat, but I like the rain and go on with my work. I stop only for hail, or for a thunderstorm when the horses are nervous. I only made that mistake once, shoeing a quiet little mare, but there was a big clap of thunder almost overhead and the lightning was very near. She was startled, and she dragged her foot back between my knees with a nail still protruding. It laid open the inside of my left thigh, seven stitches and it hurt like hell. I may trim feet if the thunder's not too near, but I won't nail, and I won't hot shoe either. Hot shoeing is holding the hot horseshoe against the hoof, so it shows up any parts that aren't fitting properly and burns off any rough edges so the shoe fits tight and even. It stinks and it smokes, but it doesn't hurt, and horses soon get used to it. I prefer to hot shoe, you get a better fit, but it isn't always practicable.

I've been here for four years now, and I'm doing all right. It's not just horses any more, though I'll never give that up, it's balconies and garden gates for the executive housing estates, and, sometimes, copying pieces of iron work for antique restorers, or people who seem to spend every penny they earn keeping vintage or veteran cars on the road. You may know the type, turning up in the evenings with some bit of machinery, hoping, as they say, they're not disturbing me, and enquiring about the cost almost with the next breath. Sometimes I can help, but I rarely work for nothing. Children with something they've broken perhaps, or a pensioner's garden fork, but not cars. I had to fight for this business, and it nearly killed me; I remind myself of that when I'm tempted by the anxious expression on the face of someone who's trying to bring the first flush of youth back to the appearance of his One True Love, a 1910 Daimler Benz, or a seventy-year-old traction engine. If the machine means that much to them, then they can save up for a couple of months, and polish their darling's brass headlamps in the meantime.

I still dream of the Children of God sometimes, and then I wake up crying, but it's getting better now. Dr Mantsch said I should try to write it all down, it would help. For six months I've been saying I will, and I suppose it's time to try, but even writing the name's making my hand shake. I didn't know many of the people they killed, but if I had been pretty enough to be a sacrifice I would certainly have been one of them. This time, being rejected saved my life.

1

Uncle Henry and Aunt Ruth bought the forge at Anford and invited the three of us to come and stay. They had no children of their own, John never married, and Gloriana and I were the only members of the new generation. We'll probably be the last.

My mother didn't like the place or, more probably, didn't like Uncle Henry, who was not noticeably affected by her air of pretty helplessness. She used to say that Henry was sexless, and Ruth ragingly jealous. Glory was frightened of the animals. She'd found, by the time she was six, that expressions of fear won attention, petting, and bribes, and anyway we'd both been told that men like to feel protective. What men liked and did not like governed the way we lived. By the time Glory was eighteen she had quite a handy little collection of phobias, one for almost every occasion, large animals being one of the first. So Lucille, Gloriana and Antoinette went to the forge together only once, and a thoroughly rotten weekend it was, with Lucille alternately bored by having nothing to do, and shocked by Ruth's ideas of entertainment, not only for herself but for the girls. Particularly appalling was Ruth's suggestion that we might like to ride the pony. Riding, as everybody knows, leads to bow legs, ugly, disfiguring. Glory cried, silently and beautifully, huge tears rolling down her cheeks from the drowned blue eyes. She was frightened of Fag End, and terrified of bow legs, whatever they might be.

Two weeks later I was back at the forge, on my own. Ruth met me at the station, thanked the guard for looking after me, and gave me a big, welcoming hug. Back at the cottage my pink summer dress was hung carefully in the wardrobe with a sheet over it to protect it from the dust, and for the next month I usually wore nothing but my knickers. Aunt Ruth fed me, and Uncle Henry said I could stand up straight if I liked, and not bend my knees or hunch my shoulders.

I was five years old, and six inches taller than Glory, who was seven. She was blonde and delicate; I was dark, bony, and awkward. She called our mother 'Mummy Darling', or 'Mama'. I called her Lucille, so that some people at least might not realise we were related. I was bony because Lucille was trying to diet me out of my rapid growth. By then, I knew a great many things that men were understood not to like, and at the top of the list came women being taller than them. Also, men did not like sulks, scowls, and stubbornness. Lucille, depending as she did upon men for almost everything, was bound to try to bring up her daughters in the same mould.

At the forge I was not Antoinette, I was Ann, or Annie Love, and I was liked. There were always animals around, and I got on well with them, not because I was sweet and gentle, but because I understood from the first that they were animals, not subnormal children. I was allowed into the forge, a place barred to other children, and that made me special. Uncle Henry got me a sort of canvas smock to wear, high necked and long sleeved with close fitting cuffs to protect me from sparks and bits of sharp metal. If you want to see a blacksmith stripped to the waist as he pumps the bellows of the forge and works red-hot iron you'd better go to the cinema, although I do admit that most of us roll up our sleeves. When I said I wanted to ride Fag End, the Pony Club Jumble Sale supplied a pair of second-hand jodhpurs and a hard hat. I hated the hat, but Aunt Ruth put her hands on her hips and glowered, which meant no discussion. We were risking the bow legs anyway, skull fractures were Taking Things Too Far, a crime in Aunt Ruth's code.

And so for two weeks I ran around the forge and the cottage, wearing as little as possible, getting even browner, chasing the chickens until the rooster chased me, and pecked and buffeted my legs so badly I screamed from pain and fright and promised Aunt Ruth I would never be a bully again. I rode Fag End, at first with Uncle Henry leading him, and then on my own, inevitably, on that first visit at least, straight back to his stable from wherever it was we had been taken off the leading rein. I cooked in the kitchen with Aunt Ruth, and she and Uncle Henry ate what I had made and affected to like it.

And I made a wrought-iron butterfly.

I still have it. It's a rather surrealistic creature, and the wings fall off if it's handled too roughly, but the memory of my first efforts, with Uncle Henry holding a spare piece of flattened iron onto the anvil with the big tongs, and me hitting at it with the hammer, is a true treasure. It's never been anywhere other than the forge, stuck to the wall with a big piece of putty. We all knew that Lucille would not have received it well, believing as she did that I spent my time with Ruth in the cottage. When I went back to Reading, in the pink summer dress that would no longer do up at the back, to be met at the station by Lucille and Glory ('Oh, Antoinette, you've *grown*!') I bent my knees again, and hunched my shoulders, and thought of my iron butterfly. To me, it was a talisman, and as such desperately important. Whenever I went back to the forge, the butterfly was the first thing I looked for, and when the forge was mine, and I walked through these great black doors for the first time as its owner, and saw the butterfly still stuck to the wall, my anxiety was, for a little while at least, replaced by a feeling of triumph and exhilaration.

Glory and I were sent to boarding school when she was nine and I was seven, almost eight. I was the tallest in my class by almost a foot, and the class mistress's opening remark, 'My! Aren't you a big girl!' gave me a sinking feeling. Lucille had said, over and over again, that men wouldn't like it if I grew too tall, and I knew that girls who men didn't like were failures. On Glory, an air of fragile helplessness was sweet. On me, it was grotesque, but Lucille, trying to do her best for both her daughters, the fairy princess and the troll, trained me to flutter my stubby eyelashes, to listen to inane conversation with an air of enthralled expectation, to smile shyly if a man or a boy happened to look at me, and never, ever to express an opinion of my own if one of the sacred creatures happened to be present. In Lucille's house, at least one of them was nearly always present.

At school, Miss Leonard's well-meant remark told me I was marked for failure, and so I didn't bother to try. I sat at the back of the class and gazed out of the window and wished I was in the forge with Uncle Henry. I thought of riding Fag End through the park, and I wondered if Aunt Ruth had made a stew out of that vicious rooster, as she had threatened. History and geography floated over my head, the sublime perspicacity of Shakespeare left hardly a mark, and English grammar and mathematics lost themselves in the face of my dreaming fantasies. Only at games, a generic term covering gymnastics, hockey, tennis, netball and swimming, did I take an active part.

It started one afternoon in the gymnasium, where Miss Holbrook was trying to teach us to climb a rope in the approved manner. I was, and am, an uncoordinated type, with no eye for ball games and a poor sense of balance. I was hanging from the rope, flailing around with my feet trying to get the rope wound around them as Miss Holbrook had instructed, and everybody was laughing. I was getting angry, and frustrated, and then Miss Holbrook snapped at me.

'Antoinette, for heaven's sake! Just get up that rope!'

And I did. Hand over hand, my feet still dangling free, faster than anybody else had done it, simply by the strength of my arms. I got to the top of the rope, and looked down, and then I felt frightened, not by the height, but by the fact that I had been defiant, and probably rude and disobedient, three of the things that men didn't like, and I was going to get into trouble.

Everybody was looking up at me, open-mouthed. Miss Holbrook did not seem to know what to say. There was quite a long silence, and then Carol Sturbank spoke, and seemed to express the general feeling.

'*Jesus Christ!*'

It was Carol who got into trouble, and in the uproar that followed her blasphemous comment I managed to descend the rope almost unnoticed.

That evening I was summoned to the headmistress's study.

Miss Oakroyd was a small woman, with white hair and a very quiet voice. She was gentle, sometimes seemed a little vague, but the questions she asked were nearly always the ones whose answers reached the heart of the matter. It's a rare gift, and invaluable when dealing with unhappy children.

She sat in an armchair on one side of the fire, tea in a bone china cup on a fragile table at her side, and I sat on a footstool on the other side, milk in one of the school's white china mugs clasped in my hands.

'Why do your friends call you Leather Jacket?' she asked.

'They're not my friends, they're horrible.'

She was looking into the fire. She turned her head, smiling enquiringly. Her question had not been answered.

'They say I'm like a big ugly insect.'

'Ah. Actually, a leatherjacket is the larva of the crane-fly, which is a rather beautiful creature. It does damage grass, unfortunately. Yes. Rude, and misinformed. That would have been Felicity Hunt, I assume.'

'Yes. She says I'm probably a nigger, too.'

'Does she indeed? Do you know what a nigger is?'

'A black man?'

She was looking into the fire again, and she nodded, vaguely, more in agreement than confirmation.

'A term of abuse for a negro, yes.'

There was quite a long silence. She stirred her tea, and I drank my milk. I felt more comfortable on that hard footstool by the fire than I had anywhere other than at the forge. I felt accepted.

'Miss Holbrook says you're a gymnast. She's really quite excited about you, she says she doubts if she could have climbed that rope faster herself. That's high praise, Antoinette. Would you like to be a gymnast? It's probably rather a short career as such, but no doubt you could do something else afterwards. What do you think?'

'I don't know.'

'Perhaps you have other plans?'

21

Failures don't have plans. I shook my head, not looking at her.

'When were you happiest, Antoinette?'

'When I made my iron butterfly.'

'Did you really? An iron butterfly? Tell me about it.'

'There are lots of sparks when you hit it, but if it's cold it breaks and you have to start again, Uncle Henry says iron's quite fragile if you don't treat it right. If it gets too hot it goes soft and sort of runny. When you hit it it gets flat. Then you put it in a bucket of water and there's steam. Uncle Henry put my butterfly on the wall with some putty, he says it's the forge mascot, and he's wanted a forge mascot for years. It's a good butterfly, it's got four wings, like a real one, but I couldn't do the legs. Uncle Henry says it doesn't matter, wings are what matters on a butterfly. It's black, so it's quite rare. There aren't many black butterflies in that part of the world, Uncle Henry says.'

Miss Oakroyd was smiling at me, her eyes sparkling.

'There aren't many seven-year-old girls who can make black iron butterflies, either. So, you're a metal-worker, are you?'

'A blacksmith.'

'Yes, I see. Well, Antoinette, I don't think a girl who can work black iron needs to worry about silly insults from the Felicity Hunts of this world, do you? But perhaps you could think about being a gymnast too. Miss Holbrook would be so pleased.'

I was in the gymnastics team, and Miss Holbrook was pleased, but I had no real talent, I was just very strong.

Miss Holbrook told Lucille gymnastics would be good for my figure. In the junior school events strength was enough, but later, when we went on to the expensive public school Peter, John and Henry paid for, I was too clumsy and uncoordinated. But by then, it didn't matter.

Felicity Hunt and two of her friends cornered me in the art room and told me I shouldn't be in a school with proper children, there were special schools for things like me. I thought about my promise to Aunt Ruth not to be a bully. I was bigger and stronger than them. Then I wondered if I was bigger and stronger than all three of them put together, and I decided I wasn't. I picked up Felicity Hunt, quite high, over my head, and then I dropped her. There was a dreadful fuss, with her being taken to the doctor in one of the teacher's cars, but I didn't get into as much trouble as I thought I would.

In the maths class, the teacher gave us a problem about how quickly a piece of hot iron would cool. In English, there was a comprehension question about shoeing horses. In geography, we had a map showing where iron was mined. School was becoming interesting.

I was never popular. I was still an ugly great insect and I never had a real friend for more than a few days. I can't say it didn't matter, I was unhappy and lonely, but I was never bullied again, and I stopped daydreaming quite so much. I learned enough to pass the examinations for the next school.

By the time I left Harts Hill I was eleven years old and only two inches short of six foot tall. I was round-shouldered, and I rarely raised my head. Lucille had taken me to doctors, pleading for something to be done, her distress increasing with every half inch I grew. There was nothing wrong with me. I was healthy, I was just very big and tall. Most of the doctors responded to Lucille's misery, and tried to comfort her with reassurance about my health, but I think she hoped they would find something wrong. Even if it was something incurable, there would be an excuse. Some of the doctors were brusque. They had genuine patients, children with deformities and disabilities. Sometimes Lucille cried, just from looking at me.

'Antoinette, please try to be a little more feminine! I know you can't help being tall, but you don't have to be so . . . so . . .'

Thirteen years old, six foot one, eleven stone. I was dark and swarthy, with wiry reddish hair and dark brown eyes, the only good feature I have. My shoulders were massive, and heavy. At school someone dared me to tear a telephone directory in half, and I did. The house mistress was annoyed, replacing the thing would be a nuisance, but she did agree not to tell Lucille.

Her name was Elizabeth Mullins, and she was one of the best teachers I ever knew. She taught English, and despite my complete lack of interest in the subject she got me through the syllabus and the examinations. Once we had mastered the grammar of our own language to her satisfaction, she allowed us to break the rules in our own writing, but not before. Sometimes she even accepted new words, if we could define them accurately, and there were no existing words that fell within the definition. 'Femininny' was one of her own, and I listened to her explanation of it with fascination.

'A femininny is a woman who glorifies her failings, and justifies them on the grounds of her sex. She regards not understanding electricity, and therefore not being able to change a plug or a fuse, or even a light bulb, for herself, as an asset. Not being strong enough to carry a suitcase, not being tall enough to reach a shelf, and, worst of all, not being *clever* enough to do, or understand, something, because she is *only* a woman, all these are the hallmarks of a femininny. Some of them are very successful, they wield considerable power, but only by manipulating men. The damage they do to women who wish to be independent is incalculable. They reinforce men's belief that they are entitled to judge women, not on their merits, skills, qualifications, talents, but on their personal appearance, their charm, their femininity.'

Fifteen years old, six foot three, twelve and a half stone, and many times judged by men. Poor Lucille! No wonder I spent so much time with Uncle Henry and Aunt Ruth down at the forge. Lucille tried to take Glory and me to parties, but how do you dress an Antoinette? Lucille cried sadly, tried flared skirts to party dresses, dark colours, flat shoes. Glory, with her tiny waist and her thick blonde curls, was never at home, always being whisked off to parties, taken out to dinner; Glory could wear anything and look lovely. Glory, in Lucille's eyes, had the world at her feet, her feminine, sparkling little feet. What was to become of Antoinette?

And what might become of Gloriana, if men realised that the huge, miserable creature trying to smile shyly at them from the darkest corner of the room was the Fairy Princess's sister?

Glory failed all her O levels except art. Pretty Glory could paint in water-colours, landscapes, flowers; she could play the piano too, a little. If Glory stayed on at school for another year, she might perhaps get a few more O levels, and then she could go to art school and study dress design.

Antoinette was doing quite well at physics, but this was not to be mentioned. Antoinette was to listen enthralled as Glory's boyfriend explained the internal combustion engine to Lucille, who found it quite incomprehensible, but how interesting! And Antoinette was *not* to offer to change the wheel when the MG got a puncture on the way back from the party, even when Glory's boyfriend had wrestled with the wheel brace for half an hour trying to turn a stubborn nut. Men do *not* like women who can do that sort of thing. Lucille and Gloriana and Antoinette will wait politely in the freezing cold for an hour until another car stops, and another *man* shifts the wheel nut.

There are double gates at the entrance to the forge, and I made them. They hang properly, and I dug the holes for the posts, and set them straight, and painted them. Those gates are closed on Sundays, and you can climb them, or vault them, or sit on them, and they will not sag. I made them when I was fourteen. The cross bars are not quite straight, and they are plain, but they do their job, and do it well. Uncle Henry and Aunt Ruth liked my gates.

I saw the look of contempt in the eyes of Glory's boyfriend, who couldn't change the wheel on his own car, but who could lecture Lucille on the internal combustion engine. How could I blame him? I was contemptible.

I was smiling at him as winningly as I could, I was dressed in my pretty, dark blue taffeta, and my face was made up to the best of Lucille's considerable ability. I was wearing false eyelashes. My fingernails were painted.

I was nearly six foot four, and I was utterly ugly, my smile a travesty on a face made for scowling.

Fag End dozed out his days in the paddock, and Ruth and I rode a gentle old hunter through the park. Ruth was old, I noticed she was thin, and she coughed. Her hair was getting whiter, but she was tough, and said she was fine. Henry didn't change at all. We worked together, he and I, comfortably and happily. I wasn't really aware that I was learning, but it was a fine apprenticeship I had with Henry Mayall. As he ran his hands down horses' legs, felt their feet, looked at them, even smelled them, as he watched horses walking and trotting along the wide concrete path between the forge and the stable yard and listened to the beat of their hooves and the different rhythms they made I stood beside him, watching, listening, and learning. I listened as he talked to vets and racehorse trainers, breeders and dealers, and, as another child might learn of camshafts and valves,

brake horsepower and compression, I learned of pha-
langes and flexor tendons, of fullering and frost nails. I
was still Annie Love, allowed in the forge when the
other children were not, able to handle all the tools now,
big and small, allowed to use the forge if Henry
watched, with her own leather apron with the traditional
cut made by the jealous tailor's shears in the time of King
Alfred. At the forge I wore jeans, and men's shirts, and a
canvas smock of the type Henry had first had made for
me, and I still do, although now I wear Western-style
chaps instead of an apron. I helped Ruth in the kitchen,
and learned to make bread almost as well as she can,
but I liked the forge best and she knew it.

Most of Henry's work was with horses, and he had a
good name. He knew a lot about corrective shoeing, and
horses were brought to him from a long distance for that
work. He had notebooks on a shelf in the living room
filled with drawings of horses' feet and notes he had
made on the shoes that had helped to correct faults, and
the shoes that had failed. When I was still a child, about
nine I think, I had gone into the forge and seen two
horse's feet lying, bloody and covered in flies, on the
bench. I had been upset by the sight, but Uncle Henry,
seeing my distress, had sat me up on the bench and
talked to me.

'I knew this horse, Ginger his name was, he was a
good old friend. But he's dead now, he doesn't need his
feet any more, he wouldn't mind me having them. See,
he always had a problem, he never could keep his hind
feet straight, always a bit tilted over at the fetlock here, I

never could put it right for him. But if I can see what it was, maybe I can put it right for another horse. Old Ginger, he would have liked that.'

Sentimental rubbish it might have been, but for a child, upset at the sight of a dead horse's feet, it was ideal. Half an hour later we were both probing at those feet and discussing the bony growths that had developed in the joint, and I was learning about the bones, and how the wall of the hoof grew down from the coronet, and the difference between sand cracks and grass cracks. As I touched and searched and probed those feet, oblivious now to the blood on my hands, I learned something else from Uncle Henry. I learned a sense of wonder at the beautiful engineering and the intricate design of bone and tendon and muscle. Now, if I have a horse with problem feet, I always ask for those feet if the horse is destroyed, and my books of drawings and notes are on the shelf in the living room alongside Henry's, but I never cut open a horse's foot without an echo of the wonder that I first felt at Henry's side, sitting on his work-bench and watching him searching for the cause of old Ginger's problem.

That last time I went to the forge I think I knew Ruth was dying. Her face was thin, with a frightening, blueish look, and she staggered when she stood for more than a few moments. Henry was spending more time with her, and his work was falling behind. They wanted to be together for as much time as they had left, so I worked alone in the forge, except with the horses, and never thought I was a blacksmith myself, I was still just Ann, helping Uncle Henry. There were gates to mend, plough shares to sharpen and reset, bits and pieces of farm machinery, broken garden furniture, nobody questioned the fact that it was me writing down the orders in the big ledger, I suppose they thought, as I did, I was still just helping, only a bit more now.

Fag End's teeth were giving him trouble, he was getting thin. We three decided it was time to send him to the knackers. I went with him to make sure nobody was rough with him. I cried when he sank down into the straw when the man pulled the trigger on the humane killer, and the poor man was horrified, he hadn't realised I was a child. He tried to make me leave, but I wanted to stay with Fag End, and I sat beside him patting his old head as the light died out of his eyes, then I went out and caught the bus back to the forge. I didn't want to see the rest of it. We were all sad, we all missed him. That afternoon I cleaned out the stable, and washed down the walls. I wanted to get rid of everything that would remind me of the old pony. We had already given his saddle and bridle to a riding school that taught disabled children, we hadn't ridden Fag End for two years. Ruth had a photograph of him on the wall of the living room taken just after they came to the forge. I couldn't look at it then, but I have it now, and I'm glad of it.

I was at school when Ruth died. The housemistress called me up to her room and told me, and said that my mother had given permission for me and my sister to go to the funeral. Glory refused, saying she didn't know them anyway, and funerals gave her the creeps.

Henry met me at the station, he seemed pleased to see me. A lot of people came to the funeral, the village church was crowded. He and I sat together in the front, me in my school uniform, he in his dark suit with a black crêpe band around the sleeve. I hated the service, I felt people were looking at me, and for the first time down there I stood as I did at home, my knees bent, my shoulders hunched, my head lowered. We watched the coffin being lowered into the grave, we threw our handfuls of earth, we went back to the forge in the hired black limousine.

Uncle John was there waiting for us, the first time I met him, a tall, thin man with grey hair receding from a high forehead, and the same blue eyes that Henry had. He shook my hand and smiled at me. I left them together, changed into my jeans, and went into the forge. There was work to be done. I assumed I was to stay and help.

I was wrong. Lucille telephoned, and told Henry I was to go straight back to school, even though it was the weekend. I thought he must have misunderstood, so I telephoned her back.

'Darling, now Ruth's dead it's impossible, you can't stay at the forge any more. What would people think?'

'But Henry needs me here. I can go back on Sunday, I can't leave him alone, he's . . .'

'Antoinette, don't argue, please, you know I hate arguments. It won't do, now just say goodbye nicely, and catch the next train back.'

I hung up on her, and went back to the forge. Lucille

had never known what I did there, I had always allowed her to believe I helped Aunt Ruth in the kitchen. We all knew what her reaction would have been if she had found out I was working in the forge, she would hardly have thought it a suitable occupation for a young girl. But with Ruth dead, and Henry dazed with grief, I no longer cared what Lucille found out, I was needed there. I was unhappy too, so I just started work on straightening out some bent garden tools that somebody had brought in.

The police arrived. The sergeant was very apologetic, but 'the mother' was insisting that 'the child' leave immediately, and go back to school.

I never worked with Henry again.

2

I was seventeen years old, almost six foot five, and fourteen stone. I was in the sixth form at school, and, according to Lucille, on the shelf and lost to all hope everywhere else. At least I'd almost stopped growing, just in time to stay out of *The Guinness Book of Records*. I had five O levels, in the unfeminine subjects. I was a prefect, and the captain of the school lacrosse team. I was sullen and unpopular, and I looked at the future with misery.

Glory had left school the year before, with just enough qualifications to get her into art school. She was studying fabric design. Lucille remarked that even Glory might find a job useful some day. I was destined for secretarial college.

We did visit the forge sometimes, Lucille and I, because I begged her to let me go, and she wasn't unkind. However, a young girl and that old man with no woman present wouldn't do, and therefore she came too. It was almost worse than not going at all, sitting in

Aunt Ruth's living room drinking tea and talking about how I was getting on at school, when all Henry and I wanted to do was go into the forge and get on with our work. I wanted at least to go and see what was happening in there.

'Oh, darling, no! All that dust, and that dress shows every mark.'

We did talk about my progress in physics and chemistry, and how I was getting on in zoology, where I'd been dissecting dogfish. I'd been learning how to draw the diagrams properly, and I'd brought some of my drawings to show Henry. It was the best I could do, the closest I could get to him. He was very quiet.

We'd never needed to talk much before, we'd spoken if anything needed saying, otherwise we'd just worked together. This new business of making conversation sat awkwardly, and I think we were both relieved when the time came for our visits to end, and sad that it should be so.

Lucille was always rather irritable on the way home. All this talk about physics, and those disgusting drawings of the insides of dead fish, and why on earth should Henry think we could be interested in him having had to repair the bellows? Such a boring old man, nothing to say for himself! And the cottage wasn't very clean, her gloves had dirty marks on the fingers.

I sent Henry a set of dissecting pins for Christmas. He telephoned that afternoon, delighted with them, wondering why he'd never thought to buy a set for himself and had always made do with a hammer and tacks.

I hadn't heard him so animated since Ruth had died, and we talked quite happily for nearly half an hour. It seemed we had plenty to say to each other after all, if we were on our own. I said I would telephone him on New Year's Day, when Lucille and Glory were going to lunch with one of Glory's boyfriends' parents.

He died on New Year's Eve, shoeing a horse. He had the horse's foot between his knees, and he just folded quietly over, laying down his hammer as he fell, and never moved again.

I hadn't even realised he was old.

This time when I went down for the funeral it was Uncle John who met me at the station. I'd forgotten him, and didn't recognise him. He didn't seem surprised, and certainly wasn't offended. We drove straight to the church together in his car. Even though it was the holidays I was wearing my school uniform, I had nothing else that seemed suitable. Uncle John and I sat in the front pew, where I'd sat with Henry for Ruth's funeral, and I listened to the shuffling and whispering as the church filled. There was a strong smell of incense, which was new, and more candles than before.

It was a new vicar, a soft, plump man with a round pink face and curly pale grey hair. He wore a lace surplice, and I immediately thought it looked like a maternity smock over his large stomach, and was anyway rather ridiculous and inappropriate for a funeral. I was nervous, as I always am in crowds, feeling that people are looking at me, and the appearance of the vicar irritated me, and made me even more uneasy.

He spoke of the ancient and mystical nature of the craft Henry Mayall had practised, of the merging of the elements, fire, water and iron. It all seemed rather silly. He hadn't known Henry if he could talk like that about him, as if he had been some sort of latter-day sorcerer. Henry's love for his God was very real, but it was the love of a craftsman for the genius of the creator, a complete trust, but very little blind faith and no mysticism at all. I could feel Uncle John sitting stiffly beside me, and knew he was disapproving.

Henry was buried beside Ruth. It was sleeting quite heavily, and not many people stayed at the graveside, just me and John and three farmers for whom Henry, and I, had done some work, and a racehorse trainer, who I thought I remembered. The vicar got through that part of the service as quickly as he decently could, shook hands with us, and hurried away. The farmers and the trainer said a few awkward words, and one of the farmers smiled at me and said the job I'd done on his barn door hadn't fallen apart yet. I smiled back, grateful for the well-chosen words and the friendly face.

Uncle John and I both seemed to feel we should be the last to leave the graveside, and so we stood together in the sleet, watching the sextons shovelling the earth down onto the coffin while the cars backed and turned and drove off towards the main road.

'Do you think we could go to the forge?' I asked. 'Have we got time?'

'Oh, I think we should. There are a few things to talk about.'

The forge was cold, the only time I ever knew it so. Cold, and quiet, and dead. The iron butterfly clung to the wall, and I touched it briefly as I wandered through the familiar place, running my hands over tools, stroking the new leather of the great bellows, looking at the shining dissecting pins in their case and remembering what Henry had said about them, less than two weeks before.

'He used them,' said Uncle John from the door. 'He was using them the day before he died. I cleaned them up and put them back in the case. I had to throw away the specimens, I'm afraid.'

There were files and rasps lying on the bench, and a dirty hoof-knife on the anvil. It must have been the one he had been using on the horse just before he died, he would never have left a sharp knife lying like that, dirty, and where somebody might cut themselves on it.

'Uncle John, do you mind if I tidy up? Are you in a hurry to get back to London?'

'No, take your time. I'll make us something hot to eat before we go.'

My smock and my apron were hanging on the peg at the back of the forge, where I'd last left them on the day of Ruth's funeral, when the police had come to take me back to the station and see me onto the train back to Surrey, and school. I took off my uniform jacket, and put them on. They still fitted. They were dusty, but they fitted, and they were mine. I cleaned all the tools, and then I oiled them, thinking it might be a long time before anybody else would come and care for them. I raked out the ashes and clinkers from the forge, swept the floor, scraped the dust into the rubbish bucket, closed the shutters over the two windows, hung up my apron and my smock, and left the place I loved. I closed the massive doors, and snapped the two big padlocks shut on the hasps.

Uncle John had made soup, and there were fresh rolls heating in the oven. He was wearing an apron over his dark trousers, his jacket hanging on the back of a kitchen chair. I'd thought him a rather cold and stuffy man, not the sort to go to the trouble of making chicken soup. I laughed in surprise, and he smiled at me. I saw the likeness to Henry in the crow's feet around his blue eyes and the way his mouth turned down, rather than up, when he smiled, and I felt more comfortable with him. I felt I could ask.

'What will happen to the forge now?'

'It's yours. Henry left it to you.'

He was pouring soup from the saucepan into Aunt Ruth's big blue mugs, very steadily, without spilling any. His hands were thin, and long, where Henry's had been square, but Henry had had steady hands, too. They were quite alike, these brothers. Ruth's mugs were a pretty blue, like cornflowers, and big, with comfortable handles. And the table was scrubbed pine, very scratched and scarred where she and I and Henry had cut and chopped things. It was a working kitchen. We were a working family here.

Uncle John's words were sliding around in my mind as I watched his hands, and the soup, and the mugs, the table, then the warm bread as he took it out of the oven. He'd been thoughtful, and known I would be hungry;

he'd bought bread, and things to make soup. I stood, and watched.

'Hadn't you realised he'd do that?' he asked at last.

I drew in a deep, shaky breath, and then the tears came, and I was sobbing and gasping, and sitting at the table, and he handed me a big, white, practical handkerchief and sat down opposite me.

'I hadn't ever, *ever thought* he would *die!*' I said.

He didn't tell me to cheer up, he didn't say never mind, he didn't try to pat me on the shoulder, he just sat opposite me, his hands around a mug of soup, as though he had all the time in the world, and as if there was nobody he would rather be with than a huge schoolgirl crying and sobbing about his brother. And when my sobs finally subsided, and I was quiet, he pushed my mug towards me, and smiled again.

'Drink that before it gets cold. Are you warm enough?'

I was freezing, and hadn't realised it. I heard him go upstairs, and when he came down he was carrying the thick blue blanket that had been on my bed. He wrapped it around my shoulders.

'Shock,' he said. 'Do you want a doctor?'

'Oh, no. No, I'm all right. I'm just cold.'

He laid and lit a fire in the living room while I drank my soup and shivered inside the warm blanket. I went to the door, and watched him as he crouched at the grate, piling coal onto the pyramid of wood, and then lighting the paper so that the flames licked up around it and it caught quickly, crackling and flaming, and the coals began to glow.

'That's good,' I remarked. 'You're quite practical!'

'I haven't always been a solicitor.'

I thought I'd been rude, and tried to apologise, but he smiled again.

'No, no. I'm pleased you think I'm practical.'

I drank some more soup, and it was very good, very thick and warming. I began to feel better. It was growing dark outside, and the sleet was turning to snow.

'Lucille may be worried,' I said. 'She might telephone soon.'

'The telephone's been disconnected.'

I considered that for a moment, looking into the fire, which was glowing brightly, yellow flames over red coals.

'You *are* practical,' I said, and we both laughed. 'Is the forge really mine?'

'Under certain conditions, yes.'

'Oh. What conditions?'

'You can't sell it until you're thirty, and you can only let it under the terms of a lease Henry and I drew up, and to a tenant who meets with my approval.'

'I will *never* sell it!' I protested. 'Never *ever*.'

'Quite,' he replied, expressionlessly. 'And under the terms of this will, nobody can make you do so.'

I thought about that. I wondered how Lucille would take the news that Henry had left me the forge. I looked up, and saw Uncle John watching me, and knew he'd read my thoughts.

'The machinery and the tools are yours, too, and the furniture and books, but there's no money, not in cash anyway. Your education's provided for, but what's left after that goes to a charity.'

'There was a horse,' I said.

'He was too old. I sent him to the knackers. I hope that was the right thing to do.'

'Yes, I'm sure. And Aunt Ruth's cat?'

'I've got her. Henry said you'd ask about the animals. Don't forget the goldfish.'

'There aren't any . . . Oh. You're laughing at me.'

'No, Ann, I'm not laughing, just thinking how well Henry knew you. He said you wouldn't be interested in the money, only the animals and the tools and his notebooks.'

'And the forge.'

'And that,' he agreed. 'And the forge.'

It was late when we got back, and snowing heavily, and Lucille was angry and upset. She said she'd nearly called the police, she had been so worried, and she couldn't imagine what could have kept me so long, with the funeral scheduled for early in the afternoon. The telephone to the forge had been disconnected, surely I must have realised she'd be worried, I should have been home hours ago, what on earth had I been doing? And why was I wearing my school uniform? People would think I had no other clothes, at my age nobody would have expected me to wear black, there was that nice lavender dress, it would have been quite suitable. What had I been *doing*?

I told her I'd been talking to Uncle John and she grew

even angrier, and said he was a dried-up, sexless old stick with nothing to say for himself, and a solicitor should know better than to keep a young girl out until all hours of the night. What had we been up to?

I was getting quite angry with her. I was unhappy about Uncle Henry, and pleased I'd got to know his brother, and in a complete muddle about the forge and what to do about it, and very, very tired, and dreading the next day, when we had to go to a party and I would have to try to be feminine again only a day after I'd been where I belonged and able to be myself, so I spoke very rudely to Lucille.

'I raped him,' I said. 'It's dead easy when you're big and strong, ask any of Glory's precious boyfriends.'

'*Antoinette*! How *dare* you speak to me like that!'

'We had to talk. It took a long time. Anyway, he brought me all the way home, and he's very nice, he was very kind to me.'

'I think you must be a bit unbalanced. I shouldn't have let you go to that funeral, so morbid and unnecessary. You'd better go to bed, you'll look a complete fright tomorrow if you're not careful. I'll make allowances, Antoinette, but I will *not* be spoken to like that. John is not a suitable companion for a young girl, any more than Henry was, and if John was being nice to you, I dread to think what he had in mind.'

'Henry's left me the forge. And the cottage, and the land, if it comes to that. And I think it was super of him, and I loved him very, very much, and what John had in mind was explaining about the will and that's all. As you keep telling me, men don't like women who are bigger than them, and Uncle John is a six foot *midget*, and my guardian now I come to think of it, and Glory's too, so just what the hell do you mean, not a suitable companion?'

She sent me to bed. She was slightly mollified by the news about the bequest, and said she supposed it might fetch quite a good price, enough to see me through a secretarial course with a bit left over. I didn't bother to explain about the will. I knew the forge was safe in Uncle John's hands, and I knew there was nothing Lucille could do about it. I was not going to be a secretary, I was going to be a blacksmith.

I lay in bed in the dark staring up at the lamplight on the ceiling. I was going to have to find a farrier to take me on as an apprentice, there was a lot I had to learn, all the things Uncle Henry hadn't taught me, and many of the things he hadn't known. Blacksmithing is the oldest of the crafts, but it isn't stagnant, and it had been a long time since Uncle Henry had learned it. I had to learn about the new metals, and the new ways of working them. Uncle John had suggested I take a metal-working course first, and I had to think about that. But I was going to learn my craft, and I was going to be myself. I made a lot of decisions that night, and some of them were the right ones.

I went a bit crazy for the rest of the school holidays. At the party the next day I drank too much champagne, and asked a stockbroker if he didn't think that shuffling money around wasn't a rather childish and unproductive way for a grown man to spend his life. Then I challenged Glory's sneering boyfriend to an Indian arm-wrestling contest, which alarmed him considerably, and which he wisely refused. Lucille made our excuses and took us home in a taxi, crying with mortification all the way. I was ashamed of myself, but defiant as well. The day after, I took all my silly, pretty clothes to the Oxfam shop, and swapped them for men's shirts and sweaters, and I went to Lucille's dressmaker and ordered three pairs of jeans for myself, and put them on her account. She promised she'd do them right away, and she did. Lucille screamed at me, and called me an ungrateful troglodyte and a changeling. She'd found out about the terms of Henry's will, and Uncle John had told her of my plans to be a blacksmith. She was hysterical, and viciously abusive, and it was then that she told me Peter had taken one look at me in my cot and walked out.

Glory gave me a gold bracelet, and said I should sell it because I was going to need money, and also mentioned she had a few other bits of jewellery if things got too bad. She'd dropped the sneering boyfriend, she'd told him she loved her sister and didn't like hearing nasty remarks about her, and also that if he had taken up my challenge he might be short of an arm by now, and it was a pity he had been too much of a coward to find out.

I was really startled by that. I'd always thought Glory did exactly as Lucille told her, and speaking to a man like that was strictly against the rules. But Glory was almost nineteen, and although she was frivolous she was not a complete fool. I hugged her, and thanked her.

Lucille locked me in my room and said I'd have to stay there until I came to my senses. She called a doctor, and asked him to give me a sedative. He came up to my room, and we talked for a while. He left me some pills, which I flushed down the lavatory. One of my decisions had been never to listen to anybody fool enough to look at me and talk about occupations suitable for my sex.

I stayed in my room for three days, hoping to make my peace with Lucille on my own terms, but it was impossible, as I had suspected it might be. Poor Lucille, the perfect example of Miss Mullins' femininny, how could she accept that her daughter, *her daughter*, was going to be a blacksmith, was rejecting everything she had ever believed and had always taught about the role a woman should play, and the life a woman should lead? Lucille was distraught, and angry, and frightened, and, like most people in that state, she was entirely unreasonable. It was not possible for her to listen, or to think. All she could do was scream, and demand, and plead, and when those ploys failed, she refused to accept anything, anything at all, except complete surrender.

The day before I was due back at school I took my trunk down from the top of my wardrobe and began to pack. Lucille told me that I wasn't going back to school, I'd already learned more than enough. I tried to talk to her again, and she slammed my bedroom door again, and locked it, and screamed that it was not going to be unlocked until I listened to reason, and I could pee in my pants or burst my bladder or come to my senses, whichever I liked. I heard her telephoning the school to say I wasn't coming back. I knew that the fees were paid through Uncle John, one term in advance, and so I continued my packing, and made a list of the things I needed that weren't in my bedroom. I've always been quite methodical.

The door was only thin plywood on a frame, and the lock not designed to stand anything in the way of force. I had to kick it only once. Lucille stood at the top of the stairs, tears streaming down her ravaged face, screaming, and screaming, and screaming.

'I'm going back to school,' I said. 'If you touch my things, I will break up your dressing table and tear up your clothes.'

She gaped at me, saliva running down her chin, her pretty face red and blotched.

I collected everything I'd written on my list, and finished my packing. Lucille stood on the landing and watched, shaking. At least she had stopped screaming. Glory came back from a dinner party, looked at us both, looked at the broken door, and went into her room. I sat on my bed, watching Lucille, waiting for her to speak. I waited a long time, but at last she did.

'If you go back to school I'll never have you back, you'll never come into this house again. I've put up with you all this time, I've tried to help you, but you've just got uglier, and uglier and uglier.'

She was starting to scream again. I got up, and pushed the door shut. She threw it open again, and stood, leaning against the frame, screaming at me. Her voice was becoming hoarse, her eyes were staring, and she was shaking again. I watched her, and knew what she would look like when she was old.

'I wish I could have left like Peter did. When I looked at you, like he did, I wish I could have gone and left you, like he did. You were *hideous*. You are deformed, I don't care what the doctors say, you are a *monster*, and I still took care of you, all this time I took care of you and what did you do? You got uglier every day, I could hardly bear to look at you.'

'I'm going,' I said. 'You won't have to look at me any more.'

'Go, then!' She was speaking through clenched teeth, her lips stretched wide over them. 'Go, then! And may the devil go with you.'

I went that night, carrying my trunk on my shoulder down to the station. I had enough money only for the train fare, I couldn't afford a taxi. It was three miles, and, strong though I was, it took me a long time, resting every hundred yards, and I was exhausted by the time I got there. I stared blankly at the locked ticket-office, too dazed with tiredness to think clearly, but a clerk said I could stay in the waiting room until the morning. He unlocked it for me, and I sat on the hard wooden bench, and waited for the long night to pass.

She was my mother, and I loved her. I had thought she loved me. I had been wrong. All this time she had hated me. I was so ugly, even my own mother could not bear to look at me.

I don't know how long I'd been there when Glory arrived, anxious and worried, with a pair of diamond earrings and fifty pounds. She sat beside me, her arm around my waist, mine around her shoulders, my pretty, frivolous older sister who'd heard every word and come to the rescue. She told me Lucille hadn't meant it, she'd just gone a bit potty for the moment because of the menopause.

'I know,' I said. But Lucille had meant it, the truth had come ringing through her hoarse voice and her grinding teeth, and Lucille wasn't even forty yet.

Glory fell asleep, with her head sliding down onto my lap, her arm still around my waist. I looked down at her, sleeping quietly, and waited for the night to pass, and hoped that the wounds would heal. But they never have.

3

It was a relief to get back to school, to be able to leave the problems to capable women who could, at the end of a day which had seen threats of writs and visits from the police, refer to it all as a 'kerfuffle'. As a prefect I had my own bedroom, and after I'd unpacked I spent most of the afternoon lying on my bed in an exhausted sleep.

In the evening I was woken by the matron and sent to see the Head. A summons to Miss McAuley's study was something to be dreaded as a general rule. This time, however, I was told I'd done nothing wrong, and the woman even commended me for my determination in getting back to school.

I was to stay on to take my A levels, she said. John Mayall was my guardian, and all further decisions were to be made by him. My mother was still rather distressed, and she suggested I should not bother her for a few weeks. No doubt she would come round. My choice of career was an unusual one, but no doubt quite possible, although there might be difficulties in finding a farrier who would offer me an apprenticeship at such short notice. In the meantime I was to forget everything except the work I would have to do to get my A levels.

I did try. I went to the lessons, I donned my overall for the laboratory work, I sat at my desk or at the bench, and I looked at my books, at the specimens, and at the equipment. And I saw Lucille's face, deformed by rage, and heard her screaming rejection of me. I could shut her out for about five minutes, and in that time keep my mind on my work, and then the scene came back, the lines on the pages faded, and I became, once again, overwhelmed by misery.

I cut my hand quite badly with a scalpel while dissecting a rabbit. I had to go to the doctor, who stitched it, gave me an injection and told me to be more careful in future. I broke a set of scales in the physics laboratory, and was snapped at for my carelessness. I was told that, if I didn't pull myself together, I would fail my exams.

My housemistress called me to her study, and tried to talk to me. I listened to her, but there was nothing I wanted to say. There was nobody to whom I could repeat what Lucille had said to me. Even when I thought of it, I could feel my face flaming with shame. I could hardly bear the thought that anybody else should know those terrible words.

Two weeks after the beginning of term there was a lacrosse match. It wasn't a great challenge, the school we were playing was small, with only a mediocre team, and my opponent was nearly a foot shorter than me, a slim and pretty girl, quite friendly. Almost at the end of the second half, when my team was leading by four goals, we were both reaching for the ball and I was getting to it first, my reach being longer than hers. She was breathless, and she laughed.

'Wow! Aren't you *tall*?' and I spun towards her, my lacrosse stick cracking down across her head in a short, hard blow.

She stumbled and fell to the ground, and I stood over her, sick with horror at what I'd done, and wondering frantically if I'd killed her. Then, as the whistle blew, and the referee came running up, she sat up, her hand to her head, and climbed slowly to her feet.

She was helped from the pitch, and I watched her go. The referee seemed so astounded by what had happened that she couldn't believe it. She looked from me to the injured girl, to the reserve now running onto the pitch, and then back to me.

'I suppose you lost your footing, did you?' she asked at last. 'I mean, you slipped? Is that how it happened?'

I couldn't answer, and at last she walked away, blowing her whistle, and calling out instructions.

The reserve reached me, and stood alongside me, waiting for the game to begin again, and looking at me contemptuously. Throughout the rest of the game she said not one word to me, and when the final whistle blew, and everybody else shook hands, she turned her back on me and walked away.

The next day Uncle John arrived at the school. We met in the library. There was a fire burning in the grate, and when I went in he was standing in front of it, staring into the flames.

'I've spoken to Gloriana,' he said as I closed the door behind me. 'She told me what your mother said to you.'

I bent my head and closed my eyes, feeling tears welling up, my face growing hot. I had liked Uncle John, but now he knew, and I could no longer bear to be with him.

'I'm sorry you've had to come down.' My voice was unsteady. 'I'll try to work harder. I'm sorry.'

'Ann, sit down, please. I'm not here about your work, that's your business. In view of Lucille's behaviour, I think it's time you knew the truth.'

'I don't think I can talk about Lucille,' I said. My throat felt tight. 'I nearly killed somebody yesterday because she was a bit like Lucille.'

He threw up his hand impatiently.

'She's got a bump on her head, girl. Please don't dramatise, I haven't time for it. Now, sit down and listen.'

I sat at one of the library tables, my eyes lowered to the polished wood, my hands stuffed into the pockets of my skirt, where I kept Glory's diamond earrings. I should have handed them in as soon as I arrived at school, but I'd kept them, and when I looked at them I remembered her generosity, and was comforted.

Uncle John was still standing by the fireplace. I couldn't look at him, but I felt his eyes on me.

'What I have to tell you may come as something of a shock. Please hear me out, and I'll answer your questions when I've finished. Will you do that?'

I nodded, still staring down at my reflection in the table.

'Most of what Lucille said were just insults, very hurtful I imagine, but untrue. You are not ugly, certainly not hideous, so I hope you can put all that nonsense behind you. It was the rantings of a hysterical woman who had failed to get her own way. By the way, she is both insisting that you return immediately without completing your schooling, and asserting that she will never have you in the house again. That's an indication of her frame of mind.

'Gloriana told me that Lucille said Peter had walked out because of your appearance. In fact, you were a very fine-looking baby. Peter left because you were, rather obviously, not his.'

I took the earrings out of my pocket, and laid them on the table. They glittered and sparkled, and I turned them with my fingers, round and round on the shining wood, watching the firelight flash on the stones. John, not even my uncle, just John Mayall, the brother of my mother's husband, was silent, watching me.

Brown eyes, I thought, I have brown eyes. Lucille's eyes are blue, so are John's, so were Uncle Henry's. Henry's, not uncle. Henry Mayall. Fair hair, blue eyes, slim. Brown eyes, I have brown eyes, I am dark, and heavy. I am brown-eyed, and dark, and heavy, and illegitimate. I am not even Glory's sister, just her half-sister.

I picked up the earrings, looked up at John Mayall, and held them out to him.

'Gloriana gave me these,' I said. 'There's a gold bracelet, too, and fifty pounds, but I had to spend some of that. Would you give them back to her?'

'If you like. The money, at least. She wants to help you if she can. She'll be hurt if I give back the jewellery, but if that's what you want, I will.'

I laid the earrings on the table again, and nodded.

'Gloriana told me she thought you might not be Peter's daughter. She said she's suspected it for several years. Did you never wonder about your brown eyes?'

I shook my head. Perhaps I was stupid as well, something else I could not have inherited from the Mayalls.

'Henry and I didn't want Peter to marry Lucille. Not because we didn't like her, we did, rather. She was very young, in fact she was still at school when Peter first met her, but she was great fun during the war. She always knew of a party to go to, or something like that, and it was important to have fun when you were on leave then. We were all under a lot of pressure. Peter had a narrow escape on his last convoy, that sort of thing can upset your balance, so he decided to marry her on his next leave. He told us, and it was obvious opposition wouldn't stop him. Lucille said she was pregnant, too. She wasn't in fact, though I suppose she might have thought she was.'

I listened to him. I knew Lucille could be fun. I had seen her at parties, sparkling and delightful, in the centre of a laughing group, and I had so wished to be part of that group. She could lie, too. She might easily have lied about being pregnant if she'd wanted to marry Peter, she would have seen nothing wrong in the trick. She'd often lied to me and Glory, and had been perplexed by our anger when we'd found out, pointing out that if she'd told us the truth, we wouldn't have done what she wanted. We'd forgiven her. Everybody forgave Lucille.

'Is Glory Peter's daughter?' I asked.

'I'm sure she is. She looks quite like him. Her concern about you, that's like Peter, too. She telephoned me the day you came back to school. I was in court, and she couldn't reach me. She spent all day trying to get hold of me, she got me in the end at about ten that night. Peter would have done that. He would have sat with you through that night in the waiting room, too.'

'Who's my father, then?'

'Probably an American serviceman. We tried to find out, but Lucille just insisted it was Peter.'

'Oh. I see.'

'Lucille had to be loved, and Peter was away. Once the war was over I suppose she thought he'd come back immediately, but he couldn't. Sometimes it took years. It must have been lonely for her, on her own until Gloriana was born. Peter came home as often as he could, but he was away for months at a time.

'When you were born, Lucille said you were two months premature. But you weighed nearly ten pounds. The other thing was, even though it doesn't show now, when you were a baby it was quite obvious that you were at least partly negro.'

It was almost as if I'd been expecting that. As I listened to John, I'd been hearing Felicity Hunt's jeering voice, calling me a nigger. Then, I hadn't looked for the truth behind the insult.

'Peter set up a trust fund for Gloriana,' John went on. 'Henry and I said we'd be responsible for you. At first I must admit it was because we didn't want Gloriana growing up with the stigma of an illegitimate sister, because we didn't know you, but Henry and Ruth wanted to adopt you when you were about five. They thought the world of you, Ann. But Lucille wouldn't hear of it. She did love you, even though you may find it hard to believe that at the moment. Henry offered to take on the financial responsibility for your education if she would agree to you spending half your holidays with them. He and Ruth were concerned about the way Lucille was treating you.'

'She wasn't cruel,' I objected.

'Not deliberately, no. She hasn't done much for your self-confidence, though, has she? Any time you're faced with strangers, you crouch down and stare at the floor, except at the forge. Then you stand up straight, and you don't seem to mind how tall you are. Why should you?'

I smiled.

'And speaking of the forge,' he said, 'go and pack. We're going down there now. You're to stay for a week, at Mrs Pagham's guest-house in the village. You'll be by yourself, please don't set the place on fire. I hope a week will be long enough for you to get your muddled head straight. If not, you'll have to have extra tuition during the Easter holidays, your work's a catastrophe just now, and you haven't got all that long before the exams. Miss

McAuley thinks a break might help. We don't want any more bruised heads, either.'

A week was long enough. I fired up the forge, to warm the place up rather than for work, although I did use the time to make a set of garden tools, just to see if I still could, and because there was some iron in the store. I packed up Uncle Henry's notebooks too, and took them back to school with me. Mrs Plant, our biology teacher, was fascinated by Henry's drawings and notes, and incredulous when I told her he'd had no training in zoology. She got a bullock's foot for me to dissect, to compare with the horses, but after that we had to get back to the dogfish and the rabbits, and we just browsed through the notebooks sometimes in the summer evenings.

I spent the Easter holidays staying with Mrs Pagham again. The cottage had been let, to an artist and his wife, Steve and Susan Adams, nice people who had no objection to my going to the forge, which in any case wasn't included in the lease. They kept sheep in the paddock, and a couple of pigs in the stable. They were trying their hands as smallholders, seeing whether they could make a success of it first on rented ground before they committed themselves to buying a place of their own. I made an iron trellis for their roses, but I spent most of the holidays doing school-work. I did it in the forge because it was a place in which I'd always been able to concentrate happily on what I was doing. I sat at the bench with my textbooks propped open against a tool rack, and, when I needed a break, I used the rasps and files to do a bit of wood carving. During those holidays I learned, very clearly, that I had no talent for it. I kept a little fire going in the forge, just for the comfort, and to keep the place dried out and warm. I oiled the tools, and sharpened the knives on the grindstone.

Glory came down for a weekend. She was as pretty as ever, but somehow less fluffy. The fashion was more for a sleek look by then, and it suited her. She still had the helpless, fluttery mannerisms that Lucille had taught us both, but now nobody would take her for a fool. In response to her teasing I tried to make some iron jewellery. It was a complete failure. When she caught the train back on the Sunday night I felt she was more my good friend than my sister, and in a way I was glad of the change. We had hardly mentioned Lucille during the whole weekend.

The summer term passed in a sort of calm frenzy of hard work. By the end of May we'd completed the syllabus, and were simply left to work and revise on our own, helped when we needed it by the staff. We had the freedom of the reference library, and the laboratories were ours in the evenings. It would have been a stressful time, if it hadn't been for the rules, enforced only when necessary, banning school-work after a certain time in the evening, and encouraging instead tennis, or swimming. My memories of that time are more of summer evenings on the tennis court, or swimming up and down the pool, than of school-work, although when I think seriously about it I know that every day I was in the library revising, and working, and keeping my mind supple, and many of the evenings were spent the same way, too.

I did pass my exams, and I got good grades, too. The letter with the results came one Saturday morning before I left for the forge, and I sat on my bed turning the envelope over in my hands for a few minutes, gathering up my courage, before I opened it. Then I telephoned Uncle John with the news, as he'd asked me to, and he invited me up to London.

'I think we should celebrate this,' he said. 'Can you come this afternoon? I'll get hold of Gloriana and we'll paint London red.'

He took us out to dinner at some wickedly expensive restaurant, and we had champagne. He was an entertaining host, and we both relaxed and enjoyed our evening. Glory giggled, and told him that the last time I'd had champagne I'd challenged her boyfriend to an arm-wrestling contest. Uncle John was amused.

'Did he take you up on it?'

I was blushing, and staring down at my plate. I shook my head, but I couldn't help laughing at the memory.

'He said something about it being an extraordinary idea,' I said.

'It was a very good idea,' retorted Glory. 'He was an arrogant slob, and a wimp besides.'

'A short term boyfriend, may one assume?' enquired Uncle John.

'But it was *such* a nice sports car,' explained Glory, and they both laughed.

We went on to a night club, where a marvellous New York jazz band was playing, and it was noisy, and friendly, and everybody was happy and laughing. There was more champagne, and at one point Glory was dancing on the table, being cheered on by the waiters. At about four o'clock in the morning we went back to Uncle John's flat in Kensington. Glory and I were both rather drunk, but Uncle John didn't mind, even though the night porter seemed politely scandalised as he summoned the lift. It just made Glory and me giggle even louder. It was a wonderful evening.

I went back to Anford the next day, still happily humming 'Sweet Georgia Brown', and with only the mildest of headaches. Glory came to the station with me.

'I told Lucille about your results,' she said. 'Do you know, she rang up nearly everybody she knew to tell them? She said something about Antoinette being the *brainy* one of the family.'

'Not a bad excuse, I suppose,' I replied, and she wrinkled her nose at me. She knew exactly what I meant.

I had eventually decided to take Uncle John's advice about the metal-working course. The only farriers who were willing to take me as an apprentice at that time were both in Scotland, so I decided to wait for two years until I could go to an old friend of Uncle Henry's, Peter Andrews, and take the course at Hereford. It's a four-year apprenticeship, and I didn't want to be so far away for such a long time.

I started my course at the technical college that September. There were twenty students in the course, only three of them female. We were all about the same age, school leavers with A levels, most of them planning careers in civil engineering. I had digs on the outskirts of the town, an attic room, long and low, over a house owned by a rather crazy woman who thought the local airfield was a launching pad for alien flying saucers, and spent a lot of her time searching the skies with a pair of binoculars looking for them. The house was clean and comfortable, and Miss Lugens was quite kind and reasonable, except on the subject of aliens. She had dogs, two whippets, and I used to walk them for her on evenings when she had to stay in because of a suspected flying saucer launch.

I got Mister Plod at Christmas. He was a dog, owned by one of the students, who couldn't keep him any more. He was mostly Newfoundland, but perhaps a quarter labrador, a big, genial animal, gentle and good-natured. Miss Lugens agreed unhesitatingly that I could have a dog, provided he didn't fight the whippets, which was unlikely as they were both bitches. Plod spent his days in the garden, or in the shed if it was raining, waiting for me to come home and feed and walk him. He knew his name, but hadn't been properly trained. Luckily, he was a young dog, and quite intelligent, so it didn't take me long to teach him enough to make him controllable. He had one dislike that it took me some time to understand. Sometimes, if someone approached him, he'd walk away instead of wagging his tail, as he usually did. If that person followed him, he might even turn and growl, although I doubt if he'd ever have gone so far as to bite.

At last I realised that what he disliked was their smell. It wasn't body odour that he objected to, it was strong-smelling aftershave lotion, or deodorants. After that, if strangers asked if they could pat him, if I could smell them I warned them not to.

I could smell them very easily. I'd had to wear scent when I lived with Lucille, as had Glory, and Lucille always smelt of something meant to be lilac, but sickly. Since I'd left home I'd stopped wearing scent, stopped using deodorant, stopped using scented soaps and shampoos, and I found my sense of smell was very acute. I hated the smell of smokers, not just of cigarette smoke, but the dirty smell of their clothes, their hair, their breath. Sweat, provided it's not stale, has a pleasant smell, better by far than that of cosmetic chemicals. Plod and I liked and disliked the same smells, and, like Plod, I'm inclined to judge people by their smell.

Plod loved the forge. We used to go there sometimes for weekends, although money was short now that I had him to feed too, so I usually slept in the forge, in a sleeping bag. Once the Adamses and I were sure he wouldn't chase the sheep, we let him have the run of the place. He was road-trained, and unlikely to go far, so I never tied him up. If strangers approached he would raise his head and bark, a deep-toned but unthreatening noise. He was a grand dog, we all liked him. Susan did some sketches of him for a book she was illustrating, and later let me have one of the best of the originals.

Somehow, the college course was less demanding than school, and I found the practical work very easy. I didn't make friends with the other students. I never do make friends easily. I tell myself I prefer it that way, but I sometimes think I would like to have a few good friends. About a month after the course started, I noticed that more and more of the students were asking me to help them carry the heavier pieces of equipment or materials, and then leaving me to do it on my own. I played along with it for a little while, but then I refused. One of the students, Alec Turner, grumbled at me.

'Oh, come on, it's only a couple of yards. I'll lose a tenner if you can't.'

I didn't know whether to be amused or annoyed. I decided to remain neutral about it.

'I'm not a racehorse,' I said. 'Leave me out of it.'

And then I dragged the lathe across the floor.

'No,' whined Alec. 'You have to *lift* it.'

'Get stuffed.'

'Can't you do it, then?'

'I don't know, and I don't care. It's your tenner, not mine.'

But there was Plod to feed, and our train fare to the forge that weekend if we wanted to go there, so when somebody offered me a bet, another tenner, that I couldn't carry the lathe back to its original place, I took him up on it, and I won. Alec collected his tenner at the same time, and slapped me on the back.

'We could make some money like this!' he exclaimed.

I didn't much like him anyway, so I just walked back to my work-place, ignoring him. After that he turned against me, and I heard him making remarks about my appearance to some of the other students. When I went back to my digs that night I thought about it.

I'd accepted the remarks when I'd been living with Lucille. Then, I'd been dressed in pretty clothes, I'd had to wear make-up and nail polish, and to behave as though my one ambition in life was to be attractive to men. When I'd heard scornful whispers I'd had to pretend to be deaf, no matter how hurtful they'd been, because I'd been playing that game. I had no chance of winning it, but I'd been forced into playing anyway.

Now, I wasn't behaving as though I was trying to attract a man, I was doing my work, and I was certainly doing it better than Alec Turner was doing his.

I suppose I was just very slow-witted. I'd assumed that, because I no longer cared what men liked or didn't like, because I'd dropped out of the competition in which I'd never had a chance, men would leave me alone. Alec Turner was just the first to prove me wrong.

4

The course Uncle John and I had chosen lasted for two years, which passed quickly enough. I found the work simple compared to my A level studies, although in the last term only seven of the original twenty students were left, of whom I was the only woman. There were examinations, both practical and theory, at the end. I passed mine satisfactorily, but, since I didn't keep in touch with any of the other students, and have heard nothing from them since, I don't know how well they did.

I saw Glory sometimes. She came down to the forge for the occasional visit, and I went to London twice, the first time when she won her diploma for dress design, and on the second occasion for a party to celebrate her being offered a job with a small designer who specialised in theatre work. I went up in the afternoon to help her prepare for it, and found myself stringing coloured lights from ceiling hooks, and then trying to explain to some sleek moron that his sound system would overload the electrical system, and fuse everything. He tried to assure me that he knew what he was doing, Glory told him that I'd forgotten more than he knew about electricity, and in the end I just pushed him out of the way and wired in another circuit. I'd tried being polite, and it had failed. Lucille came to the party. I spent most of it in the kitchen keeping out of the way, Glory's friends not being my sort of people, but I was very pleased for her. She was making a success of things. Lucille was distant with me, regarding me with faint amazement, as if I had nothing to do with her and was some oddity Gloriana had picked up along the way. Glory had developed a style of her own, a bit beyond current fashion, and overlaid with something like fragility, but not helplessness.

Back in my normal world, life with Miss Lugens was predictable, if somewhat erratic. At the time of the full moon she was inclined to become excitable about the aliens, and what routine there was in that household took second place to her activities with her binoculars. I fed and walked the dogs, and made sure that her forgetfulness wasn't likely to cause actual damage. We'd once had a bad flood in the cellar when she'd left the hose running after watering the garden. She was a kindly woman, tolerant of other people's eccentricities, and only sad that they might miss an opportunity to make contact with a new form of life. Her aliens, she was convinced, meant us well.

I went to the forge as often as I could afford the train fare. There was a lot of fuel in one of the loose boxes, probably only a few months' supply if the forge had been running regularly, but enough for me to fire it up once every two or three weeks without worrying about it. Iron and steel was a different matter, expensive, and in short supply. Uncle Henry hadn't bought in materials in large quantities, and I could hardly afford it at all. The big racks in the workshop had rarely been heavily laden even when he'd been alive and working full time; usually, he bought in materials as and when he needed them. I used up what there was, and bought bits and pieces from builders' merchants, a wickedly expensive method. Sometimes there was a little work for me, from farmers I'd known, and Susan Adams would take messages and leave a list, if there was one, on the work-bench. It was still mostly broken gates, other more urgent work being sent into the town to metal-working companies there.

There was also regular work in the form of Sid's Soding Scythe, Sid being Sid Matthews, a jobbing gardener from the village, and his scythe an implement that frequently required attention. I'd find it propped against the wall in the corner by the door, with the inevitable note, 'Please fix this soding thing for me, Sid', impaled on the blade. Sid sometimes helped Steve and Susan with their garden, and Susan swore that, if there was a stone within five acres, Sid would find it and hit it with his scythe. The smallholding had been quite successful, and Steve and Susan were looking for somewhere to buy. For my part, I was only too pleased to see that they had made a large vegetable garden, and that it was weed-free and very, very fertile. The animals hadn't been such a success, so they'd sold them and decided to concentrate on organic market gardening. As a result, the paddock was unkempt and thick with thistles. Susan was apologetic about it, and Steve promised to get it mown before they moved out.

Plod came with me everywhere, except to college, when he stayed patiently in the shed, or the garden. He was slow moving and gentle as a rule, and had been easy to train. I found him a good companion, unobtrusive but friendly. I'd come to realise that animals were more likely to be my friends in the future than my own species. I preferred to be alone, or with people I knew well. If I had to meet strangers, the only place I could do so with confidence was at the forge. Anywhere else, I felt I was being judged, and that I was, inevitably and invariably, failing. As Uncle John had noticed, I was inclined to hunch my shoulders and stare at the floor, and I could rarely think of anything to say.

I'd met Peter Andrews at the forge once when Uncle Henry and Aunt Ruth had been alive, and he said he was pleased to have me as an apprentice. He was a small man, old and bent, with wiry arms and the sort of stringy look that often disguises enormous physical strength. He had two other apprentices, but one of them passed his examination only a week after I joined, and left to go to work in Suffolk. The other was Alvin, a shy young man who'd been with Peter for three years and was still producing work that made the farrier shake his head sadly when he looked at it. Peter hadn't intended to take on any more apprentices; he was almost at retiring age, and said he no longer had the patience. He did sometimes snap irritably at Alvin, but he was kind to me.

Peter had his own forge, far more modern than Uncle Henry's, fired by gas, not coal. It was much more convenient, but I liked the old forge, and had no intention of updating it, despite Peter's jokes. Peter had a portable forge mounted in the back of a heavy van, since most of his work involved travelling to his customers, rather than having them come to him. For the first year, until Alvin left to join the army, I stayed behind, working at the forge and dealing with the paperwork, halfway to being a secretary, and certainly all the way to being a cleaner. The metal-working course meant that I could do much of the work completely unsupervised, and I was at least earning my living, and, as he happily admitted, making a profit for Peter.

But once Alvin had gone, I joined Peter on his rounds, and he regretfully hired an office worker to keep the books and answer the telephone. He had to turn away work, now that I was travelling with him, but said it didn't matter. He wanted to retire anyway, and would do so in another three years.

Of the many customers we visited it was the riding schools I disliked most, with their groups of giggling schoolchildren, staring at me, and whispering together in their secretive little huddles, eyes bright and amused over the hands that shielded their mouths. Every time we went to a new customer I found myself cringing, and although I learned much from Peter, it made me hate that part of my apprenticeship. But I liked the horses, and Peter was a good farrier, quick and clever, and a good teacher, too.

Peter made most of the shoes at home, taking them with him in the back of the van and heating them in the portable forge while I took off the old shoes and cut back the overgrown hoof wall. I'd done that for Uncle Henry, and was almost as quick as Peter, so he immediately let me do that myself, unsupervised, glad to share the workload, and knowing I'd learned enough from Uncle Henry to manage it safely. It wasn't long before he taught me to nail, although he always checked my work, and often pointed out, if not mistakes, at least the possibility of improvement. I learned to work more quickly, and began to spot defects in horses' feet that I would have missed. Gradually, I needed to ask his advice less often, and quite soon we fitted comfortably into a routine on our rounds, each knowing what the other would do, and working together in an easy partnership.

I always left the talking to him, and hung back, or sat in the van, whenever he was discussing anything other than work with his customers. Peter was a friendly man, and enjoyed a joke, but although I would smile and try to be pleasant when his customers offered to see if they could find a saddle that would fit me, or suggested I carry a tired horse out to the van, I hated it. I knew I was an adequate farrier, and I intended to be an excellent one by the time I finished, but I've always felt myself to be a failure socially, and I'm still self-conscious about my size. Peter would respond to his customers' jokes about me by patting me on the shoulder and making a complimentary remark about my work, but he understood how I felt, and on more than one occasion, when somebody said something he knew would have hurt me, he turned a cold stare on the humorist and asked if he felt like shoeing his own horses in the future. Peter was more than a good master to his apprentices, he was a loyal one.

Peter's order book was healthily full, and sensible customers booked him weeks in advance for their work, keeping their fingers crossed that their horses wouldn't cast shoes between appointments, or, if they did, that Peter might, just possibly, be able to fit them in on his way to somebody else.

Racing stables are different.

There were three of them on Peter Andrews' books, and they were our most regular customers. Almost every day saw a call from one or other of them, for cast shoes to be replaced as well as the routine care of the horses' feet, and the calls had to be answered immediately. An unshod racehorse can't work, and they have to work every day if they're to reach the carefully planned peak of fitness at exactly the right moment for their next race. Peter took greater care with the racehorses than with his other charges, checking for heat in the feet, running his hands down the slim, hard legs searching for soft spots, lumps, any small sign that can give warning of impending trouble.

'A good farrier can save many times more than he costs to a place like this,' he said. 'We have to find trouble before it starts. If you can do that, you're in business. A racing stable with a good farrier will have fewer horses off work than a racing stable with a bad one, and they know it. I once had to stand alongside a trainer while he telephoned an owner to tell him his horse couldn't run in the King George because some fool of a blacksmith had buggered up his foot. I was that fool of a blacksmith, and believe me, Ann, that's an experience I don't ever want to repeat. I still go hot and cold all over when I remember it.'

I liked the racing stables. I liked the alert way the trainers watched and listened to Peter, and I loved the horses, the sense of speed and excitement just under the surface, only barely under control and never completely predictable. I liked the way the lads handled the horses, murmuring obscenities and endearments and appalling threats to them, all in the same soothing tone. Most racehorses are easy to work with, they've been handled by experts all their lives, although you do get the occasional rogue. Some of the young colts don't like standing still for long, so it's best to work quickly, with as little fuss as possible.

But it was at one of the racing stables that the incident happened which nearly made me give up all my ambitions.

Some of the students at college had never given up making remarks about me, or jokes. I had, on the whole, ignored them. I'd refused to take part in any more trials of strength, to win bets or for any other reason; carrying that lathe had strained one of my wrists, and my back had had a warning twinge the next day. Anyway, I wanted to learn my craft, not to play childish games. Never having had friends, I didn't really know how to behave in such a group, and so I'd avoided them outside the workshops and the classrooms. On the block release course at Hereford we all had more interesting topics to discuss than how tall or heavy I might be, let alone whether I could carry lathes or milling machines, but I still kept my distance. I had a reputation for being unfriendly, unsociable, even though I tried to be polite to anybody who spoke to me, but I never accepted invitations.

When you're as big as I am, and ugly as well for all Uncle John's kind words, men are rude to you. On building sites, they'll whistle at a pretty girl passing by, and I doubt if the girls ever find it offensive, for all that they usually look the other way and ignore it. When I pass a building site, I get jeers. Why not? If men are allowed to judge, they can pass judgement either way, positive or negative. If I was alone, it wasn't so bad. If I was with other people, I did find it embarrassing. It was just another reason for being alone.

At work, apart from the children at the riding stables, most people just accepted me. I was working, as they were. I was certainly not setting out to attract anybody; however else I may have behaved, and I have heard myself called sullen, morose, monosyllabic and unfriendly, I was never flirtatious. Which is why I was taken so completely by surprise, and why my reaction was so violent.

I was searching in the back of the van for something for Peter, pulling bundles of horseshoes aside, when one of the lads led a horse past me.

'There's not a mare in these stables I wouldn't rather get a leg over than you,' he said. 'Not that I could tell the difference.'

I stood up and stared at him. At first I thought I had misheard that clear, loud voice, intended to carry to everyone in the yard, or misunderstood his meaning, but then two of the other lads sniggered, and he looked me up and down, contempt clear on his face.

'Gawd!'

I hit him. I hadn't realised I was going to do it, and I'd completely forgotten I had a set of horseshoes in my hand. I felt such rage and hatred and despair that all reason left my mind, and I simply lashed out. I remember thinking that I was working, I was doing my job, in my working clothes, learning my craft, and still, *still* he thought he had the right not only to judge my appearance, but to express his judgement.

I realised I'd hit him as the horse skittered away from his crumpling form, hooves clattering on the cobbles, head thrown up in wild-eyed alarm, and instinctively I caught the rope at his head collar before he bolted. Then I burst into tears, but even as I stared down at him crumpled on the cobbles, and wondered if I'd seriously injured him, there was a feeling of triumph that overrode the fright, and that vindicated the rage.

I was still crying some ten minutes later when Peter drove us out of the yard, and still they were tears of rage. I didn't care if the damned little man was dead, I remember saying I'd go and spit on his grave. One of the lads who'd sniggered had, after a moment's aghast silence, stepped forward and taken the horse from me, backing away hastily as I turned on him.

'All right, Miss!' he said. 'I've got him, it's okay.' And he'd led the horse away, glancing briefly down at the man on the ground.

'Bloody hell!'

There'd been a great deal of activity, people running up and asking what had happened, everybody who'd seen and heard it giving their versions, staring at me and the man, exclaiming and questioning.

'She just hit him! Nearly took his fucking head off, is he still breathing? Fucking hell!'

Peter appeared, astonished and concerned, and the trainer came in from the other yard. I refused to say anything to anybody, I just stood by the van, the horse-shoes still in my clenched fist, trying to control my sobs, and fighting down the urge to hit another one. I was watching them, waiting for any hint of the same contempt I'd seen on the scarred and dirty face of the man who was beginning to stir and moan on the cobble-stones.

The trainer was asking questions, and at last I heard one of the other lads who'd seen it.

'Yeah, well, it wasn't very polite, what he said to her. But still, I mean, it was only words, wasn't it?'

'If anybody,' I said, my voice shaking, 'ever speaks to me like that again, I won't just hit once.'

They all stared at me in silence. Then Peter said perhaps, since he'd done the urgent lot, we'd better come back and finish the rest tomorrow, and the trainer told two of the men to put the lad into his car and take him down to the hospital, and everybody began to move around again. As I got into the van, I heard him speak again.

'In my book, what he said was fighting talk, and he got a fight. You'd better be careful what you say to our lady blacksmith.'

Peter dropped me off at Miss Lugens' house. On the way home I'd calmed down, but although the rage had gone, the despair remained. I said I didn't think I would be coming back to work for him, even if he'd have me. He replied he needed me until the end of the week at least, so he'd expect me the next day.

Peter and I went back to the same stables the next morning. He said nothing to me apart from his usual greeting, and we unloaded the van in silence and went back to work where we'd left off the previous day.

I was rasping down the hoof of one of the horses when someone approached. I didn't look up. I saw a pair of brown jodhpur boots, which came to a halt alongside me.

'In case you're interested,' a voice said loudly, 'you broke his jaw in three places, and he's . . .'

'I'm *not* interested,' I said flatly.

There was a silence, and then a cough.

'Right. Well, then. Okay.'

And the brown jodhpur boots retreated.

As I led the horse back to his box one of the lads passed me, carrying a saddle. He nodded in my direction.

'Nice morning.'

I nodded back.

The injured lad was back at work two months later, but he left shortly after that, and he and I never spoke to each other again. But word got around, at least in racing circles in that area, and I was treated with studied politeness from then on. Even the filthy language was moderated a little, although I'd never expected that. In stables, you either get used to it, or endure it, or leave, it's part of the scenery.

But I nearly gave up then. I'd been naive, I suppose, thinking that I was immune while I was working, except perhaps from children. I sat on the lawn in Miss Lugens' garden, Plod lying beside me, and I scratched his back and pulled his ears as I thought about it. There wasn't anything else I could do, no other way I could make a living that I could think of. And even if there was, I'd probably get even more insults. At least I had my forge. In there, with one of the big hammers in my hand, nobody had ever insulted me. I honestly wondered, for a little while, whether violence might not be the answer. I pictured myself again, confronting the dirty little man with his scarred face and his filthy tongue, and this time it wasn't horseshoes I hit him with, it was a pickaxe, and it went straight through his head and out the other side.

JENNY MAXWELL

It was a regrettably satisfying fantasy, and it never really left me. I can still smile when people joke about me, and perhaps it's as well they can't see the pictures I have in my mind as I do so.

I did decide not to travel. People who wanted their horses shod would have to bring them to me. I knew it would mean losing most of the horse business, and certainly all the racing work, but still it seemed the right decision. I'm not quick-witted, I've never been able to think of a fast answer, so I'm helpless when people insult me. I'd either have to accept the insult, and the hurt that goes with it, or I'd have to be violent, and, as I said, I thought about those alternatives quite carefully. Violence had worked once.

But I'm not stupid, either. Once, I'd got away with it. I might not be so lucky twice.

The rage remained. I still find my fists clenching when I remember that little man and his filthy remark, and I've never regretted hitting him. I was relieved that no trouble came about as a result of it, repeating what he'd said to a policeman, or in a court, would have been a horrible experience, but apart from that I was indifferent. When the trainer mentioned that he was recovering, that there'd be no permanent damage, I just looked at him coldly, and, like the one who'd challenged me, he dropped the subject and went away. Peter made no comment at all, nor did he ask if I'd changed my mind about working with him. He simply accepted me when I turned up for work on the following Monday, and we worked through the day as though nothing had happened.

78

In the end we worked together for four and a half years.

I passed my exams at the end of the fourth summer, with Honours, and this time when I went up to London to celebrate with Glory and Uncle John, I took Peter with me. He told Uncle John I was the best apprentice he'd ever had, although he did give some of the credit for that to Uncle Henry.

Glory had made me a dress as a present. It was full-length, sweeping the floor, styled like a medieval robe, in brown velvet faced with gold. I stared at myself in the mirror, surprised, seeing a stranger, tall and command-ing, certainly unfeminine, but female nonetheless, and perhaps even magnificently so. Wondering, I turned my head and looked down at Glory.

'Pre-Christian earth goddess,' she said. And when we went into the restaurant that night I drew many eyes, and most of them were admiring.

I worked with Peter for six more months, until the Adams' lease on the cottage expired. Peter had sold his business to a farrier from Belfast, and for the last few weeks took him in the van on his rounds, leaving me at the forge to make sure all the papers were in order, and to overhaul the machinery.

Peter gave me a magnificent set of tools when we said goodbye, and I'm still using most of them, although the best of tools wear out eventually. He and his wife bought a cottage by the sea, where she happily watches birds, and he tries to grow roses in the teeth of the gales that blow off the English Channel. He judges at farriery competitions, and sometimes tries to persuade me to take part, but I laugh, and say I've had enough of him looking over my shoulder and criticising my work.

He was a good master to me.

5

For the first time, I went into the cottage before the forge. I'd been in the forge many times since I started college, but had left the cottage strictly to the Adamses. Once or twice I'd been in the kitchen, where Susan had made me a cup of coffee, but I'd not seen the other rooms since they'd moved in.

Nothing much had changed. The walls were white painted, where Aunt Ruth had preferred a pale green, and there were patches where pictures had hung. The carpets had been cleaned, but were now very threadbare. I decided to take up the stair-runner, there were holes, and it looked dangerous. There were more scratches and dents on the furniture. That didn't matter to me. None of it was valuable, and signs of use made no difference.

Susan and Steve had left a nice letter for me. Once again, they apologised about the state of the paddock, and said they hoped that the vegetable garden, which they had planted, would compensate. I felt it was a more than fair exchange. It was proving to be a hard winter, and I hadn't managed to save much money. I'd used most of my wages on driving lessons, and once I'd passed the driving test I'd bought a van. I've always hated public transport, and Plod, being so big, had been difficult on buses and trains. The van had cost me most of my savings. I might find myself relying on what I could get from the garden if the business was slow to pick up. Plod was my real worry; I could manage on vegetables, but a dog would quickly lose condition and become ill without meat, and tinned dog-food was expensive.

I telephoned the farmers Uncle Henry had worked for, and told them I was back. They were friendly, but not very enthusiastic. Most of their work was now done in town, but they promised to keep me in mind if anything came up. Clearly, I was going to have to turn out excellent work, and at the right price, if I was to compete.

There were saws and drills, and some other metal-working machinery in the workshop. I'd used it only rarely as a child, under Uncle Henry's supervision, having always been more interested in the forge, with the roaring fire and flashing hammers. Welding torches had never had the same glamour. Now, with far too much time on my hands, I decided to overhaul it all, and see how well it worked after its long hibernation. But I lit the fire in the forge, and threw open the doors. Word might get around that the blacksmith was back, and it would do to be prepared. The cottage could be cold, but the forge had to be ready, had to look as if it was in use.

I cannot remember a time when I was happier. I had no money to speak of. The cottage was bitterly cold as I didn't dare to use my precious fuel and it was early in February when I moved in, cold and snowy. The motor on the big saw had burned out. I looked ruefully at the hacksaws on the rack, and thanked God for work-calloused hands and the vegetable garden. I had no customers, my stock of iron and steel was down to rock bottom, and there was only half a cylinder of oxygen for the welding torch. I spent most of the time with an idiotic smile of sheer happiness on my face, and I sang as I worked in the vegetable garden.

Not that much was growing at that time. Leeks and kale are vegetables that I've never really cared for, and they didn't become acquired tastes that winter. There was a little broccoli, and the last of the Brussels sprouts, and I grew heartily sick of them all. Plod ate biscuits, and stale brown bread from the travelling baker, and I counted, carefully, the dwindling supply of dog-food tins.

I raked over the paddock, dragging the cut thistles and nettles into heaps. The ground was frozen hard, so I had no chance of digging out the roots, but I could at least make the place look tidier. I trimmed the hedges, and layered them where they seemed thin. One day, I thought, I'd like to have a horse again, and I had no desire to spend time chasing it around the countryside when it got out through the bad hedges. I found an old gate that had been pushed between the beech bushes to strengthen a weak spot, and I dragged it back to the forge and repaired it. The sounds of hammering were cheerful, and spoke of industry rather than idleness. New work standing outside the forge was at least some sort of an advertisement. I repainted the gates, marvelling at the crooked crossbars, but remembering my pride at that work, and even then conceding that at least they were strong, and hung straight. The paint was half-dried and lumpy, but I strained it through an old curtain. Much of what I did was very time consuming, time being the only commodity I had in plenty. The habit I'd learned of calculating the financial value of it had to be set aside until I had work.

My first customer arrived early one morning after I'd been at the forge for ten days. He was riding a grey hunter, and he was in a hurry and a filthy temper. The horse had cast a shoe.

'Get this damned thing back on his stupid hoof!' he was yelling as he threw himself out of the saddle, thrusting the shoe into my hands and striding back down the drive to listen. In the distance, a hunting horn whined through the thin winter air.

'God! They'll be miles away.'

The horse was excited and restless, but well trained. I refitted the shoe, working as fast as I'd ever done, and handed the reins back to the rider.

'The other three are loose,' I warned him.

'Send me the bill,' he shouted back over his shoulder,

and he kicked the horse into a fast canter and clattered onto the road in pursuit of the hunt. I had no idea who he was. I swore, but hoped he'd spread the word.

About a week after that, a commotion of drumming hooves and a shouting voice brought me and Plod running out of the workshop into the yard. A tiny man on a little dun pony was brandishing a pistol and shouting in an appalling fake American accent as the pony spun in circles on his hind legs, wild-eyed, his bit dripping with foam.

'They shot him!' the little man yelled. 'The low-down critturs shot the best gol-durned pal a man ever had!'

He was dressed in Western clothes, a fringed poncho thrown back over one shoulder, a stetson hat crammed onto his head. He saw me, yelled again, tried to rein in the pony, and pointed the pistol at me.

I plucked him out of the saddle, taking the pistol out of his hand, and sat him on the bench. The pony, freed of his rider, bolted into the paddock. I closed the gate behind him, hoping that the half-repaired hedge would hold him. I put the pistol on the ledge over the forge doors, and contemplated my captive.

He stared back at me, round-eyed and silent, his mouth working in and out. His little hands gripped the edge of the bench. He was quite old, I saw, wrinkled and white-haired. I watched him for a moment or two, then, as he seemed to be all right, I went back into the workshop. Plod, trained never to bark when horses were around, permitted himself one disapproving rumble, and followed me back into the warmth.

A few minutes later I heard a car on the gravel. As I walked out, two men got out of it.

'Come on, Mister Osborne,' one of them said. 'Time to hit the trail.'

The other one looked around.

'Pony?' he asked.

'In the paddock.'

'Sorry about this. Did he do any damage?'

I shook my head.

They took the little man by the arms and led him to the car. He watched me all the way, wide-eyed, his mouth still working in and out. As they drove away he was still watching, turning his head back over his shoulder to keep me in sight until the car turned the bend behind the beech trees.

I caught the pony. It was too cold to leave him long in that state. He was still nervous, throwing up his head and showing the whites of his eyes as I approached, and I noticed there was blood in the foam that was drying on his mouth. I spoke to him, and he stood his ground, although he trembled as I took the bridle. I took him back to the yard, unsaddled him, and threw a rug over his back before walking him around to cool him down.

About half an hour later a woman drove up in a Land Rover towing a pony trailer.

'*Bloody* little man!' she said as she got out. 'He's perfectly all right so long as he takes his pills, but one never knows if he has. Poor Teddy! Is he all right?'

I shrugged. It was impossible to answer. The pony's

legs were cool, but they might easily be swollen the next day.

'His mouth's cut,' I said.

'Poor little beast. We'll just have to see, won't we? At least he didn't try to shoot anybody this time.'

I thought about that final remark as she drove away, and I took the pistol down from the ledge. I hadn't noticed before how heavy it was. I'd assumed it was a toy, a cap gun.

It was real, and it was loaded.

First I started to laugh, remembering the look on the little man's face as I took the gun out of his hand, and then, as I recalled he'd been aiming it straight at my head at the time, I began to shake. I unloaded it, and put it on the shelf over the doors, but this time inside the forge. I needed a little time to think about this before I decided what to do. In the end, I completely forgot about it.

Uncle John came to see me the next day. I stood in the drive and watched as he stepped out of his shining new Rover, a stupid grin plastered across my face.

'Morning, Madam Blacksmith,' he said. 'Where are all the customers?'

'Staying away in their hundreds,' I replied happily. 'Shall I shoe that stinking old heap for you? Or do you want wrought-iron doors fitted on it?'

He said that coffee would be adequate, and that he'd come to talk finances. We drank our coffee in the forge, the cottage being too cold. He seemed perfectly happy sitting on the anvil, and somehow the pin-striped suit wasn't incongruous. I propped my hip on the work-bench and waited. I was ridiculously pleased to see him.

'There's about fifteen hundred pounds,' he said.

'Wow! Wealth beyond the dreams of Everest, or wher-ever it was.'

He ignored my feeble joke.

'Get yourself a horse and ride it round Gorsedown Park.'

I stared at him.

'I can't *possibly* afford a horse,' I protested. 'I've got twenty-seven pounds to last until my first paying cus-tomer, and we're down to ten tins of dog-food. Oh, I hope you like kale and broccoli soup, that's what we've got for lunch.'

'Start looking for a horse,' he said. 'Let it be known that you're here. Make a noise about it.'

I sighed, and drank some more coffee.

'Is it really twenty-seven pounds and ten tins of dog-food?' he asked at last.

I nodded.

'You've got to get a horse,' he said, as much to himself as to me. 'The Gorsedown estate's up for sale again. I want you riding around the park and well-established before anybody starts anything clever with the deeds. Bugger it, we'll have to use some capital. Unless you know anybody who'll lend you a horse for a while?'

'No.'

He thought for a moment more.

'No, neither do I. Anyway, get a shotgun licence. I can

lend you a gun and the paddock's full of rabbits. That'll help keep Plod on his feet, and you too, come to that.'

'I can't shoot.'

'Anybody can shoot. Rear sight, fore sight, target, all in line and sitting still, squeeze the trigger and pick up your supper. Get the form from the local police station, I'll countersign it.'

It was a good idea, and his gun kept Plod and me in meat all through that winter and spring. As he said, anybody can shoot, unless the target's moving. I still never try to shoot anything that's running, or on the wing. I'd far rather be unsporting than injure an animal, and anyway, I shoot what I need to eat, not for fun. Plod learned to retrieve, which was a help.

The day after Uncle John's visit I got my first firm order, a pair of double gates for a farmyard entrance. Uncle John had left me thirty pounds, the last rent payment from the Adamses, and half of it went on the materials. I made the gates that afternoon, and hung them the next morning. It was good work, and I knew it. The farmer whistled through pursed lips when I named my price, but he looked hard at the gates, swung them, leaned on them, and at last nodded in satisfaction.

'Yes. Well, at least I can say they'll last.'

And then came my guardian angel in the unlikely form of Lord Robert Halstay, grinding into the yard in an old Mini, unwinding his feet from around the pedals and steering wheel and levering his extraordinarily long body out of the seat.

'Dear lady!' he exclaimed. 'So glad to find you in. Can you come? Horse cast a shoe, other fellow on holiday. Do bring the dog, dear chap most welcome.'

'I don't travel,' I said. 'Can you bring the horse here?'

'No trailer. Can't walk that far. Dear lady, do please come, poor old Blackie, feet hurt. Can't do without his shoes.'

I looked into his worried, kindly face, thought about the cost of dog-food, and shrugged. Lord Robert smelt of hay, and tweed, and Plod was waving his tail. We all climbed into the Mini, not without difficulty. Lord Robert searched for reverse, ground the gears, and jolted us out of the yard.

'Silly little car!' he exclaimed. 'Wonder whose it is?'

He'd borrowed it. It had been in the stable yard, with the keys in the ignition. Lord Robert saw nothing wrong in borrowing whatever he needed. The staff at the Hall took care to lock their cars, but the Mini was owned by a visiting plumber. Lord Robert himself owned a splendid Jaguar, which was later used in an armed robbery. He explained to the bemused detective who telephoned him that it had been missing for a week, but he hadn't reported it stolen because he thought somebody must have borrowed it.

'Horse of your own?' he demanded.

I shook my head.

'Got to have a horse. That's the forge with the right to ride in the park. King Henry's Deed. Better get a horse, dear lady. Can't have Blackie, he's lame. Can't have Lizzie either, nearly thirty, old Lizzie, and anyway,

Blackie's pal. Can't let you have a horse, sorry. Got to find one, though. Think about it.'

We came to a junction, and he peered earnestly to either side before pulling out into the road almost under the wheels of a grocery van, which screeched to a halt, blaring its horn, the driver mouthing furiously at us through the windscreen.

'Jake Brewer, Jake's got horses. Trains them. Breeds them. Sells them. Good man, Jake. Jake'll sell you a horse. Tell him I sent you. Don't buy that weedy great chestnut. It's mine, it's useless, he'll never sell it.'

I reflected that, with Lord Robert telling everybody it was useless, he was probably right. I wondered if Jake Brewer knew.

'Not far now. Nice dog. Like dogs. Got labradors, and the cook's got a dog. Nice little thing, mongrel. Like animals. You like animals? Good.'

There was a groom waiting for us in the stable yard, and the man I later learned was the plumber. A tall horse was tied to an iron ring set into the stable wall.

We climbed out of the car, and Lord Robert performed vague introductions, waving his arms at us.

'Ha! Plumber chap, all done? Good, good, splendid. Stephens, dear chap, this is our lady blacksmith, come to see Blackie, very kind. Right, leave it all to you, try and patch him up. Get him ready for the autumn sales if you can, can't have him eating his head off here, never earn his keep like that.'

He glared defiantly at Stephens, and strode off towards the house.

I nodded at Stephens, who was grinning, and ran a hand down the horse's neck. He snorted softly, and turned a kind and friendly eye back towards me.

'Blackie?' I asked. The horse was a bright bay.

'Black Bear. You know old Black Bear. Champion old horse, Blackie. Three mile chaser, sixteen wins in two years, old Blackie. Then he done his fetlock, now he's history, my old lad.'

I ran my hand down the horse's foreleg, and he lifted his foot. The fetlock and pastern were thickened, sunk low to the ground. The tendon had given way.

'That's chronic,' I said.

'Course it is. Been like that for four years. Mind, he can still hop around, doesn't hurt, dot and carry one, old Blackie. Lord Robert hacks him around, two old crocks together, he says.'

'Lord Robert said I should patch him up for the autumn sales.'

Stephens threw back his head and crowed with laughter.

'Sell old Blackie? Never! Blackie's all right if he's shod right. Needs his funny high-heeled shoe, though. Listen, Lord Robert says he's got no time for sentiment where animals are concerned, likes to think he's hard-headed. This place is full of pensioners, there's a Muscovy drake we've been fattening up for Christmas for the last three years, tough as a brick, couldn't carve him now with a chainsaw. You just put Blackie's funny old shoe on and tell Lord Robert he needs a bit of time.'

I nodded, and started work. Stephens watched me,

carefully. I've never minded that. A good horseman should always watch what's done to his horses. Somebody had been careless with Blackie, the horn had grown unevenly, and there must have been a gap between the shoe and the hoof. I rasped it down, and fitted the cast shoe back in place.

'Better if I could hot shoe him,' I said.

'No box,' said Stephens. 'Still, I'll have a word. You've done a good job there. That bugger Greg's getting lazy. I reckon we need a new farrier. Getting cheeky with His Lordship, too. I don't like that. Lord Robert's a good man, I don't like lazy bloody farriers getting cheeky with him.'

I straightened up, and Black Bear tested his foot on the ground. He was a lovely old horse. I checked his other feet, and decided they'd do.

'Lizzie?' I asked.

'Told you about Lizzie, did he? Right, why not? The old girl's not shod, mind, but you could take a look, cut her toenails for her.'

I blinked at him, and he grinned, and trotted off round the corner of the stables. A few minutes later he came back, leading an old grey mare. She was shaggy and muddy, with sunken hollows in her face and a deep sway-back.

'Lives in the orchard,' said Stephens, tying her alongside Blackie. 'Blackie goes out with her when it's not too cold. We don't get many apples, I can tell you. Lizzie likes Cox's Orange best.'

I rasped the mare's feet, but Stephens had obviously

taken care of her. They were well tended and healthy, and I smiled at him as I stood up. He was a good groom, the two horses were as fit as they could ever be. Lord Robert was well served.

Lord Robert came back as Stephens was untying Lizzie, announcing his arrival with the explosive bark I was to learn to expect.

'Ha! Finished? Good, good. What do you think?'

Stephens stared me hard in the face, and I dropped my eyes. I'm not very good at lying, and old Black Bear would never be sound. I hoped Lord Robert knew it, and that this was just a game.

'Needs a bit of time,' I mumbled.

'Time, yes? Right. Good old Blackie, that's better, bit of time. Now, get you home. Car?'

He looked around the yard as though expecting one to materialise at his command.

'Farrier says Blackie should be hot shod,' said Stephens, leading Lizzie away. 'She's right, and she's better than that Greg Wotsisname. Have to hire a trailer and take him to the forge.'

'Whatever you say, Stephens. Good chap. Now, find a car. Stephens? Dammit, where's he gone? Taking Lizzie back. Right. Oh, yes, dear lady, Jake Brewer, go and see him, got lots of horses. Got to have a horse.'

Stephens drove me home in his own Land Rover, having declined, rather emphatically, to lend it to Lord Robert. He paid me in cash, for which I was grateful, and said we'd be meeting again soon, Blackie being a great one for kicking his funny old high-heeled shoe off.

He also told me Jake Brewer was as honest as most horse traders and better than some. Lord Robert's name would help.

I had two paying customers, a rabbit in the larder, and almost enough money to put in an order to the steel mill for materials. Plod and I danced around the paddock in celebration. I thought of telephoning Uncle John with the good news, but decided to send a postcard instead.

Jake Brewer sold me Lyric, although I nearly bought the skewbald cob who looked more like a weight carrier. Lyric was a lovely mare, but I couldn't believe she could carry my weight. He told me her story and said that she was a better buy than the cob, even though he wouldn't guarantee her soundness. He asked me if I'd be interested in a tall chestnut hunter, and when I said not he sighed, and asked if Lord Robert had warned me against it. I agreed he had, and Jake laughed. I said I wanted time to think about the two horses.

Lyric was beautiful, the way only a thoroughbred can be, every line spelling speed and sheer breeding. Class, I suppose. She was tall for a thoroughbred, sixteen and a half hands, and she had an intelligent head. I felt her legs carefully, and they were cool and hard, despite her history, and the risk Jake frankly described that her knees weren't right. The cob was ugly, and laid his ears back as I approached him. But he was strong and sound, and certainly a safer ride for somebody who was by no means an expert. Common sense said I should buy the cob, but I yearned for the shining racehorse, crazy though it was.

I did telephone Uncle John that night, and he advised me to get the better-looking horse. I needed to look prosperous, he said, and it was true that a thoroughbred was a good weight carrier.

I hadn't realised he knew about horses. He was always full of surprises, Uncle John.

6

It took me two years to build up the business to the point where I knew I could make a success of it. During that time Plod and I lived on rabbits and vegetables, stale bread, and unbranded tinned dog-food. I don't suppose it did either of us any harm. At the end of those two years the racks had enough iron and steel of various types stacked on them to meet most demands, the machinery was in good working order, there was coal enough for the cottage as well as the forge, and almost every day saw me working, and working hard.

I'd modernised the forge, too, although I'd left the old leather and oak bellows in place. Many people asked me to leave it as it was, they said it would be a shame to spoil the old look of the place, and I had to agree. But the electric fan's hidden by the old bricks, and if you're working alone, as I do, pumping the bellows takes time. Some of the customers enjoy working them, and they bring back memories for me, too. It was one of my first jobs for Uncle Henry. I keep the leather oiled and supple.

I'd even been able to buy a new saddle for Lyric. Jake had sold me an old one when I bought her, but he warned me that the tree was broken and I'd have to replace it eventually. Where Lyric was concerned, the saddle wasn't my main worry.

The day after she'd been delivered I'd saddled her up, taken her into the paddock, and, not without misgivings, mounted. She accepted me quite quietly, and we set off, walking along the inside of the hedge. It was when I wanted to urge her into a faster gait that the trouble started, because I made the mistake of kicking her, as I'd always had to do with Fag End and the old hunter. Lyric immediately bounded forward, was in a gallop within two strides, and moving faster with every passing yard. I pulled on the reins, and she threw up her head, jerking them almost out of my hands. She was completely out of control. Luckily, we came to the corner of the paddock quite quickly, and I managed to pull her to a halt before she tried to jump the hedge. It was a discouraging introduction, and I decided to put in some practice in the paddock before we ventured into the park.

It was probably a good idea in theory, but I never did really learn to control her. Once she broke out of a walk she tried to gallop, and all too often I couldn't stop her. I'm not nervous with horses, and I did find riding her quite exhilarating, although there were moments when it was alarming. The first time I took her through the park we covered the two and a half miles from the paddock to the eastern boundary in less than six minutes. After the first half-mile I gave up pulling at her mouth, and just let her run, hoping she'd tire quickly under my weight and stop of her own accord. Eventually she did, and it became my practice when riding her to make sure I had plenty of room to let her wear herself out. Even tired, however, she was unpredictable. On more than one occasion when I'd been riding her home after a long hard hack through the park she suddenly took off with me, sometimes on the roads, when all I could do was try to steer her and hope she managed to keep her footing.

But at least I was keeping up the tradition of the blacksmith riding in the park, and I became fond of my flighty racehorse. Plod enjoyed our outings too, although he quite often got left behind. I'd have to dismount once I'd succeeded in stopping Lyric, and wait, and eventually he'd catch up, panting a little, but still with his lovely plume of a tail gallantly high and waving a greeting. He'd flop down at my feet, and we'd take a ten-minute break before going on with our ride.

Lord Robert Halstay told some of his friends about the Dear Lady Blacksmith, who'd done such a good job on old Blackie, and some of them brought horses to me, partly I suspect from curiosity, and stayed because they liked my work. It was this that led to an unpleasant confrontation with the other farrier in the area, an Australian, Greg Wilson, who'd telephoned me to accuse me of poaching his customers, and who'd later turned up at the forge shouting threats. He accused me of under-cutting his prices, and threatened to report me. There was, he said, only work enough for one farrier in the area, and he was that farrier, he wasn't going to be put out of business by some great slut of a monster cow. At that point I whistled up Plod, and told the man to leave. He did, but swore he'd be back. I never saw him again, and someone told me he'd returned to Australia. Some of his customers came to me, and a few of them endorsed Stephens' opinion that Wilson was lazy and rude. They also told me his business was already failing, and my arrival on the scene was only the last straw.

There had also been a most peculiar interview with the vicar, the corpulent and overdressed man who'd conducted Uncle Henry's funeral. I expected to dislike him, remembering his strange eulogy, and I was right. He smelt of rose-water.

I'd assumed, when he arrived at the forge, that he wanted some work done, but that was certainly not the case.

He opened the conversation by asking me if I was aware of the ancient traditions of the craft I was practising, if I even knew how old it was. I puzzled over his question for a moment, wondering if he wanted me to make something using only Iron Age tools and techniques; I'd heard odder requests than that, and could probably comply, if there was some village history society project that needed Iron Age work. But the point he wanted to make was that the elements I used, fire, iron and water, were not suitable for women, had always been worked by men and men alone, and indeed in most cultures an oath had to be sworn in which the apprentice craftsman vowed never to divulge any of the craft secrets to a woman. He went on to deplore the loss of ancient traditions, and to demand whether I thought it was morally or ethically right to destroy them in the transient cause of something so frivolous as women's liberation.

It was obviously a speech he'd written, memorised, and perhaps even rehearsed. I heard him out in silence, as I usually do, and wondered if he seriously expected me to give up years of planning and work in the cause of superstitious bigotry.

He then wanted to know if I had nothing to say for myself. It all seemed a rather stupid waste of time, but in the end I replied that I believed the pre-Christian tradition of worship in Europe was that priestcraft was handed down from mother to daughter.

He denied it furiously, and accused me of stealing work from men. I excused myself, and went back into the workshop, where I was cutting lengths of piping. He followed me, but I ignored him, switched on the saw, and got on with my work. I had ear protectors; he had none, and so eventually he gave up shouting at me, and left.

I thought that would probably be the end of it, but then I heard he was preaching against me. I telephoned Uncle John to ask his advice. He suggested I write to the bishop, and I did. The sermons stopped, but the animosity increased. Luckily, the church was no better attended than those anywhere else in the country, and the vicar's influence was limited.

I was asked to make a cage for a fox cub for the local mother and toddler group, who'd decided the animal was an orphan and needed their protection. I said nothing, made the cage, and waited to see what would happen. Sure enough, within a week one of the toddlers was badly bitten, and Our Woodland Chum promptly returned to his proper environment. There's nothing wrong with rescuing wild animals provided people remember that they're wild, and won't know the rules.

Quite a lot of my work was one-off jobs of that sort, and I tried to help if I could. The fox cub cage led to a job reinforcing the old stage in the village hall, a week's work, and the director of the village amateur dramatic society was an ironmonger in Gloucester. His goodwill put more work on my order book. I'd learned from Uncle Henry that I should never turn down a job, no matter how small or daft, because I could never tell where it would lead.

One of my first customers was Glory, tearful and anxious about a design which she'd been told was impossible.

'It's important!' she insisted over the telephone. 'And they won't do it. They say it can't be done.'

'What is it?' I asked.

'Wings. Well, sort of. Can I come? I can't explain, I'll have to show you.'

I met her at the station. She stepped off the train carrying a roll of drawings under her arm. As always, she looked beautiful, even though she claimed to be wearing her tatty working clothes, sweater and slacks that fitted as only expert tailoring and craftsmanship could make them, and her curly hair was tied back with a broad silk headband.

But there was an anxious, strained expression on her face.

'It's this freaky play about angels,' she explained as we got into the van. 'It's bound to flop, but I don't want it to be my fault. Oh, Ann, please do them for me. Please.'

'Of course,' I said. 'Calm down.'

'We've only got three days before the dress rehearsal.' There were tears in her eyes. She brushed them away impatiently, and turned her head to look out at the passing houses as we drove through the suburbs. She was silent, apart from the occasional muffled sniff, for a long time.

'I've got to be back tonight,' she said at last.

'We'll manage.'

'Maybe he's right. Maybe it can't be done. He's been saying all along I was too inexperienced for this job. Too young. He wants us to lose the contract. The assistant told me, he wants his cousin to get the contract, he's put money in the firm, his cousin's firm, I mean. How can I start again with only three days? He only told me yesterday, he said it was impossible, it's far too complicated, he said. I've done all the gowns around this design, I can't start again now, and I've spent all the budget except for what I set aside for the wings. Why didn't he say before? I gave him those drawings two weeks ago. He's done it on purpose, left it so I haven't got time to do it. He said they'll be too heavy, but the actors don't mind. They've been sweet. They said up to forty pounds, they could cope, and they would, too. They won't be as heavy as that, and it's only for the first two scenes, then they start getting lighter.'

We unrolled her drawings on the big table in the workshop, under the bright strip lights, and Glory explained.

'They start off as angels, you see. Conventional, white robes, big feathery wings, but they're not angels, they're demons. Throughout the play you're supposed to start to realise. They get darker, and thinner, bits of the robes come off and under them it's all black leather. And their faces, the make-up girls don't know whether to laugh or cry, they have to work so fast, you see, in between the scenes.'

'The wings,' I reminded her.

'Oh, God. The wings. Well, I wanted them to come apart, so they can take off some of the feathers at the same time. In the end they're not wings at all, they're whips. Four stages, you see, first of all feathers everywhere, then you take off this layer, then the next, they should clip together, and then when you take this off, it's just these long whips.'

It wasn't impossible, but there were eight angels in that play, and when I'd made the metal frames Glory still had the feathers to glue into place. She took three pairs back with her that night, and I worked throughout the night and the next day on the other five. I sent them up by taxi, as she'd insisted, but the cost made me wince. The last two pairs weren't ready for the dress rehearsal, but she finished them in time for the opening night. They weighed twenty-five pounds, she told me when she telephoned, and the actors said they were fine.

She sent me some of the cuttings.

Even Gloriana Mayall's excellent costumes could not disguise the essential banality . . .

The best efforts of a good cast, and the sure touch of one of the country's most promising young designers, Gloriana Mayall, were totally insufficient to rescue a boring . . .

The play was taken off a week later, as everybody had expected, but the producer asked Glory to look at another script he was considering, and the cast gave her a bouquet of roses.

'I want to buy you a present,' she wrote. 'You saved my career. What would you like?'

'Toenail polish,' I wrote back flippantly. 'Well done!'

Two days later a parcel arrived, a thick winter rug for Lyric, padded and lined. There was a small bottle of silver nail varnish with it, Elizabeth Arden's 'Angel's Wings'.

It was Lord Robert Halstay who sent the gypsies to me, four of them with six horses, strong and sound animals, but with their shoes worn as thin as paper. Many farriers don't like working for gypsies; farriers don't like to haggle over prices, and a gypsy loves a battle for a bargain. Lord Robert telephoned me to ask if I'd do the work, and I agreed. Six sets of shoes took nearly all day, but the gypsies were patient, sitting under the tree and talking as I worked, sometimes coming in to watch, bringing buckets of water for the horses. They'd shod them themselves, replacing the old shoes after rasping down the overgrown hooves, but they admitted making horseshoes was work they'd never learned, although their fathers had done it.

Lord Robert brought Blackie in the next day. The old horse had kicked off his high-heeled shoe again. I was shoeing a cob for a farmer, Peter Salson, when he came, and he asked if the gypsies had been.

'They been with Maggie Ripley?' asked Peter.

'I should think so, wouldn't you? They usually stay there.'

I'd met Maggie. She lives about five miles away, on a few acres of land, in a caravan, and she breeds horses. She has three brood mares. She can't read or write, and the telephone's a mystery to her. When one of her horses needs attention, she leads it to the vet, or to the farrier, and simply waits until something's done. It's no use trying to explain anything to her; she just smiles through her broken teeth, and says they'll wait.

Lord Robert patted the cob and murmured 'Yes, yes,' a few times.

'She likes a bit of company now and then,' he said. 'Her own kind, mind. They look after her a bit, fix up the wagon. Yes.'

'Why doesn't she go with them?' I asked.

Lord Robert looked unhappy, and Peter coughed.

'Old story,' he said. 'Best forgotten.'

'Oh, no, my dear chap! No. Best *not* forgotten, definitely, best not. Poor Maggie, she's a bit touched, as they say, perfectly harmless unless provoked, but not normal.

'It must have been nearly fifty years ago, was it? Do you remember? Between forty and fifty. Horse country here, you see, dear lady. Not just the races, but hunting, driving, everything. Horses, yes, very important here. And there were gypsies, many more than now, not always popular. Well, no point denying it, poultry does go missing when the gypsies are around.

'Maggie's father, Moses. Moses Ripley. Now, he was a horseman. There was nothing he couldn't ride. Big man, too big for a jockey. Pity, he'd have been a champion. But he was a rider. Anything with hooves, they used to say.

'My father had a hunter, bought him in Ireland, Falcon, he called him. Beautiful animal, unmanageable. The vet chappie said he'd probably been drugged when my father saw him in Ireland. Possible, I suppose. Nothing to be done. Dangerous animal. Very.

'Tony de Vere bet my father Moses Ripley could ride Falcon. The de Veres were hunting people. My father wasn't happy, but it all blew up, big event, Moses to ride Falcon, four miles, Lower Japley to Anford, choose whatever route he liked. Bets laid, local feeling, sporting event. In the end my father agreed. Never was happy, though.

'One Sunday it was. Summer, lovely day. So they set off, Moses and that damned hunter. Everybody thought they'd go across the hill and down through the park, but

Moses had a better idea. He was going to ride Falcon down the river, it's not too deep there. It's an old gypsy trick, break a wild horse by riding it belly deep in water, I've seen it done. Everybody was watching at the park, you see. Watching to see Moses riding Falcon, if he could. There wasn't anybody at the river, except Maggie. She knew where he'd go.

'He made it, that half-mile down the river, and he rode the horse up the bank to get into the park. But there was barbed wire on the top of the bank. They'd only put it up a week before, he hadn't known. Nobody thought he'd go that way.

'Falcon tried to jump it, but he hit it, and came down, his feet tangled up in the wire. They both fell down the bank. Maggie was there. She tried to drag the horse off, you see. She couldn't. His feet were still tangled in the wire, and Moses was under him. Moses drowned, and Maggie couldn't save him. She was only about ten years old. There wasn't anybody else there. She's never been the same since.'

I rasped the last of the clenches flat on the cob's hoof, straightened up, and nodded to Peter Salson.

'Just walk him up the path, please,' I said.

He led the cob away, and I watched, crouched down to see the way the horse set his feet, as Uncle Henry had done, and had taught me.

'Maggie's mother was a parson's daughter, from Suffolk. She wasn't a gypsy. Silly story, damned silly, romantic nonsense, running off with a gypsy. He was no good to her, she was certainly none to him. Too many silly novels, silly folk songs, wild gypsy rover stuff.'

Lord Robert ran his hands through his thin white hair in exasperation, and watched as the cob turned back towards us.

'Her people wouldn't have her back, nor poor little Maggie, and she'd had enough of life on the roads by then. My father gave her that little bit of land. Not much, but enough for the horses. Maggie's horses are all descended from Moses' horses. Maggie hasn't travelled since Moses died.'

Peter Salson rode his cob away, and Lord Robert unloaded Blackie and tied him to the ring, while I mused on the strange association between men and horses, and the dangers of the exploits it brought with it.

Gorsedown Manor stood empty, with For Sale signs gradually growing dilapidated at the gates. At first the house itself was kept in good repair, but the grounds were neglected. It was difficult to sell large houses with grounds, except to developers, and the park was green-belt land, with no immediate chance of planning approval for building. A local conservation group was watching very carefully.

Nobody questioned my right to ride in the park. A few people asked if they could ride with me, but King Henry's Deed only applied to the blacksmith and his family, for which I was very thankful.

There was a policeman in Anford, Constable Harris, a sour, middle-aged man who'd been there for about three years and seemed to resent it. He came to see me one morning to check that the shotgun was being kept in a safe place. I'd made a gun cabinet, copying the design from a mail order catalogue, and had bolted it to the workshop wall. He looked at it, and asked if I'd made it myself. When I said I had, he told me the police didn't usually approve of home-made gun cabinets. I thought about that in silence, wondering if the insult was deliberate. He checked the lock, grunted, and reminded me that I shouldn't keep the cartridges in the cabinet with the gun. I'd already shown him the two boxes of cartridges, in a locked drawer in the work-bench. I said nothing, and he stared at me, and then looked at the tools, picking them up, hefting them in his hand, laying them down, wandering around the workshop as if he had all day to spend there and every right to do as he pleased.

'Right,' he said at last. 'That'll be all, then. Mind you keep this place locked up, these tools could come in handy to a burglar. You need a dog in a place like this.'

'I've got a dog.'

'Not much of a watch-dog, is it? Letting me come in, never even barking.'

I whistled, and a moment later Plod appeared at the workshop

'Barking frightens horses,' I explained. 'He won't let strangers in if I'm not here.'

Harris snapped his fingers. Plod ignored him, as I had known he would. Harris smelt strongly of deodorant.

'What's his name, then?'

'Mister Plod.'

There was a long and heavy silence. Then the police-man walked towards the door. He turned when he reached it, and pointed a finger at me.

'That's what passes for a joke with you, is it? Laughing at the police? Typical of your generation, that. Until you need us, then it's a different story. Then it's please, Officer, yes, Officer, no, Officer, thank you very much, Officer. Makes me sick.'

I watched him drive away, and then I went into the workshop and sat on the bench, wondering what I'd done to antagonise him. I could think of nothing. I had no friends, but I was certainly not looking for enemies, least of all in the police.

I worried about it for some days, and wondered if I should do anything. I even tried to compose a letter to Harris, explaining that I hadn't named my dog myself, and hadn't meant to offend, him or anybody else, but after a few drafts I gave up, threw the last one to join the earlier rejects into the waste-paper basket, and decided to forget it. His attitude was Harris's problem; I would just have to hope it would never become mine.

People were rumoured, off and on, to be buying Gorsedown. There was a plan to turn it into a golf course. I thought of Lyric's hooves tearing up the mani-cured grass of fairways and greens, and hoped most fervently that it would fail, and it did. It was then to be a conference centre, a convalescent home, a private school. The park became even more overgrown, and I had to be careful of rabbit holes. An Arab sheik was said to be planning to buy it, but then dropped the idea when his scheme to erect high voltage electric fences was vetoed by the County Council. It was to be a rifle range for the Ministry of Defence, and then a stud farm, and a private zoo.

I heard all this from customers bringing horses to be shod, and I listened, grunted when a response seemed to be expected, and wondered who could possibly afford to keep up a place like that in the 'seventies. Even empty, repairing the roof and keeping the house dry was said to cost thousands every year, and the land was going to ruin. Woods that had been clear and open were choked with brambles and fallen branches, grassland was scattered with clumps of nettles, thistles rose in jagged spikes over matted tussocks, somebody abandoned an old car in a wood beside the boundary road, and then rubbish was heaped around it; broken glass, tin cans, a ruined mattress. One night some people rode into the park on motor cycles. The roars of the engines could be heard for hours, and the next day there were broken windows, and paint had been sprayed on the walls. After that, the gates into the park were chained, but the hedges were in such poor condition that nobody believed it would stop the vandalism. One of the local riding school instructors told me that the insurance company was refusing to renew cover on the house.

Glory got a short term contract with the Royal Shakespeare Company to design the costumes for a production of *The Merchant of Venice*. She drove down to see me in a little red sports car, her own, and, as she proudly announced, paid for. She brought a sketch book with her first drawings. I bought wine in the village shop, and we toasted each other's success. The drawings were lovely, like frost patterns on black glass, but muted. She said they were a background for the play, not intended to distract the audience; you don't try to upstage Shakespeare, not unless you like making a fool of yourself.

I had made her a copper belt-buckle, not really knowing what else to do for her, and while I looked at her sketches she drew a design for the belt. I was fascinated; I had seen the buckle as something to attach two ends of a leather strap, but Glory designed the belt in folded chiffon, so the buckle looked like a clenched fist crushing the fabric. It was dramatic, and very original. I could see why she was making such a name for herself. She said if I'd been a silversmith we could have gone into partnership together, and then we both looked at my big, calloused hands, and laughed.

Lucille, she said, almost refused to have my name mentioned in her presence since I'd taken over the forge and become a blacksmith. If anybody asked about me, she put on a faintly wondering expression, as if she could not remember, and would then sigh, and change the subject. She still lived for her social life, still regarded the likes and dislikes of men as being of paramount importance, still maintained her air of helplessness and dependence.

'I wonder why she never remarried,' I said.

'I don't think she and Peter were ever divorced,'

replied Glory. 'I suppose he's still supporting her. I've tried to ask her how she manages, but she just says, "Oh, darling, let's not talk about money, it's so boring and vulgar," so I don't know.'

'Is he still supporting you?' I asked.

'No he isn't, not since I got this job. I'll tell you something, Ann, I may marry one day, and I may look like one of these femininnies you talk about, but I'll never let myself depend on a man for money, never. If my husband wants to breed he'll pay for a nanny and like it.'

There seemed to me to be something not quite straight about that argument, and Glory saw it too, and grinned at me.

'Do you ever wonder who your father is?' she asked.

'Yes, sometimes, but it's only curiosity. I think of Uncle Henry as my father, I suppose. He's the closest I ever got to having one.'

'You were lucky. I wish I'd known Peter. I asked Lucille who your father was. She snapped my head off, of course, said it was Peter, threatened to sue Uncle John for libel. I'll ask again if you like, but I doubt if she'll tell me.'

She's so beautiful, my sister, so beautiful and so loyal. I love her very much.

I had a riding stable and the dude ranch as customers. I was always a little puzzled by the dude ranch, it seemed such a strange way of spending a weekend, dressing up in cowboy clothes and trying to learn how to throw a lariat. The harness they used was magnificent, tooled and embossed leather with brass or silver fittings and decorations. I was asked to shoe the horses Western style, but I didn't know how. I knew some young farriers had been sent on a visit to the United States, so there must be different methods, but I had no idea what they were. Neither had the owners of the ranch, a couple called Laverton. It had been Mrs Laverton who'd collected the little pony, Teddy, when the crazy old man had ridden off with him. I went to the ranch to watch some videos of Western riding at their request, and there were two scenes showing horses being shod, but not in detail. I said I thought they looked very similar, but I suspect any differences are because of the work the horses do, and the terrain, which would make nonsense of using Western-style shoeing on hacks in the south of England anyway. I became quite used to groups of colourfully dressed cowboys and cowgirls standing around the yard or sitting on the iron bench while I shod Pinto or Palomino horses for them. The horses were well cared for, and at least nobody suggested I put on fancy dress while I worked.

It was Mrs Laverton who told me about the sale of Gorsedown Manor. She'd arrived with two horses in the trailer, and she was dressed prosaically in slacks and sweater.

'At last,' she commented. 'Maybe they'll get the place in order again, though it'll cost a fortune, I should think. Yes, yes, bound to. What's the park like now? You're the only person I know who ever sees it.'

'Bad. Nettles, brambles, rabbits.'

'Yes, well, we'll have to see. A four-square-mile bramble patch, yes. No joke, if you're signing the cheques, yes, I hope they've got the money for it. And those big Victorian houses, they weren't built with economy in mind, were they? Still, it'll be lovely if they can put it right. Yes. Bloody shame it's got in such a state. Have you seen the house?'

'Broken windows. Graffiti.'

'Hell! Still, only to be expected. Yes, it'll take a bit of cleaning up, I suppose they know what they're buying.'

'Who's bought it?'

'Some religious order, I think. Monks or nuns, I suppose. Still plenty of money in the church, it seems. Yes. I don't know much about them, it was Peter Gadd who told me, his firm handled the sale. Not him personally, one of the partners. Yes, that's right. What was it he said? Oh, yes, the Children of God. That's what they call themselves, the Children of God.'

7

They moved in almost immediately, one bright autumn day, lorries and cars backing up from the drive onto the road as people argued about the chains and locks on the gates. Eventually, one of the drivers came to me to ask if I could cut the chains for them. I thought about it for a moment or two while he complained and argued, wondering whether it was possible that they might be well-organised squatters, and then took a pair of bolt cutters and sheared through the chains. They were young people, mostly wearing jeans and anoraks, no sign of the monks or nuns Mrs Laverton had mentioned. They thanked me for my help, and I nodded to them, and went back to the forge.

That afternoon we heard them out in the grounds, the muted crashing of axes and slashers in the brambles, voices calling to each other, a few of them singing. They sounded happy. The rotted 'For Sale' signs, which over the last six weeks had sported the triumphant proclamation 'Sold!' plastered across them, were pulled down and taken away, and in their place a neatly lettered board was raised.

> *'Blessed are the Peacemakers, for they shall be called the Children of God.*
>
> *Matthew V, v IX.'*

Underneath it, a smaller notice, black on white.

> *Private property. Please do not trespass.*

I rode through the park the next morning. Already, there were clear signs of work on the land, dead wood having been dragged out of the stands of trees, clumps of brambles cut down. There was no sign or sound of machinery, only hand-tools. I pulled up on the crest of the hill opposite the manor house, and looked at it. New glass glittered as men replaced broken windows. There were about a dozen people working, some on ladders, cleaning the paint-sprayed graffiti off the grey stone walls, while others dug the garden or repaired the old brick wall that surrounded the big vegetable plots.

I rode on towards the eastern boundary, Plod trotting at Lyric's heels. It was a beautiful morning, cold and clear, an early frost crisp underfoot, the sky a pale, clean blue with faint lines of white cloud. I could hear people calling to each other from the house and the garden, their voices carrying in the still air. There was the smell of a bonfire, and I saw a thin column of grey smoke rising away to my left. The leaves were turning gold and yellow, red and brown, brilliant against the sky, some already falling so that Lyric's hoofbeats, muffled in the leaf mould underfoot, rustled when we rode through drifts of them lying across the open track where the wind had dropped them.

I came across them unexpectedly as I turned a sharp bend, five of them, standing in a line across the track about thirty yards in front of me, heavy slashers in their hands, staring expressionlessly. I reined Lyric in, and she stopped, ears pricked. Plod trotted up beside me, his tail high, sniffing at the wind. I saw the hackles begin to rise on his shoulders, and I spoke his name quietly. He stopped, and stood motionless, a soft growl rumbling in his throat.

They did not move. They were silent, watchful, hostile. I looked at them, looked from one to the other, five young men in jeans and sweaters holding sharp and dangerous tools, the signs of their work clear on either side of the track, their faces blank, their hands tense and hard on the wooden handles. They were completely still, waiting and alert, the only movement the wind gently lifting the leaves around their booted feet, the only sound the rustle of those leaves, and Plod's menacing growl.

Lyric, sensing my unease, shifted under me, turning away, trying to pull her head free, and I checked her again, feeling her tugging at the bit, knowing I would not be able to hold her for long. Plod, still standing beside me, growled again, and then lifted his voice in a sharp, threatening bark, once, twice, and again.

I rode forward, calling him to heel. Lyric tried to turn again, her powerful quarters bunching under her, ready to bolt. Plod followed, his head high, hackles raised and teeth bared, growling. I kept Lyric reined in very tightly, her chin almost touching her chest, and wondered if I could ride her through them if they stood their ground. I was beginning to feel frightened; the steel blades of the slashers glittered along the edges where they had been freshly honed, the faces of the men who held them were turned to mine, and were cold.

The man in the centre of the line turned his head to each side, saying something I could not hear to the others. Without taking their eyes off me they stepped back to either side of the track, leaving the way clear, standing side by side and watching me.

As I rode towards them I could feel the hairs on the back of my neck rising, the muscles in my shoulders tensing. Lyric's eyes were wild and white-rimmed, her ears flicking in fright, sweat breaking out on her shoulders. Plod paced beside us, stiff legged, a snarl lifting his lips.

They stood on either side of the track, their eyes on my face, expressionless, holding the slashers, waiting for me.

I forced myself to speak as we rode between them, turning my head to look down at the man who had given the order.

'Good morning.'

My throat was dry and tight, and my voice was hoarse. He gave no sign that he had heard me as he stared back into my face, unblinking and silent. They all watched me, not one of them shifting his eyes to the horse or the dog, their heads turning to follow as we walked on down the track, and then Lyric plunged, dragging at the reins, and broke into a gallop, racing flat out in panic within a few yards.

I looked back over my shoulder. They were standing across the track again, five in a line, watching me, five young men, holding sharp and heavy slashers.

I reached home about three hours later, having come the long way round by the roads rather than through the park. I was feeling very shaken, and I telephoned Uncle John and told him what had happened. As I described it, I began to feel foolish. He asked me questions, and I answered them. No, they hadn't threatened me. They hadn't even barred my way. Yes, they'd been working, bushes had been cleared from beside the track. They hadn't tried to stop me, they'd stood aside as I rode up.

'Sorry,' I said at last, feeling stupid and miserable. 'It's just they seemed so horrible. Sort of menacing. I don't know, I can't really describe it. Maybe I'm being a fool . . .'

'Ah,' he replied, 'but you're not a fool, are you? Let me know if something like this happens again.'

I telephoned him again that afternoon. When I had taken Lyric out to the paddock I'd found the gate between it and the park had been chained, and a notice like the one beside the main gate had been screwed to the post.

Private property. Please do not trespass.

He sent me a letter to sign. It explained my right to ride in the park, and gave details of the case Uncle Henry and Aunt Ruth had won against the estate owners nearly twenty years before.

'Send it by registered post,' he said in a covering note. 'Give them two days, and if they haven't taken down that chain by then, cut it. Don't stop riding in the park.'

I followed his advice. Two days later I shut Plod in the workshop, cut the chain on the link next to the padlock, and rode Lyric through the gate and into the park, looking around to see if anyone was watching me. Since I'd sent the letter I'd thought about what I should do, and had decided to try to make my peace with my new neighbours. I felt the best way would be to call on them, and explain. I took the chain with me, and rode over the hill along the track beside the drive, straight to the main door of Gorsedown Manor.

I dismounted, looped the reins over my arm, and rang the bell.

As I waited, people began to gather in the drive behind me, standing some distance away, but watching. I turned to look at them, and saw on their faces the same cold hostility that had marked those of the five young men in the woods. Some of them were carrying garden tools. They were all young, dressed in jeans and jackets or anoraks, and they all stood in silence, staring at me, not looking at each other, not approaching, standing motionless on the gravel drive, watching.

I rang the bell again, and at last heard footsteps approaching, softly and slowly. A bolt was drawn, and the door opened. I looked down into the face of a thin young man who stared back up at me, dark eyes narrowed under heavy brows, hostile. I took the chain and padlock out of my pocket, and held it out to him.

'I'm the blacksmith. I wrote to you. This is yours.'

He made no move to take it, did not even look at it. His eyes were fixed on my face.

I waited, holding out the chain and the padlock. Still he said nothing, simply stared up at me, his face blank.

I looked around, saw a small table just inside the door, and reached in to put the chain on it. As I did so, he dropped his hand onto my arm, gripping my sleeve and pushing me back. I stopped, looked into his face, and then thrust past him to lay the chain on the table. He resisted for a moment, and then stood aside. His expression did not change, and he said nothing. I stepped back, and looked down at him again.

'Don't chain my gate,' I said. 'I'm allowed to ride in the park.'

'We are a religious order,' he replied at last. 'You are not welcome.'

'I'm allowed to ride in the park,' I repeated. 'I'll try not to disturb you.'

But he was already closing the door, and I heard the bolt slide back into place. I turned to face the people standing in the drive.

'I'll try not to disturb you,' I said again. 'If someone will tell me when you have your services, I'll stay away from the house at those times.'

Nobody spoke, nobody moved. They were not as

menacing as the men in the woods had been, but their silence, and the blank hostility on their faces, very clearly echoed the words of the man at the door. I was not welcome.

I mounted Lyric, and looked around at them again.

'I'm allowed to ride in the park. Don't chain my gate.'

I rode away, not back towards the forge, but northwards, alongside the garden wall towards the beech woods. I could feel them watching me. When I reached the track I looked back, and saw them, still standing in the drive as they had been when I was at the door. I waited and watched, and gradually, in ones and twos, they walked away, back to their work, and I heard their voices as they spoke to each other.

It had begun to rain. I turned up the collar of my jacket, and rode on along the track, feeling depressed.

In the village, people speculated about the Children of God, and many came to see me on various pretexts, wanting to know what I'd seen in the park, and whether I'd spoken to anybody there. I answered their questions as briefly as I could without being rude. There was in any case little I could tell them. My gate wasn't chained again, but the notice stayed in place, screwed to the post. I decided to leave it where it was. The main gates to the park, and those in the north-western boundary, had been repaired, and new, strong locks fitted. The hedges all round the park were also being strengthened, with new thick saplings being planted in the gaps, and the older plants were layered, the slashed and bent branches woven amongst those of their neighbours to make a strong barrier. One of the farmers told me the boundary of the park is nearly twelve miles long, and it seemed they were making every inch of the surrounding hedges impenetrable. When the villagers spoke to the young men and women as they planted the saplings and layered the bushes they were answered politely, but requests for information about the Children of God were rebuffed. It was, they were told, a closed order, and visitors were forbidden.

I rode in the park at least twice a week, Plod trotting behind us as before, but I stayed away from the house. Unless I came upon them unexpectedly, I tried to avoid the people. Sometimes, when Lyric ran away with me, we passed quite close to them, but nobody tried to bar my way. Plod, running after us, always avoided them, sometimes going quite a long way off our trail in order to do so. They stopped working and turned to watch as we went past, always silent, always with the same blank and unfriendly look on their faces.

I could no longer ride through the northern gates to the park, since the locks had been fitted. I wrote to Uncle John to ask about that, wondering whether King Henry's Deed spoke of access, and he wrote back saying the Children of God would have to let me have a key. The smith had been given access to collect Fitzallen's horses, and the deed remained unchanged. Once again, he sent me a letter to sign, to send on by registered post. A week later an envelope arrived, also by registered post. In it was a key. There was no letter, no explanation, simply the small, flat, heavy key, plated brass with grooves and rollers, to fit an expensive modern lock. I took it into Gloucester to try to get it copied, but the locksmith told me it was a security lock, and no copies could be made without the authorisation card. He told me to be careful not to lose it. I clipped the key to one of the D-rings on Lyric's saddle.

September passed, and October was cold, with high winds and heavy rain. The tracks across the park were deep in mud. I stayed off them, taking to the cleared woods and the grass-land instead. Dead trees had been cut down and dragged away, the stumps low against the ground, chippings from axes lying around them. I hadn't seen or heard any machinery, apart from the lorries that brought them, since the Children of God had arrived. They had worked hard, and fast, too, considering they only used hand-tools.

The hunting season was beginning, and steeple-chasing was taking over from flat racing. Two of the farmers in Anford had horses in training, hunter chasers and point-to-point horses, and they brought them to me to be shod. One of them told me the hunt had been told to stay off the park, and it seemed nothing could persuade the Children of God to let them back. Now, I was the only outsider ever to set foot on Gorsedown Manor lands. Groups of people came out of the park every morning, and caught the bus into Gloucester. Sometimes they shopped in the village, but there were never less than four of them together, and they spoke as little as possible to the villagers, although they were always polite. None of them ever came to the forge. Because I seldom went into the village I never met them except when I rode through the park, and when I saw them there they always reacted in the same way; they stopped what they were doing, turned towards me, and watched, silently, as I rode past.

Mrs Laverton rode over, leading two ponies. Her damned fool husband, she said, had turned the trailer over and smashed it up and would I please change my mind and come to the ranch to shoe the horses; Teddy had nearly dislocated her elbow dragging on the leading rein. I shook my head, and she sighed in exasperation.

'The Children of God,' she told me, 'are beggars, prostitutes, thieves and blackmailers. Yes. Also drug-dealers, white slavers and gangsters.'

'Yes?' I picked up Teddy's foot and began to clip off the risen clenches, the turned-over ends of the nails.

'So various village gossips have it. Ann, how does one make you talk? You could dine out every night of the week if you'd only say what you see in the park.'

'I don't see anything.'

'But what do they do in there? Any sacrificial virgins? Black masses on Thursdays? They sent the vicar away with a flea in his ear, did you hear?'

'No.'

'Oh, but yes, and bloody glad I was to hear it. Yes. Don't you want to know? I'll tell you all about it if you'll give me just one little snippet about the Children of God. Just one. What do you say?'

I smiled, levered the shoe off Teddy's hoof, and reached for the knife.

'They're clearing the dead trees out of the woods,' I said.

'Yes?'

Teddy turned his head to nuzzle my back, and I pushed it away with the back of my elbow. He'd been known to nip.

'Is that it, then? Is that my snippet? God, you drive a hard bargain, you mean cow. Dead trees in exchange for the vicar being called the Whore of Babylon. Who was the Whore of Babylon, anyway?'

'I don't know.'

'I wish they'd write an index for the Bible, there are all sorts of things I'd like to look up, Whore of Babylon, Witch of Endor, have you noticed all the really interesting characters are female? Yes. Anyway, Father Chalmers galumphed up to them in the Post Office and invited them to come to Harvest Festival, wouldn't take no for an answer, you know the way his voice carries. Yes. According to Mr Comfritt, who says he was buying stamps but I bet it was gin, one of them turned on him with a real fire-and-brimstone speech, very biblical, and ended up with the Whore of Babylon gibe. Father Chalmers was very put out, yes, pink as a carnation and lost for words, which is a first for someone. Are Teddy's feet all right?'

'Yes.'

'Don't get carried away, you chatterbox, what about that corn, any sign of it? Or has it healed up?'

'It's gone.'

'Thank you so much. Yes, well, there were four of

them, there always are, aren't there? Except when there are five, or six. Yes. And only one of them spoke, have you noticed that, when you're in the park? How it's always only one in the group who speaks?'

'No.' I began to work on the other pony, and Mrs Laverton laughed.

'I'll tell you something else, though, they do beg. Yes. I saw them in Gloucester, that tall fair-haired man, and three girls. They all had collecting tins, some charity called Reconcile, have you heard of it? I hadn't. Yes, Reconcile. Something to do with refugees, or political prisoners. Do you know anything about it?'

I straightened up, and pretended to think about it. I was fairly sure I had never heard of Reconcile, but I didn't want to seem unfriendly; I like Jane Laverton.

'Reconcile? No, I don't think so.'

'No, odd, that. I thought I knew most of the charities. Yes, Clive says there are thousands of them and most of them are tax dodges, but he would, he's a cynical rat as well as a lousy driver. Yes. I could shoot him for smashing up the trailer, it's a complete write-off, and it wasn't even insured. Thank God there weren't any horses in it.'

Everybody wanted to know about the Children of God, and few of them were as honest about their curiosity as Jane Laverton. Most people assumed that, because I rode in the park, I must know what they were doing, but apart from the man who had opened the door, not one of them had ever spoken to me. When I was asked, I said they were clearing the land, taking out the dead wood and the brambles, working in the gardens, mending hedges and walls, and cleaning and repairing the house. That was, quite truly, all I knew, all I'd seen. Nobody seemed to believe me.

In the eyes of the Children of God, I was an intruder, an unwelcome trespasser they had to endure. Of all the people in the village, I was the last to whom they would willingly speak.

I saw no signs of any religious activity, none of them wore crucifixes or amulets that I could see, when I heard them singing in the distance it seemed to be folk songs. I heard no hymns or psalms that I could recognise. When they called to each other their voices sounded friendly, and I sometimes heard laughter.

Lyric seemed nervous in their presence, but I think that was because I was uneasy, and Plod never passed them without growling, his hackles raised and his lips curled up over his teeth.

There was nothing I could complain about. Since they'd received my letter nobody had tried to prevent me riding in the park, and they were under no obligation to welcome me. If I enjoyed my rides less now than I had when the manor house stood empty, there was nothing I could do about it. If, when I encountered the Children of God, I felt uneasy, felt their hostility as clearly as did my dog and my horse, my options were clear; I could stay out of the park, or I could ride in it, and try to ignore them.

In November, a letter arrived from an estate agent in Gloucester, Fletcher and Agnes, a small company that sometimes handled sales in the village. The letter said that the company was acting for a third party, who wished to buy the forge, the cottage, and the land that went with them. The offer was for fifty thousand pounds.

I was surprised at the amount, nearly a third higher than the last offer Uncle John had received shortly after Uncle Henry's death. I wrote back to the agent, saying I wasn't interested in selling. Almost by return of post, another letter arrived, increasing the offer to seventy thousand.

This time when I replied, I explained that I'd inherited the forge on condition that I did not sell it until I was thirty, that I was at that time only twenty six, and that in any case I had no intention of selling.

I thought that would be the last I would hear, but within a week there was a third letter. His clients, wrote Mr Agnes, would be prepared to pay thirty thousand pounds for an option to purchase the forge for a further seventy thousand pounds in four years' time. There was one condition.

The right to ride through Gorsedown Manor lands would be forfeited upon receipt of the thirty thousand pounds.

8

'It's a lot more than it's worth,' said Uncle John when I telephoned him. 'Thirty thousand to give up the right to ride in the park? It's an extraordinary offer. What do you want to do?'

'Can I sell it?'

'Oh, yes. You can sell anything except the freehold. We didn't mention the assets, it would have been too complicated. It might have caused difficulties in letting machinery go in part exchange when you bought something new. Do you want to sell?'

'I don't know. I just wanted to know if I could, before I even start to think about it.'

I didn't need any more money. Many people would have regarded that statement as a vicious heresy, I know, but I had enough. I lived where I wanted to live, did what I wanted to do, paid my own way, and had enough to keep myself free of financial anxiety. What, I asked myself, would I do with thirty thousand pounds?

It was quite clear that the Children of God were

behind the offer, and I was fairly sure I could reach an agreement to sell the right to ride in the park without committing myself to selling the forge later. All they wanted was complete privacy, and it seemed they saw my rides through their land as an invasion of that privacy.

Earlier, I'd telephoned Peter Gadd, Jane Laverton's friend whose company had handled the sale, and asked him about Gorsedown Manor. He'd been quite happy to tell me about it.

'Actually, it was exactly what they were looking for,' he said. 'They wanted a big house, lots of land and no rights of way, condition immaterial. Lots of houses like that around, of course, but the rights of way made a problem. Four or five square miles without a single public footpath, actually you'd probably have to go to Scotland and the trespass laws are even more complicated there.'

'Money no object?' I asked.

'Ah, no, sorry, that's confidential.'

'What about King Henry's Deed?'

'Yes.' He sounded a little defensive. 'Well, it isn't a listed right of way, of course. Actually, we didn't know about it. It's one of those blasted one-off things that plague the business. They did contact us a few weeks ago, rather annoyed, you know. But what can one do? I mean, it's hardly turned the park into a tripper route, has it?'

It wasn't through Peter Gadd's company that the Children of God were trying to persuade me to sell the forge. It seemed they'd lost the account. I wondered if they knew.

By then, I was beginning to feel thoroughly resentful of the Children of God. I didn't want their money, I wanted to ride in the park in peace. If I gave up the park, I'd have to sell Lyric. She was too unpredictable, too difficult to control, for me to be able to ride her safely anywhere else. I liked my horse, I even liked the way she ran away with me at any opportunity; it added the spice of risk to our rides. But running away in the park, with miles of safe countryside in every direction, and running away on farmland, where I might encounter barbed wire fences, grazing cattle, and even busy roads, were two completely different matters. Quite simply, I couldn't risk riding her anywhere other than in the park. I'd have to sell her, and either give up riding, or buy something boring, like the skewbald cob.

I shrugged away the idea irritably, picked up the telephone and dialled my suppliers with an order for some horseshoes. After that I listened to the messages on my answering machine. That machine was an investment Glory had persuaded me into making, and I'd never regretted it, even though it had been expensive, and some of my customers still didn't seem to understand it was a machine they were talking to. Almost everybody seemed to assume I was available day and night for their horses, and I saw no reason why it should be true. But I did telephone Jake Brewer to ask after one of his point-to-pointers who had developed ringbone. He sounded depressed.

'My own bloody fault,' he said. 'I didn't rest him long enough after that fall. Shit. Did you know Ashlands is going to be built over next year? Bloody executive housing estates, one of the best rides in the county going under concrete. Where the hell am I going to train my eventers now? You don't know how lucky you are, having Gorsedown Park.'

I telephoned Sir Robert. Blackie had loosened his funny old high-heeled shoe again according to my answerphone, and needed, as always, immediate and urgent attention. In fact the old horse was perfectly all right unshod for a day or so, it was Sir Robert who became fretful and querulous. He, too, was unhappy.

'Lizzie's dead,' he said sadly. 'Laminitis came back, poor old girl. That vet chappie said better make an end. Right, of course. Still, sad. Blackie misses her.'

'I'm sorry,' I said, and I meant it.

'Well, never mind. Right, Stephens and Blackie at your place tomorrow, ten o'clock. Fine, thank you, dear lady. How's the dear dog?'

'He's well, thank you.'

'Always looks fit, the dear chap. Must be those runs through the park. Wonderful place for a dog.'

I took out my typewriter, and wrote a letter to Mr Agnes of Fletcher and Agnes Ltd., Estate Agents. It was a very pompous letter, and it said that I was not interested in selling any of the rights of the forge, and that this correspondence must cease. A carbon copy was sent to Dr John Mayall, LL.D., Messrs Freyer and Mayall, Solicitors, Holborn. Then I walked down to the village post office and sent it off by registered post.

I saddled Lyric, and rode into the park. She was fresh, and the wind was cold. As a result, she got away from me almost immediately, and we covered two miles at a thrashing gallop before I managed to bring her under control. I was laughing with exhilaration, and we were both plastered with mud, and breathless. Nothing, I thought, as I trotted her up the rising ground towards the beech trees, could compensate for this, no money in the world could buy what I already had. Bloody awful rider I might be, as Jake said, but here I could ride my lovely racehorse, and it didn't matter that I looked like a sack of saddles with elbows in all directions, it was nobody's business but my own.

I turned her at the crest of the hill and looked across the misty valley at the big grey house. I would not be turned off this land by the Children of God, would not be tempted by their money nor intimidated by their hostility, nor would I leave the forge, the only place where I had ever been loved, my home, where I could stand up straight and not mind how tall I was.

I watched Plod galloping into view, his nose low to the ground as he followed our tracks, and I stood up in the stirrups and called to him. He raised his head, and turned off the trail to cut across the grass towards us, his tail high and waving and his thick, shining coat rippling in the wind.

I would ignore the Children of God, and enjoy the company of the two animals. I would not nod to them as we passed, I would either look straight ahead or stare back at them, and damn them all.

Lyric bent her head and snorted at Plod as he reached us, and he responded with the snuffling half-bark he reserved for friends, panting happily and wagging his tail, before jumping up at me and licking my boot.

I was too busy to ride much in the next few weeks. One of the racehorse trainers just outside Gloucester had been reckless enough to sack his farrier without finding a replacement first, and, according to one of the lads who brought me my first consignment of hurdlers at five o'clock in the morning to fit them with racing plates on their way to Plumpton, no amount of apologies and grovelling was tempting the affronted craftsman back. Jake Brewer, a minor rival, had given me advance warning.

'Ulverton, his name is,' he said. 'Make the bugger come to you, don't relax your rules. He's a sod, but he's got good horses, damn his eyes. If Brass Rags goes lame before Cheltenham, I'll give you a hundred quid.'

I laughed, but there'd been some bitterness in Jake's voice. One of his horses had had to be taken out of a good race that week because the farrier had driven a nail in crookedly, and he'd suspected it had been no accident. It wouldn't have been the first time such things had happened.

Ulverton telephoned within half an hour of Jake's warning call, his tone hectoring.

'I'll expect you tomorrow morning at eight sharp,' he said, after the briefest of introductions. 'Don't be late.

Four sets of racing plates for Saturday, we'll look at the others when you get here.'

'I don't travel,' I said. 'I only work here.'

'Rubbish! This is a racing stable, smiths come to us, how the hell do you think I can manage, bringing horses to you? No racing stable takes horses to the smith.'

There was a long silence.

'Well?' he demanded.

'I'm sorry, Mr Ulverton. I don't travel.'

'Bloody hell!' he yelled, and slammed down the telephone.

He was back on the line a quarter of an hour later.

'If one of my lads picks you up and takes you home afterwards,' he said. 'How about that?'

'No. I'm sorry.'

'But why not? I've got thirty horses in training here, I pay my bills, I'm a bloody good customer. For God's sake, woman, I'll pay your travelling costs, time, mileage, whatever, come by blasted taxi if you like, just get here.'

'I only work here. I'm sorry.'

'God *damn* it!'

Once again, the telephone was slammed down. I wondered how often he broke them.

The next time, it was his travelling lad who spoke to me, amused, and with a Welsh accent.

'Can you be up at five o'clock in the morning?' he asked.

'Yes.'

'Good. There'll be four hurdlers turning up for their

early morning cups of tea and their running shoes the day after tomorrow. You be ready, now.'

I was ready, the yard lights switched on and the forge fire roaring. The horse-box swung into the yard, followed by a big Jaguar, and Ulverton jumped out of it and began issuing orders.

'This is ridiculous!' he snapped at me. 'What sort of preparation is this for a day's racing, in and out of horse-boxes on the way? Just get on with it, don't just stand there gawping, woman! I don't want them standing around in the cold.'

The first of the hurdlers was still being led down the ramp, the lad crooning into his ear, his breath steaming in the frosty air.

It was awkward, shoeing the horses with their travelling bandages on, it made their fetlocks stiff, but I managed. Two of the sets of plates were dangerously thin, the edges sharp. I hoped no jockey would be unfortunate enough to be kicked or trodden on by either of the horses wearing them. I pointed them out to Ulverton, who snorted, and told me to get on with my job before the bloody horses got frostbite.

When I finished the last horse, it was the travelling lad, Alec, who thanked me, and asked if they could call in on their way back for the working shoes to be replaced. Surprised, I agreed, and he smiled. Ulverton was already climbing into his car.

'He's not a bad trainer,' said Alec, following my gaze. 'Regrets half of what he says as soon as he's said it, but I don't know of anything he's regretted more than sacking Forbes. I'll be bringing a few horses next week, but, mind, you won't keep this job once he finds a farrier who'll come to him, so don't go counting any chickens.'

They came back late that evening, happy and smiling. A win and a second, they announced, as they led their tired charges down the ramp, and no falls. A good meeting, no injured horses, happy sponsors and the bookmakers thrashed. There was laughter and ribald jokes between the lads, and even Ulverton was grinning.

One of the thin plates fell in two pieces onto the concrete as I levered it off the horse's hoof. I looked up at Ulverton.

'Lucky it didn't turn,' I said.

'If it's nailed on properly, it won't turn.'

'Lucky I'm a good farrier, then.' I refused to drop my eyes, and he nodded.

'All right, throw those two sets out. Monday morning, ten sharp, there'll be four horses here, plus any that cast shoes in the meantime.'

I couldn't check the horses' legs through their bandages, but I'd looked closely at their feet and felt carefully for heat in their fetlocks. Ulverton had watched me, a half-smile on his face. The horses were as they should be after a day's racing, tired but sound.

When I went into the forge to put away my tools I found a bottle of beer on the anvil, with a note. I was to drink the healths of Pancake and Diskus Thrower, as well as that of the jockey, Tony Ridger, who'd ridden them both. It was a friendly gesture, and I appreciated it.

For the next four weeks until after Christmas almost every day brought some of the horses from Ulverton's yard to the forge, for cast shoes to be replaced, racing plates to be fitted or removed, as well as routine shoeing. It was good to be dealing with racehorses again. On New Year's Eve the head lad telephoned to ask me yet again if I wouldn't reconsider travelling to the yard, and when I said no I heard him sigh.

'Sorry, then. Forbes has agreed to come back.'

I'd known Ulverton would eventually find a smith who'd travel to his yard, even if the self-righteously indignant Neil Forbes had continued to refuse to work for him. I had come to know most of the lads, and at the forge we got on quite well, but I still didn't want to work on somebody else's land. Somehow, I could cope with the initial startled glances, and even the odd sniggering whisper behind my back, if I was at home, while those same glances and whispers anywhere else made me cringe. If I went to Ulverton's yard I might find myself travelling to the riding school, or the dude ranch, and I remembered from my days with Peter Andrews how much I'd hated such places.

Ulverton himself telephoned later to tell me about Forbes, and to thank me for the work I'd done.

'We might still send Trafalgar to you,' he added, and we both laughed. Trafalgar was a steeplechaser who'd three times managed to get his teeth to my shoulder. Luckily, I'd been wearing my thick padded jacket, but he'd still left bruises. He wasn't even a good jumper, he fell on average once in every four races, so he was nobody's favourite. But I would be sorry to go back to the hunters and the ponies after the racehorses.

I took Lyric and Plod into the park that afternoon, taking a few hours off from my work as I knew I'd have time to catch up on it the following day, with Ulverton not bringing any more horses. Lyric was stiff and stuffy after a long time with too little exercise; I felt guilty for having neglected her. Plod ran happily through the woods, nose to the ground, searching for rabbits and setting off in pursuit when he found one. In the distance, I could hear the Children of God calling to each other, and a voice raised in song. I turned eastwards to ride along the southern boundary in order to avoid them.

Lyric moved sluggishly, her head low, the mud sucking at her hooves. It had been a wet December, and the ground was waterlogged. It began to rain, slowly and steadily under the low grey sky, the heavy drops splashing into the deep puddles on the track, turning them a dirty yellow from the rutted clay. I turned up my collar, wondering whether to turn back. I quite like the rain, but Lyric was clearly not enjoying our ride, labouring through the mud, her ears low. She was dispirited, hating the weather.

It began to rain harder, straight into our faces, and I ducked my head to try to keep it out of my eyes. Neither Lyric nor I saw the log, half-submerged in the mud, and when she stumbled over it, her shoulder dropping, I was taken completely by surprise, and fell off, landing on my back in six inches of filthy rainwater and clay.

I clambered to my feet, swearing, feeling the cold water soaking through my clothes and running down my legs into my boots. Lyric stood with her head low, sullen and miserable, her mane plastered to her wet neck, rainwater streaming down her face.

It was then I heard laughter, high and delighted, an exuberant giggling and chuckling interspersed with whoops of indrawn breath. I looked around, and saw a tall black woman standing on the bank under an oak tree, her head thrown back in uninhibited joy, her body shaking with laughter.

'Oh, I sorry!' she gasped at last, wiping tears from her eyes, her white teeth brilliant against her black skin. 'Oh, but that *so funny*! You coming down that path, all grumbling and muttering, and then next moment, splat! You lying in the mud like a great big beetle, you arms and legs waving, and that *swearing*! Ain't like no beetle I ever heard before.'

I smiled politely, feeling she was overreacting, and that set her going again, whooping and giggling, until at last she collapsed against the tree and slid down it to sit on the root, gasping helplessly, tears of delight running down her cheeks.

'Oh, I sorry!' she said again. 'You all right? You not hurt?'

'Wet,' I said, and she laughed again, dropping her face into her hands, her shoulders shaking.

Plod galloped up through the trees, attracted by the sound of our voices, and stood looking at us, water dripping from his coat. He had obviously been swimming in the pond. After a moment's hesitation he trotted over to the laughing woman and sniffed at her. Startled, she jumped to her feet, and then Plod began to shake the water out of his thick pelt, great sheets of spray flying off his coat. She screamed, tried to push him away, and then flapped her hands, ineffectually trying to shield herself from the dirty water that was soaking into her clothes.

'Go *away*!' she shrieked. 'Stupid great dog, get away from me! *Look* at my skirt now, stupid animal!'

She ducked behind the tree, and Plod followed, wagging his tail, ready for a game. As she shouted at him and tried to push him away he jumped up at her, and she slipped, and slid down the bank to land at the bottom splattered with mud and furiously indignant. I began to laugh.

'What you laughing at?' she demanded. 'This your dog? Look at my clothes!'

And then suddenly she fell back against the bank, once again whooping with laughter, rolling around in the mud hugging herself with glee.

At last she got herself under control, although every time she looked at me she had to struggle not to laugh again. We were both soaked with rainwater and mud, and the wind was getting up. She began to shiver.

'Oh, my!' she said. 'I don't get out these wet clothes I get pneumonia.'

'Are you trespassing?' I asked.

'No! Are you?'

'You're not one of the Children of God?'

'No. We just staying with them.'

It was nearly three miles to the house from there, less than half that distance to the forge.

'You'd better come home with me, and get dry.'

She nodded, and we set off down the track, me leading Lyric. The mud was deep and sticky, and at my suggestion she took hold of one of the stirrup leathers to help herself along.

'You must be the godless blacksmith woman,' she said, glinting at me mischievously. 'We been told not to speak to you. So you take note of this, I not speaking to you, I talking to your horse. Okay?'

'Okay,' I said. 'Her name's Lyric.'

'Well, hello Lyric, and thank you for your help through this rotten English mud, what's a nice lady like you doing in a dump like this? My name's Emily Peters and I come from Liberia, and I do *not* like your English weather. What you got to say to that?'

We reached the forge about twenty minutes later, squelching slowly through the clinging mud. Emily, on the way, had told Lyric that she was a doctor, and a refugee, and had been in England for about six months. She was by then shivering quite badly from the cold, so I showed her into the cottage and ran hot water for a bath, leaving her to herself while I dealt with Lyric and Plod. When I went back into the cottage she was sitting in front of the fire in the living room wrapped in a towel.

'You still in those wet clothes?' she demanded. 'You a damn hardy race, you imperialist slave-trading honkies.'

I grinned at her, dropped my jacket on the kitchen floor and kicked off my boots.

'Hot drink?' I asked.

'You get warm and dry first. I'm a doctor and that's an order. Bad enough you a godless heathen, without you being a *sick* godless heathen. And I can make tea, you get dry.'

'You're talking to me,' I commented as I went upstairs to the bathroom. 'That's forbidden.'

'That's true enough,' she called up after me. 'You get good and dry now, you hear?'

I heard her, busy in the kitchen, as I had a bath and dressed in dry clothes, wondering as I did so what I could give her to wear. She was quite tall, but still she only came up to my shoulder, and she was slim, with narrow hips and a neat, supple waist. I took her a thick towelling dressing gown, and she gave me a friendly grin and dropped the bath towel on the kitchen floor before slipping into it. It almost swamped her, but she rolled up the sleeves and went on stirring a pot on the cooker. Something smelt of beef and spices. There were jars and packets scattered around the kitchen, long-forgotten oddments dug out from the backs of cupboards, and the lid of the freezer stood open. Emily's idea of tea was making my mouth water.

I took her clothes out to the forge and hung them on a line there; they would dry quickly, and then the worst of the mud could be brushed off. They were good quality clothes, but old, a heavy printed cotton skirt, a thick Arran sweater and very clean white cotton underwear that smelt faintly of sweat and lavender.

We sat in front of the fire and ate the spicy beef broth

she had made. There was only one armchair, deep and comfortable, with the leather worn thin on the arms, that had been Uncle Henry's, and I sat in that. Emily seemed happy and comfortable on the padded footstool, wriggling her bare toes in the sheepskin hearthrug. I realised to my surprise that I was happy to have her there, in my home; usually, I tried to avoid inviting any-body into the cottage.

She talked a lot. She had a squeaky voice and an accent that I sometimes had difficulty in following, but I was content to listen to her, and to answer her questions when she asked any.

'We still on Gorsedown Manor lands?' she asked at one point, and I shook my head.

'No. This is Anford Forge. It's mine.'

She rolled her eyes, and grinned.

'Ooh, I'm breaking *so* many rules today! We supposed to stay on Manor lands, we not supposed to talk to strangers, we *particularly* not supposed to talk to you.'

'Why not?'

She shrugged.

'Holiday, religious retreat, sort of. We relax, we forget our troubles, we leave everything to the Children of God. We leave the world behind, outside the gates, and the world don't trouble us. Why do they say you a god-less woman? What they got against you?'

'They don't like me riding in the park. But I have a right to ride there, I won't give it up.'

'Tell me,' she commanded,.and so I explained about

147

King Henry's Deed, and the Children of God trying to buy the forge. She listened, her eyes round.

'Whee!' she exclaimed at the end. 'Lotta money! You sell, give me the money, I build a hospital in Maryland County.'

'Why are you a refugee?' I asked, and Emily laughed. Emily, I found, laughed at everything. Sadness, anger, even grief made her laugh.

'My father was a politician,' she said. 'Big man. Big, big man. Very important, you know? A political leader. But he quarrelled with an even bigger man in his party, and he left, and started up his own party. Same sort of thing, just different people, few policies changed, you know?'

'Splinter group?' I suggested.

'Right! Splinter group. So they shot him. They told him they going to kill him, and his whole family. They put a price on our heads, you want to earn big money, you go and kill a Peters. And they damned near done it too. They got him, and his brother, and my sister and my aunt, and they came looking for me.'

I stared at her, and she laughed again, a high, whining sort of laugh, grief and anger in it.

'Well, I don't want to get shot, so I ran to the Red Cross, and they put me on a ship and here I am. Maybe I'm the last, I don't know where my mother is, or my brother. Maybe they got them too.'

'Emily, that's horrible.'

'Yuh. Well, I got political asylum, at least, I hope I got political asylum. Up to the lawyers.'

'Do you need a lawyer, Emily? My uncle's a lawyer.'

She shook her head and grinned again.

'Reconcile, they got me a lawyer. They paid for him, too.'

Reconcile, I thought, and then remembered Jane Laverton had told me the Children of God had been collecting for a charity of that name.

'They sent me down here, too. Sometimes the Children of God, they help refugees, fix things up so they can go home again. That's what Reconcile does too, if they can.'

'Are they trying to do that for you?'

She shook her head emphatically.

'Me? No chance. How they going to do that? They going to speak to maybe two or three hundred gunmen? Tell them the price is off my head? How they going to find them all? How they going to *know* if they found them all? No chance. I'm staying here, I'm not going back. Maybe I can practise medicine here, too, if I can pass these exams. I hope so. You sick, or something? Maybe I can practise on you.'

And she threw back her head again, laughing at me.

It was almost like a shock when I realised that I had, at last, found a friend.

9

A week after Ulverton made his peace with the affronted smith, Forbes caught viral influenza. The head lad telephoned me on the Friday afternoon and told me, in his cheerful Welsh voice, that we were back in business, four sets of plates for the Saturday meeting at Hereford, they'd be with me at ten, it not being far to Hereford. I said I was glad to hear it, but in truth I'd been rather enjoying a slackening of the workload. Sighing, I buckled a New Zealand rug on Lyric and turned her out into the paddock; I wouldn't have time to give her enough exercise until Forbes recovered.

The next morning the familiar horse-box turned through the gates to the forge, bearing the dreaded Trafalgar as well as the pride of the stable, Brass Rags, and two of Ulverton's hurdlers. Trafalgar clattered down the ramp with his ears back, and swung his head at me, ears flattened and teeth bared, as his lad tied him to the iron ring.

'Does he ever kick you?' I asked, and the old man shook his head, sucking on the cigarette that was nearly always stuck to his lower lip.

'He sometimes,' he wheezed, 'kicks the place where I recently was.'

It seemed a good comment on his job, and on the expertise he brought to it. Ulverton, who'd arrived as usual in his Jaguar just behind the box, grinned appreciatively.

It was as I was taking the shoes off the second of the two hurdlers that I found the problem, heat in his knee, and a slight swelling.

'Trouble,' I said to Ulverton, and immediately he was beside me, hands probing gently.

'Oh shit!'

The travelling lad hurried up, ran a careful hand down the inside of the horse's knee, and looked up at Ulverton.

'Fred said he'd bumped it on Thursday,' he said. 'When Flight swerved, it threw him off line, he said he thought he'd knocked it on one of the uprights.'

'That's right, he did. It should've been spotted this morning, I'll crucify that girl.' Ulverton was exasperated. He straightened up, and looked at me, hopefully.

'He shouldn't travel far on that leg,' he said. 'Can we leave him here? Pick him up on our way home?'

I nodded. Lyric's box was free anyway, and it wasn't the first time I'd stabled his horses. He'd left two of them with me overnight only a fortnight earlier, during a busy week when he'd been short of transport, and he and the local horse-box hire firm had spent most of the day ferrying horses around the south of England.

We turned the hurdler into Lyric's stable, one of the lads staying behind to toss fresh straw onto the floor and fill buckets and hay nets, and the horse-box set off while Ulverton borrowed my telephone to contact the hurdler's owner, and the vet, who promised to call in during the morning. The lad fussed at me while waiting for Ulverton, telling me not to feed the horse chocolate or beer or he'd fail a dope test, and to put an extra rug on him if it got cold. I was used to the affection the men who worked with racehorses lavished on them, so I nodded, and agreed to do, or not do, everything he asked. He hovered at my elbow, wondering if he'd forgotten anything, until Ulverton came out of the cottage pulling on his gloves, and they set off on the trail of the horse-box.

I looked in on my visitor after I'd cleared up the yard and the forge. He was standing with his head over the door, watching for me as I turned the corner. I rubbed his ears and fed him half a carrot. He didn't seem to be favouring the injured knee.

The vet arrived quite early, saying he'd thought he might as well get this visit in before his usual rounds. I held the horse's head while he checked the knee. It was, he said, a bruise, needing rest, and perhaps cold compresses. There was no sign of anything worse, but I should tell Ulverton he'd X-ray it on the following Monday if it was still swollen. I promised to pass on his message. I padlocked the box door when we left;

customers did sometimes wander around, and children in particular were inclined to leave doors open.

It was a busy day. I had an order for four window grilles to finish that morning, and horses booked for shoeing in the afternoon. The riding school had taken to saving transport costs by getting the older children to ride the ponies to me on Saturday afternoons, something they were only too glad to do. On the whole, I wasn't very happy with the arrangement; not only do I not like children, shoeing half a dozen ponies takes time, and children get bored. That was when the giggling and the whispering started, and also the mischief. I found two of them in the hay store that afternoon, jumping around on the bales, not only breaking them up but dirtying them, too. I turned them out, telling them horses didn't like eating dirty food any more than they did. As I turned away, I heard one of them speak.

'Bloody great sow.'

'You,' I said, turning back to them, 'can both leave now. Go on, get off my land, and don't come back. You can walk. I'll telephone Miss Forrest and tell her to send somebody else for the ponies.'

I did telephone Miss Forrest, and she suggested I was overreacting. I was in no mood to argue the point, and quite angry enough to risk losing her custom.

'No more unsupervised children,' I said.

'Honestly, Miss Mayall, if I didn't think they were capable of handling the ponies I wouldn't . . .'

'I'm not arguing, Miss Forrest. They're spoilt, arrogant and insufferably rude. No more unsupervised children.

And please send somebody to collect the two that Samantha and Tamsin were riding.'

'There are other farriers, you know.'

'Good,' I retorted. 'Find one.'

I suspect she spent the next half-hour trying. I told the other children to take the ponies into the stable yard while I shod a hack for a nice woman who'd asked if I could fit her in that afternoon. They looked surprised, and one of them remarked that they'd been there first, but they led the ponies into the yard, talking in their loud, bored voices, and slapping at their boots with their crops. I started work on the hack, and one of them came back again.

'Did you know that the horse in Lyric's box isn't Lyric?' she demanded.

'Yes.'

'It isn't even a mare, you know. It's a gelding.'

'I know.'

'Oh, well. I just thought I ought to tell you.'

She waited for a response, and when I didn't reply, sighed heavily, and walked off.

'Who are they?' asked the woman.

'Riding school brats.'

'And Lyric?' asked the woman, after a pause.

'My horse.' I felt I was being rude, so I looked up and smiled at her. 'She's in the paddock, I haven't got enough time to exercise her at the moment. There's a lame hurdler in the box, he comes from Kingsdown. I think he's called Fools Gold.'

She smiled back, and made a comment about the

damned silly names racehorses were given.

Miss Forrest telephoned as I finished.

'Would you please tell Jennifer to ride Shadow and lead Mischief, and Petra to ride Kerry and lead Pablo. Paul can ride Donny and Sally can ride Prince. Samantha and Tamsin have just got back, they're both very upset and Tamsin's got a blister.'

'Right,' I said. 'I'll get started, then.'

'Haven't you done them yet?'

'I thought you were looking for another smith.'

'Oh, really! Do, please, hurry.'

Emily arrived just as they were leaving. I was very pleased to see her. She was wrapped in a heavy cloak in dark red wool, and she looked warm and exotic, and mischievous.

'I sneaked off,' she said, in her high, squeaky voice, grinning at me. 'Am I welcome?'

'Always,' I said. 'I'm busy, you don't mind? I'll have to work.'

She shook her head.

'Can I help? I better not be standing out here, the Children of God might see.'

I picked up the tools and took them into the forge. Emily followed, looking around curiously, and then went to stand beside the forge. The firelight flickered on her face, making her eyes and teeth gleam. I started to clean the tools, and she watched.

'What would the Children of God do if they knew you were here?' I asked.

'Oh, I don't suppose they do anything. It's just, they

my hosts, you know? They say don't go in the garden, tread on the dug-over earth, I don't go. Stay on Manor lands, I stay. Don't go into the chapel, I don't go. Don't talk to heathen blacksmith, I think, you go to hell, I talk to whoever I like.'

I laughed.

'But I don't rub they noses in it, you understand? So, better I stay in here, or in the cottage maybe. Not outside. Besides, it's still your rotten English winter and I hate it. What you doing?'

I was spraying the hoof knife and the rasp with disinfectant. I'd never bothered to disinfect my tools before Ulverton started bringing his horses, but he was paranoid about infection, and it did no harm. I washed down the concrete outside the forge where the horses stood every afternoon as well. I told Emily about it, and she was interested.

'Do you like horses?' I asked her.

'Don't know much about them. I suppose so. Where's that dog?'

'In the workshop. Children keep messing him about, I lock him in there when those brats come.'

I opened the door to the workshop, and Plod came through into the forge, wagging his tail at the sight of Emily. She patted him, smiling. I looked past them through the door, wondering how long it would be before Ulverton turned up for the hurdler, and whether I should feed his horse or leave it to him. Jake Brewer was supposed to be sending three hunters, and he was late. Lyric needed a feed as well, and it was beginning to get dark.

Plod lifted his head, and a moment later I heard a horse-box. Emily glanced over to the door, and stepped back into the shadows. I smiled at her, and she grinned back. Apart from her teeth, she was invisible.

Two of the horses Jake had sent were thoroughly awkward, one badly trained and fidgety and the other a sour tempered mare who bit if she wasn't tied up tightly and kicked if she was. I sighed when I saw them, knowing I was in for a difficult time, and hoping I'd have them finished before Ulverton turned up. I put Plod back in the workshop, and he threw a reproachful glance at me over his shoulder as I shut the door; he'd been locked up for most of the afternoon, and he didn't like it. Toby, the groom, started to lead the mare down the ramp, calling to me to ask if the dog was safely out of the way. He tied the horse to the ring, and I bent down, warily, and lifted her foot, watching for her teeth.

I'd just started work on the second horse when Plod barked. I stopped and listened; he barked again, and then started baying, angry and alarmed, and I heard a clatter as he knocked some tools off the work-bench, his feet scrabbling at the door. The horse threw up his head, and Toby swore, reaching for his head collar and speaking soothingly. I started for the workshop door, dropping the pincers on the ground and running across the forge. Plod sounded frantic with rage, there were crashing sounds from the workshop, he was on the bench, trying to force his way out through the window.

As I reached the door, I heard the high, shrill scream of a horse.

For a moment I stopped, shocked into immobility by the dreadful sound, and then I heard hooves clattering in the stable and the noise galvanised me into action again. I ran through the workshop, stumbling over the tools the dog had knocked onto the floor, kicking them aside as I slammed the bolts free from the door and turned the key in the lock. Plod flew past me as I stepped into the stable yard, and I flicked on the lights and ran towards the loose box.

There was blood on the concrete, a huge pool of it, and blood down the front of the door, black against the light wood. There were thudding noises from the box, and the loud, dead thump of a falling body, a clatter of hooves against the wall, and a terrible rasping gurgling.

Ulverton's hurdler lay on the straw, shuddering as he died, his ribs heaving under his bloodsoaked rug. There was blood everywhere in the box, gouts of it splashed over the walls, the straw wet and crimson, pools of blood running together on the brick floor by the door. I could even hear it, trickling and dripping, over the sound of the horse's agonised fight for breath, and then suddenly he was still, and I saw, where he lay stretched out, the gaping wound in his throat.

'Oh, my God!' Toby was beside me, staring wide-eyed at the carnage in the loose box, his face growing pale.

'Oh, Miss! Your lovely horse, somebody's cut her throat.'

I whirled away from the box and screamed.

'Plod! *Plod, come here*!'

Emily came out of the workshop, her eyes huge and rolling in her dark face.

'Ann? Can I help?'

'Oh, no. Oh, Plod, *please, Plod, come here!*'

Toby was scrabbling at the door in his haste to reach the dead horse, not even noticing the padlock.

'Let the dog have the bastard, Miss! I hope he kills him!'

'The bastard's got a knife. *Plod!*'

And then he was there, trotting out of the evening darkness into the lights of the yard, sniffing at the blood, whining, uneasy and distressed, and I was on my knees holding out my arms to him, and he snuffled at me and licked my face.

Emily walked past me to the box, her hand touching my head lightly as I hugged my dog, and looked over the door.

'Oh, no. Oh, poor Lyric.'

I stood up, and turned towards them.

'It's not Lyric. It's one of Mr Ulverton's hurdlers.'

Toby looked at me, aghast.

'Oh, no, Miss! It's not Brass Rags, is it?'

'No. No, I think he's called Fools Gold. A hurdler, he'd hurt his knee, you see, and . . .'

'Hadn't we better call the police?'

Emily's voice was calm and gentle, the voice of reason in a scene of horror.

'Oh, yes. Yes of course, we must.'

'We can't do anything here, Miss. Come on, come away now.'

I looked again over the door at the ugly carcass that had only minutes earlier been a splendid living animal, and then followed Toby and Emily away, by the stable path towards the cottage.

I telephoned the emergency services, and told the police what had happened. They would send somebody as soon as they could.

The hunter was still tied to the ring, his head high, eyes rolling uneasily. He snorted as we approached and tried to back away, the rope tight. Toby spoke soothingly, and held out his hand to stop us. The horse jerked his head from side to side, tugging, trying to get free.

'Don't move, Miss, please. We can't get near him like this, we stink of blood. He'll break that rope in a minute.'

It was then that Ulverton's Jaguar rolled in through the gates and drew up on the gravel in front of the cottage. Ulverton climbed out, looking at us enquiringly, the expression on his face sharpening as he saw the blood.

'What's happened?' he asked. 'Is somebody hurt?'

'Your horse,' I said. 'Somebody's killed him. Just now, somebody cut his throat.'

He stared at me in disbelief, and then Toby spoke.

'It's true, Mr Ulverton, sir. He's dead, his throat's cut. Miss Mayall's just called the police. They're sending someone.'

Ulverton seemed dazed. He looked at us, from one shocked face to the other, bent and patted Plod, turned to look at his car, then at the frightened hunter still backed away to the full length of the rope.

'Killed him?' he said at last. 'Killed him? Who killed him? Why?'

I felt sick. The stench of the blood was thick in my nostrils, we were sticky and drenched with it where we had leaned against the door of the box, staring in at the murdered horse. I began to shiver, and Emily laid a hand on my arm.

'Mr Ulverton,' she said, 'please, we all go into the cottage. You all shocked, you need hot tea. I'll make it, Ann and Toby have to get out of these clothes, they filthy with blood. Please, Mr Ulverton, come into the cottage now. We can't do anything here, we frightening that horse.'

It was the last few words that got through to Ulverton. He looked at the hunter, and spoke to him calmly, and the horse's ears flicked towards him, wary, but looking for reassurance.

'One of his shoes is half off,' I said wearily. 'I can't leave it like that, I'll just get changed, I'll finish him then.'

The blood had soaked right through to my skin. Shuddering, I ran up the stairs to the bathroom, tore off all my clothes and stood under the shower, scrubbing it off, feeling revulsion and rage and sorrow. I heard Ulverton's horse-box arrive, heard voices raised, running footsteps, a shout of anger and disbelief.

I left everything to Emily, calm and assured, the doctor taking over, dispensing mugs of hot tea, telling angry men to sit down, be quiet, wait for the police. Toby had changed out of his blood-soaked clothes into jeans and a sweater from one of the lockers in Ulverton's horse-box. He and I went out to see to the hunter.

There was nothing I could do, I told myself, angrily, nothing I could have done. I bent to my work again, levering the ends of the nails free of the walls of the hoof, clipping them off, easing the shoe free, laying it down quietly so as not to startle the nervous horse, cutting the grown wall of the hoof back with the knife, rasping it flat and even, moving on to the next foot, carrying out the familiar routines automatically, yet with concentration, keeping myself occupied.

'I can bring them back tomorrow, Miss,' said Toby, but I shook my head. I was happier outside, working with the horses, than in the crowded cottage, in the little living room that had been invaded by shocked and angry men. Toby watched me, hissing soothingly through his teeth to the horse. I heated the shoes, clenched them against the hooves, cooled them in the trough, nailed them into place, turned over the nails, rasped them flat, and rubbed over the hooves with oil. Toby asked if I wanted to shoe the third horse, and I nodded. There was still no sign of the police.

Alec, Ulverton's travelling lad came out to see me, his face twisted with regret over the dead horse, and stayed to help. Like me, he was happier with horses than with people.

'Useless old bugger, he was,' he said miserably. 'Still, he didn't deserve that. Poor old sod.'

Toby swept up the used nails and the hoof clippings behind me, still hissing quietly at the horse. Alec wandered away, back to his own horse-box, climbing in through the groom's door to check on the three racehorses. Ulverton came out of the cottage and stood on the path, stamping irritably and looking around.

'Where the hell are the bloody police?'

The smell of smoke and burning hoof as I held the hot shoe in place, and the horse snorting quietly. Plod, still restless and uneasy, whimpering from his blanket in the corner of the forge. Alec's boots crunching on the gravel as he jumped down from the box. Voices from the open door of the cottage, Emily silhouetted against the yellow light in the window, the sudden roar of the forge as Toby pumped the great bellows, a hiss from the trough as I dropped the hot shoe into the water.

The other two lads wandered out into the yard, and stood kicking at the gravel, disconsolate and angry.

It was dark, and getting cold. I wanted to bring Lyric in, and now there was nowhere I could stable her. It was another anxious worry.

Toby led the last of Jake's horses back into the box, and I helped him bolt the sides and the ramp into place. He was subdued, depressed by the death of the horse and the way it had happened.

'Toby,' I said suddenly, 'would Jake take Lyric for me for tonight? I've got nowhere to put her now, and it's cold.'

His face brightened, and he nodded.

'Sure he would!' he said. '*Course* he would, he'd be glad to. You go and catch her.'

'*No!*'

Alec's voice was sharp, and we looked at him in surprise, Toby's hand still raised to the bolts on the ramp, the two lads staring. Alec looked around at us.

'There's a maniac with a knife around,' he said. 'We'll go and get your horse. Nobody goes out there alone. You go and have your cup of tea, Miss Mayall, we'll catch the horse.'

I went into the cottage. Emily smiled at me, and nodded questioningly towards the teapot.

'Whisky,' I said, and she pulled a face, but shrugged.

Ulverton was on the telephone, arguing, stamping his feet with impatience. As I walked through the door he slammed it down, swearing, and turned towards me.

'Bloody impossible! They're going to be another hour at least.'

'Saturday evening,' I said tiredly.

'Drunks and football hooligans. Sod them, let them sort themselves out, stupid bastards. Who killed my poor bloody horse? What am I going to tell the owner? Oh, shit. Where's Alec?'

I told him about Lyric, and he nodded, satisfied. Horses came first, last, and everywhere in between with him. I poured him a whisky, and he swallowed it and held out his glass for a refill.

'I could do your horses while we're waiting,' I said as I poured it. 'That is, if you'd like me to.'

'Yes, good idea, might as well, better than doing nothing. They could go on home then.'

There was the sound of hooves on the gravel, and Ulverton, restless, stepped over to the window and watched as Alec and Toby loaded Lyric into Jake's horse-box.

'I'm so sorry this happened,' I said. 'So sorry.'

He turned and stared at me.

'My dear girl, nobody's blaming you!' he exclaimed. 'Good God, woman, what could you have done? Come on, let's get my horses back into their carpet slippers before those blasted woodentops turn up.'

10

By the time the police arrived, nearly four hours after my first call, both Toby and Alec had left to take their horses home, Toby saying he'd return if necessary. Emily, too, had gone, silently, but obviously hoping she wouldn't be needed. I was puzzled; in many ways she seemed so confident, but somehow the idea of offending the Children of God worried her.

There were two detectives, and it was fairly obvious from the outset that they had more important things on their minds than a dead horse. They stepped out of an anonymous car, unremarkable middle-aged men in unremarkable grey suits, going through the routine. When Ulverton complained about the delay the senior man, who introduced himself as Detective Sergeant Royce, said they'd had an attempted murder and two muggings that evening, and had to deal with calls in some sort of priority.

I told them what had happened, and showed them the stable. They walked through the paddock and shone their torches on the gate, and on the mud around it, churned up by Lyric's hooves, and by footprints that, I agreed, might well be mine, or those of the children from the riding school. We went back to the stable, where they glanced over the half-door at the dead horse, and said we could arrange for it to be removed. Ulverton, scandalised, asked if they weren't going to search for fingerprints, and Royce replied that none of the surfaces were suitable, brick and rough, painted wood didn't yield good prints. The second man, Detective Constable Irons, fingered the padlock and asked how the intruder had got in if the door had been locked.

'The horse would have had his head over it,' replied Ulverton.

It was this that had haunted me since I had heard that shrill scream, the picture of the horse's head turned to the sound of my approaching footsteps, his friendly enquiring face as I came up and gave him a piece of carrot. He would have met his killer in the same way, trusting the human smell, and his trust had been rewarded with a knife. I very much wanted whoever had done this to be caught.

Back in the cottage, Irons produced a notebook and asked who owned the horse. Ulverton answered their questions, his voice shaking with rage at their lack of concern. I stood at the window, looking out into the deserted yard, wondering how to arrange for the removal of the carcass, which was already stiffening, and would probably be impossible to manoeuvre through the door by morning. I glanced back at Ulverton in surprise when he said the horse was called Rivet, and Royce noticed, and looked at me.

'Miss Mayall?'

'It's nothing,' I said. 'It's just I thought it was Fools Gold.'

'No disrespect to you, Ann,' said Ulverton, 'but I wouldn't have left Fools Gold here.'

'And why's that, sir?' asked Royce.

'He's one of my best horses. He's got a chance in the Champion Hurdle at Cheltenham. He's owned by Sir Roland Southerdon.'

The two policemen exchanged glances, and Irons turned a page of his notebook.

'Just how much would the horses be worth, sir?' asked Royce.

'Rivet? Not a lot, I'll have to look up his insurance.'

'And Fools Gold?'

'Nothing,' said Ulverton vehemently, 'would induce his owner to sell him. He's insured for twenty five thousand, if it means anything, and that's well under his value. Are you going to try to catch this bastard? Or are we all just putting a polite face over a complete and farcical waste of time?'

'We might be lucky,' replied Royce, unperturbed. 'Miss Mayall, how many people did you tell it was Fools Gold in your stable?'

'One,' I said. 'A customer, Miss Hancock. The children from the riding stable might have overheard.'

'May I know Miss Hancock's address?'

'I'll get the receipt book, it'll be in that.' I stood up,

wondering how much longer they were going to take, writing down irrelevant details and asking all the wrong questions. I was tired, and depressed, and I wanted to be on my own again.

By the time I came back with the book, Irons was writing down the names of anybody Ulverton could think of who might have profited from Fools Gold not running in the Champion Hurdle at Cheltenham. Ulverton was becoming sarcastic, and said that, as the Queen Mother might be entering one of her horses, perhaps her name should be on the list. I returned to my place by the window, trying to visualise the nice Miss Hancock riding her pretty Arab gelding home and getting on the telephone to a gang of co-conspirators to arrange the slaughter of a likely runner in a major horse-race.

'Something amusing you, Miss Mayall?' demanded Irons.

I decided the time had come to put my views.

'I believe whoever killed Rivet thought he was killing my mare. I think it was one of the Children of God, from Gorsedown Manor. They want to stop me riding over the manor lands.'

'How much is your horse worth, Miss Mayall?' asked Irons, and Ulverton groaned, and ran his hand through his hair.

'Dead?' I asked. 'About thirty pounds, I should think. I don't know. Alive, perhaps five hundred. She's not insured.'

'A bit far-fetched, isn't it?' asked Royce.

'Of course it's not far-fetched!' snapped Ulverton. 'It's

the obvious bloody answer, isn't it? It's got nothing to do with how much the horses are worth, or what blasted races they're entered for, nobody could possibly have known there'd be a racehorse of any description here today. The only horse anybody could have expected to find here was Miss Mayall's mare.'

He stood up and paced across the floor, stuffing his hands into his jacket pockets, and then turning at the door and pointing a finger at Royce.

'Unless it's some random lunatic on the rampage, killing anything he reaches, Miss Mayall's given you the answer. And if it is a random lunatic, then I strongly suggest you put it at the top of your so-called list of priorities, because it may not be a horse he kills next time.'

'Miss Mayall?' asked Royce, after a long silence.

I shrugged. I had nothing more to say.

'Apart from your contention that these people want to stop you riding in their grounds, why do you think it was one of them?'

'He ran off through the paddock,' I said. 'The only other way out of the paddock is into the manor grounds. I've already told you all this, my dog went after him.'

'Just go through it again for us, would you? In case something else occurs to you.'

A car pulled into the yard, tyres crunching on the gravel. Everybody turned to look out of the window, and I stood up, and went to the door. It was Jake Brewer and Toby. They'd come back with a Land Rover and a winch. Jake jumped down from the cab, and shivered in the cold evening air, stamping his feet in their heavy rubber boots and shrugging himself into the thick sheep-skin flying jacket he wore for working in winter. His shadow fell black and sharply outlined against the gravel, and I screwed up my eyes against the glare of the yard lights.

'Toby thought we'd better come and help,' said Jake. 'You'll never get him through the door tomorrow morning, he'll be stiff as a plank.'

He waved aside my thanks, and told Toby to drive the Land Rover round to the stable.

'Evening, Ulverton,' he said as the trainer followed me into the yard. 'Sorry to hear about this. Nasty homecoming for you. Any progress? Are the police here?'

Ulverton suggested I go back to explaining the obvious to the obtuse, sticking to words of one syllable wherever possible, and leave the horse to the three of them. I wished he would stop antagonising the policemen.

'Now, Miss Mayall, if we could just go over this,' said Royce heavily as I returned, 'the horse spent the day in the stable where he was killed, is that where your own horse is usually kept? Right. And you were alerted to the presence of an intruder by your dog, which was shut in the workshop at the time. You and Mr Joliot, who is a groom employed by Mr Brewer, whose horses you were shoeing at the time, went to the stable through the workshop, releasing the dog at the same time, and found the dead horse. The dog ran off into the paddock. Is that correct?'

'The horse was still alive when we got there, and the dog was chasing somebody.'

'Ah, yes. You called him back because you feared the intruder might harm him.'

'Well trained, is he?' asked Irons. 'I mean, you can even call him back when he's chasing somebody, and he obeys?'

'Yes.'

'Then I can tell you, Miss Mayall, he's better trained than a lot of police dogs I know. It's not that easy to call a dog off the chase. Unless you saw or heard the intruder, I have to tell you I think the dog just ran off, otherwise he wouldn't have come back.'

I looked out of the window. I could see the lights of the Land Rover shining on the paddock fence from behind the stable, and I heard the engine running. Then there was the rising whine of the winch, and Jake called something, and Toby answered.

'Miss Mayall?'

'Yes?'

'You haven't answered my question.'

'You didn't ask a question, Mr Irons, you gave an opinion. I trained my dog. When I'm riding I can't keep him on a lead, I've got my hands full with my horse. I have to be able to call him back, he might chase sheep or cattle. Mr Joliot's here now, you could ask him if you like. I think he'll agree with me, the dog was chasing someone.'

'Leaving the dog out of it for a moment,' said Royce, 'is there any other way an intruder could have got to the stables, other than through the paddock?'

I'd thought about that. Apart from the repairs I'd

carried out to the hedge two years earlier, the Children of God themselves had strengthened it, and the narrow front strip of forge land that ran alongside the lane was very securely fenced. If a horse got loose from the forge, I only had to shut the gates to be sure it couldn't escape; Uncle Henry had been careful about that, and I checked that fence every week, as he had done. It was, of course, designed to keep horses in rather than intruders out, and somebody could quite easily climb it, but I doubted if they could have done so without being seen. The lights had been on in the yard as soon as it began to get dark.

'I'll check the fence tomorrow in daylight,' I said. 'But I doubt it. If he didn't come off the manor lands, where he might as well use the gate, it isn't locked, he came over the fence, and I'd probably have seen him. The forge lands are surrounded on three sides by Gorsedown land. The only way in from there is the gate, and I can see the whole length of the fence along the road from the forge, except where the horse-box might have been in the way. And, also, I think . . .' I hesitated.

'Yes, Miss Mayall?' prompted Royce.

'The horse I was working on was very nervous. That's why the dog was shut in. I can't swear to this, but I'm almost sure he'd have reacted to anybody coming past if he'd heard them, and horses have very good hearing.'

Royce nodded at Irons, who folded his notebook and slipped it into his pocket. They both stood up.

'Well, we'll make enquiries,' said Royce. 'Perhaps you

could come into the police station tomorrow or on Monday and make a statement.'

I saw them out of the cottage. Ulverton was coming back from the stable, looking depressed and angry, striding towards his car, and Royce repeated his request for a statement. Ulverton grunted.

'I'll need something from you for the insurance,' he said. 'There's a form, isn't there? Just to show I've reported it.'

The Land Rover drove slowly around the corner of the stable and pulled up, Jake winding down the window and leaning out towards me.

'I've chucked an old tarpaulin over him,' he said. 'There won't be any problem winching him up into the lorry from there. If you call Johnsons, they might come out tomorrow. Tell them I said you should ask for them, mention my name.'

'Thank you, Jake. You're very kind.'

'Usual livery fees for Lyric? Get that box scrubbed down, burn the straw. You can't use the place until you've got rid of the smell of the blood, it stinks, no horse would go in there.'

I thanked them again, grateful for their kindness, and they nodded, smiling, and drove off. I noticed that Royce hadn't even bothered to speak to Toby. He and Irons walked over to their car, and I followed, to thank them, hoping by doing so to reduce the resentment they obviously felt towards Ulverton.

'You could have a word with our crime prevention people,' said Royce. 'They might be able to help.'

'I'm worried about my own horse.'

'Leave your dog loose,' suggested Irons. 'He's probably worth less than the horse.'

Ulverton was pacing across the yard, kicking impatiently at the gravel, obviously wanting to talk to me. I said goodbye to the two detectives, and went back to him.

'Look, my dear, does your insurance cover Rivet?' he demanded. 'Brewer mentioned it, I hadn't thought of it, I'm not sure mine does. He wasn't in my care, you see. It's a bit of a bugger. Can you lay your hands on your policy?'

We went back into the cottage, and I found my insurance policy. I was covered for malicious damage to my own property, but the wording was complicated and ambiguous in the clauses covering third party liability. Ulverton scribbled some notes in the back of his diary, muttering worriedly to himself, and I poured him another whisky.

Eventually, he left. I watched the tail lights of his Jaguar as he drove away up the lane, and then I went to the forge, and let my poor, patient dog out of the workshop. He ran round to the stable block, and I heard him prowling around the dead horse, growling. I cleaned and oiled my tools and swept up the concrete stand in front of the forge. Usually, my next task after cleaning up for the night was to see to Lyric, to fill her water bucket and hay net, and to muck out the stable and toss the straw into a bed for her. With my normal routine in ruins, I felt restless, tired but wide awake, and sleep, I knew, would be impossible.

I locked up the forge with far greater care than usual, whistled to Plod, and went back into the cottage. Plod was unhappy, whining and unwilling to settle down on his blanket in the kitchen. He paced around in the living room, sniffing at the furniture. Never since I'd moved into the forge had so many people crowded into that little room, and the smell of the strangers bothered him.

It bothered me, too. Royce was a smoker, and, although he hadn't lit a cigarette, the smell of his clothes lingered, along with the faint scent of cologne from Irons. The empty whisky glasses were beginning to smell stale. I took them into the kitchen, washed them, and then threw open the windows. Plod came to my side, rose up lightly on his hind legs, resting his forepaws on the sill, and we stood together, sniffing at the cold night air, and listening.

The coppery smell of the blood was beginning to fade, although it was still quite strong, a disgusting overlay on the usual scent of horses and wet earth. In the distance, we could hear heavy lorries on the motorway, and nearer the sound of music from a radio in the village. There was a glow of reflected light in the sky, and the branches of the big chestnut tree moved slightly in the wind, silhouetted against it. The wet slates on the roof of the forge gleamed.

Plod pushed his nose against my arm, dropped to the floor and walked away, whining. I closed the window, followed him back into the living room, and sank into the armchair, leaning back with my hands clasped behind my head, staring into the fire, wondering what to do. I sat there throughout the night, watching the fire die in the grate, watching the dawn light creep through the windows, and still I had no answer.

When it was light enough I went outside, and Plod followed me. I could smell the blood from the stableyard. I turned away from it, and walked down to the gate.

There were no marks on the fence, and the grass grew, strong, tufted and undisturbed, against the uprights. I looked carefully for smears of mud on the bars, and checked patches of bare earth for footprints, but I found nothing. Plod trotted beside me, sniffing at the grass, nose down and tail high and interested, but he showed no sign of alarm, followed no track across the grass towards the gravel yard. I walked back to the cottage, looking for lines of sight to the forge, or for possible hiding places.

There was a thick clump of bamboo between the wall of the cottage and the boundary hedge. I looked at it, pushing the springy stems aside, searching for signs of damage. There were none. Anybody going to the stable from the fence or the gate would have had to pass between the cottage and the forge, treading on gravel.

Johnson had agreed, reluctantly, to come and collect the carcass later that morning. Fred Johnson didn't usually work on Sundays, he said. He needed his day of rest, just like the other members of the human race, although most people didn't seem to think so. He'd had a hard week, and he was tired. I might not realise it, but his business was heavy work, he was entitled to a bit of peace and quiet one day in the week, wasn't he?

Of course he was, I agreed. It was just that Mr Brewer had mentioned him as being helpful.

He *was* helpful, said Mr Johnson belligerently. He was always helpful to his customers, wouldn't be in business otherwise. Being helpful didn't mean being at everybody's beck and call all hours of the day and night, even on his Sundays. Still. He'd have his bite of breakfast, if I didn't begrudge him that, and then he'd see what he could do. He wasn't promising anything, he'd had other plans for his one day of rest, but he'd see what he could do.

Interpreting this to mean he would be along in his own good time, expecting to be flattered and pacified, I passed the time I spent waiting for him in searching for signs of the intruder. Having done what I'd told Royce I'd do, checked the fence, I went into the paddock. This time, I opened the gate into the park, and looked at the mud on the other side.

Exactly where I'd expected to find them were two footprints, almost side by side, deep in the mud. They were smeared. Somebody had vaulted the gate in a hurry, no doubt alarmed by the sounds of the dog in pursuit, and had slipped on the uncertain surface on landing.

I crouched over the footprints, looking at them carefully. Smaller than mine and slightly narrower, with shallow treads. Not boots, then. Running shoes, probably. And yet yesterday the ground had been wet and muddy, and had been kept that way by showers. Except in the pine wood, where there was a thick carpet of needles draining away the rainwater almost as soon as it fell, the ground everywhere was heavy and sodden, and the pine wood was almost a mile away, on the other side of the park.

Plod trotted up to me, still sniffing at the ground, his tail waving. I stopped him before he came through the gate, and he lifted his head, stiffening, and barked sharply. He was looking towards the beech woods, and the wind was coming from that direction. I spoke to him quietly, and he waved his tail, but his ears were up and he didn't turn his head away from the woods. His nostrils were flaring as he sniffed at the wind. I looked in the same direction, watching carefully for several minutes, but I could see nothing, and after a while Plod lost interest and loped away across the paddock back towards the forge. The wind had veered.

I telephoned the police, and asked to speak to Royce. After a minute a woman's voice answered, and again I asked for Royce.

'He's not on duty this morning,' said the woman. 'Perhaps I can help. Detective Constable York.'

I told her who I was, and she asked me to hold on. I waited, and when she came back she said she'd found the file and asked what she could do for me. I told her about the footprints.

'Yes?' she asked. I began to feel both annoyed, and foolish.

'Isn't it possible to take plaster casts of footprints?' I asked.

'Possible,' she admitted grudgingly. 'Not easy in this

weather. They have to be quite dry. I suppose you could cover them. I'll have a word.'

'Will somebody come to try and take casts?'

'That's not up to me, Miss Mayall. I'll make a note on the file, and pass on a message.'

I found a sheet of plywood in the garden shed, and carried it across the paddock, Plod once again trotting at my heels. The sun came out briefly, sparkling on the wet grass, shining on the puddles. Where Lyric had left hoof-prints on the earth the water shone in little crescent shapes, good-luck symbols, I hoped. It was a fine pad-dock for horses, with a stand of trees for shade and shelter, and the clean stream, with a firm gravel bottom, for fresh water.

Plod barked, startling me. I looked around, but couldn't see what had alerted him. He growled, his hackles rising, and paced towards the gate, stiff-legged. I called him to heel, and he hesitated for a moment, and then obeyed, a growl still rumbling in his throat. Cautiously, I approached the gate, watching the hedge on either side of it, Plod beside me.

There were fresh footprints in the mud, and where the two prints beside the gate had been, lay the deep scoring lines of a rake.

I saw them as the sun went in behind a bank of clouds, three people standing in a line in front of the trees, watching me. One held something in his hands. He was too far away for me to be able to see it clearly, but I knew it was a rake.

They wanted me to know they had killed the horse.

They had been watching me from the wood, waiting for me to find the proof of those two footprints, and then, when they could be sure I had seen them, when they had left no doubt in my mind as to who had committed the slaughter, they had erased them. And now they watched.

I walked back to the forge, carrying the plywood. I knew I had no hope of proving their guilt, knew the police would take it no further. It was just a dead horse, not even a particularly valuable one. Just a horse, who had looked for kindness from the man who came to his stable door, because he had never found anything other than kindness from a man, and who had died choking on his own blood at the hands of that trusted man.

I telephoned the police again, and told Detective Constable York what had happened. Yes, I could be sure the footprints had been destroyed by a rake. No, I could not identify the people who had done it, they had been too far away. Yes, I did understand there was nothing they could do under the circumstances.

Fred Johnson arrived, not that morning, but late in the afternoon. I greeted him politely, and ignored his comment that I could have carried the horse down to his yard over my shoulders and saved him the trip. I smiled in response to his question as to whether I had a sense of humour. I had been thinking carefully about sharp knives and cut throats, and the throats had not been those of horses. My sense of humour was not very active that day.

I helped him fix the chains around the dead horse,

and watched as he winched it up into the back of his lorry. I gave him Ulverton's name and address, and he said he'd be in touch with him in the morning. He suggested I push the lorry back to his yard, and save him the petrol. I smiled, thinly, and thanked him for coming out on a Sunday.

I burned the filthy straw from the loose box, and the smoke rose in a black column into the darkening sky. I found I was singing, a medieval ballad about a man condemned to death through the treachery of the woman he had loved, perhaps the closest I could get to a requiem for a murdered horse. I hosed down the loose box, and sprayed it with strong disinfectant, scrubbing at the stained sandstone. The water ran red. I sluiced the concrete, scrubbing at the dried blood with a yard broom; I threw buckets full of water over the dark stains, and swept, and swept, and still the water ran red. Plod, whimpering at the smell, and at my anger, crept away. The rain began to fall as it grew dark, hard and heavy onto the ground, beating at the concrete, and the water swirled and ran, and the stench of the blood rose faintly into my nostrils, and faded, and the water was pale. I threw buckets of water against the walls of the stable, and scrubbed at the dark stains, and I was singing the ballad of the three crows, who watched over the body of the knight who lay dead in the bright green grass alongside his horse and his dog, murdered by the wife he had trusted. It was dark, and the rain fell heavily, and I shivered from the cold and from rage, my clothes soaked from the rain and the bloody water, and I scoured the door, scraping away the blood, and swept the water away, red and fading, the stink of death fainter, the water growing clean and clear. I was singing the ballad of Lord Randall, poisoned by the mother he had trusted, who had bequeathed her a rope for her own execution.

11

I telephoned Jake when I'd finished in the stable yard, and asked him if he could keep Lyric for a week. I needed time. He said he'd keep her for a year if I liked, it was my money.

I slept well that night, tiredness hitting me suddenly, and woke in the dark, restless, wondering what had disturbed me, and realising it was anger. I lay still, staring up into the darkness, thinking of the dead horse and the distress the death had caused to the people who'd cared for him. I could smell smoke in my hair, even though I'd washed it the night before, so I showered again, shivering in the cold water, and scrubbed my scalp and my skin until I felt clean, and then I rubbed myself dry with a rough towel, and put on clean clothes. The muscles in my face were tight, and my jaw ached, and when I looked at myself in the mirror as I cleaned my teeth a hard and bitter face looked back at me.

I prowled restlessly around the cottage, seeing the windows growing grey as the sky lightened in the east, and then I went out, Plod at my heels, stoked up the forge and checked my tools, looked through the order book, suddenly resenting the busy day ahead, and remembering that only months ago I'd have seen so much work as a triumph. I picked up the big hammer, the last one Uncle Henry had let me use, and let it swing against the anvil. It rang, a clear and loud tone, a humming sound hanging in the air after it. Peter Andrews had told me that Richard Wagner had written twenty-four anvils, all tuned to B flat, into the score of *The Ring Cycle*, but that nobody had ever played it that way. I hit the anvil again, and again, and it rang and hummed, and I understood why Wagner had done that. I laid the hammer down, unlocked the workshop, and turned on the lights. The machinery stood stark and angular under the bright glare, paintwork gleaming on steel housing and guards, contrasting sharply with the greys and blacks and muted golds of the old forge. It was all mine, left to me by the man who had taught me to use it, who had seen it safeguarded for me beyond his own death, who had known me well enough to know I loved it, and would earn the right to take it.

In the stable yard I winced at the sharp tang of the disinfectant, and sniffed carefully, seeking the smell of blood under it. The earth where I had burned the straw lay blackened, the grey ash soaked into the clay, dead, and dirty. Once again, I hosed down the concrete, sweeping the water into the drain, this time washing away the smell of the chemicals, and when the air was sweet again, and I could scent nothing but winter earth and the clean hay in the store, I turned the water onto the burned clay and washed that, too.

It was light by the time I'd finished, and I put away the yard broom and went into the paddock. Lyric had to have been standing under the trees when the intruder came through, the only place she could have been where he wouldn't have seen her, the dark green canvas of her rug almost invisible in the dim light of evening. I found the prints of her hooves in a patch of bare earth by a hawthorn tree, shielded from the path by the bushes I'd left in place as screens from the wind.

I looked carefully at the hedge, searching for weak spots. A rabbit would have had little difficulty in coming through it, but anything larger would have found it almost impossible. My own repairs had been thorough and careful; the Children of God had turned a normal countryside barrier into a virtually impenetrable fortification. I hadn't realised until then just how determined they were to preserve their privacy, and it shook me. My little beech saplings had been reinforced with blackthorn, not the pretty, cultivated variety that carries little white flowers, but the old type, with hard thorns fully an inch long that can tear into flesh and break off, and bring blood poisoning, too. If the intruder who'd killed the racehorse hadn't come through the gate, he'd certainly not found a way through the hedge. I crouched down, staring at the blackthorn bushes, wondering at the determination that had driven the Children of God to undertake such a task. I'd heard it said that the entire boundary had been strengthened, twelve miles of hedgerow. They'd been lucky with the winter, it had been mild and wet; hard frosts would have killed the young saplings and their work would have been for nothing.

The blackthorns stood inside the beech bushes, on the park side of the hedge. Perhaps they were being careful not to encroach on land they didn't own. I reached through the beech, grasped one of the saplings, and shook it. It was strong and hard, rooted firmly in the earth, planted carefully and professionally. The work on the hedge might have risked the weather, but everything else had been done well.

I heard the church clock strike nine, and I stood up, still staring at the blackthorn. It made me very uneasy. There are dozens, perhaps hundreds, of hedgerow plants that will make a strong and safe barrier, some of them better able to withstand winter frosts than blackthorn, and all of them less dangerous. Short of razor wire, I could think of nothing more savage.

One of my favourite customers was pulling into the yard as I returned, driving an ancient Land Rover that towed one of the widest horse-trailers in the county. I knew that trailer well; I'd reinforced the floor for Mrs Roderick to make it safe for two and a half tons of Shire stallions, a matched pair of gleaming black giants. I can never look at those horses without a smile of delight crossing my face, and Lavinia Roderick, small, square and pink-cheeked, seems to spend her days in a rosy glow of gleeful pride. Her boys, she says, are her joy, her love, and a cause of war between herself and the

Cheltenham branch of Barclays Bank. She juggles her finances between feed bills, occasional stud fees, cheques from film companies and entry money for any show with a suitable class. She lives on five acres that her mother left her, where the stables are resplendent with new paint, and where a small tree grows through the roof of her tumbledown wooden bungalow.

Tantara bounced his way down the ramp at the end of his rope, massive feet springing high under great plumes of white feathering, his mighty neck curving proudly. The top of Mrs Roderick's head only just reaches Tantara's hip joint; when she grooms her horses, she does much of the work kneeling on their rumps, or from the third rung of a small step-ladder. Everybody laughs at her, but no-one laughs louder than she does, and there is affection and admiration behind the gentle mockery.

Nothing could have been better designed to restore a sense of proportion to my confused state of mind that day than the work with those two horses and their eccentric owner. By the time I saw them on their way I was laughing, although it hurt to do so. Fanfare had given me a friendly nudge with his nose, and it felt as though he had broken about three of my ribs. How Mrs Roderick, five foot nothing in her socks and the wrong side of sixty, manages those horses is a miracle of expertise and mutual affection.

Plod, sensing the lightening of my black mood, emerged from the back of the forge hopefully, head cocked and tail waving. I swept the concrete quickly, and then threw sticks for him until my next customer arrived, late as usual, and with the same excuses about traffic jams on the bypass. I shut Plod in the workshop again. The mare had a foal at foot, who might take fright.

It must have been then that the Children of God fitted their security lock to the paddock gate. At any other time Plod would have heard them and given the alarm, and for the rest of the day he was running free. They must have worked quietly as it was; my own hearing is far from dull, and the gate is less than a hundred yards from the forge. That evening, when I'd said goodbye to the last of my customers, cleaned up the forge and sharpened the hoof-knives, I called Plod and we walked through the paddock for half an hour of fun and training before I settled down to the inevitable book work. Plod was a well trained dog, and easy to handle, but the best of dogs can forget their training, so I liked to run through the routines when we had time. I'd sent him on ahead of me, running fast, and I shouted the command 'Down!' to bring him skidding to a halt and flat on his belly. He stopped, but instead of dropping to the ground he turned towards the gate. I called 'Down!' again, and he obeyed, but he did so reluctantly, half his attention on the gate, and I saw his hackles rising. I whistled to him, and he came to me, and together we walked to the gate.

A lock had been welded to the bars and the frame.

It was the same type as those on the main gates on the southern and northern boundaries of the park, modern security locks, hardened steel, with the keys that couldn't be copied without an authorisation card. The gate itself was iron; I remembered Uncle Henry making it, about ten years earlier. It was quite a narrow gate. There was room enough for a horse, but a tractor couldn't be driven through it. Uncle Henry had fixed plates over the hinges, explaining to me that a good lock on a gate was useless if it could be lifted free at the other end.

I remembered hanging that gate with him. As I stared at the new lock, so insolently installed only a day after the Children of God had killed the horse, imagining it was mine, the picture of Uncle Henry was in my mind, and his words as he showed me how to line up the bolt with its mortice, came back to me. Henry and Ruth hadn't needed security locks, and neither had I.

The Children of God thought they had killed my horse. They knew themselves secure, knew that an investigation to discover the truth about that crime would cost too much, that the police wouldn't feel it justified. They had shown they could destroy a horse of mine with impunity, felt so assured of their invulnerability that they hadn't even waited a single day before securing the gate, and barring me from the land over which I had a right to ride.

I looked at the lock, and looked at the wicked blackthorn hedge at either side of the gate, and Plod growled beside me, obediently sitting close against my leg, but with his anger at the intruders and at the invasion of his territory only just under control.

If that lock had been installed during the night, if I had found it that morning, my reaction would have been violent rage. But I had had a day in which to recover my balance and the horse they had killed had, after all, not been Lyric. Anger I felt, certainly, but it was not the uncontrollable rage that had driven me to work late into the night washing away the signs of their crime and singing songs of revenge and betrayal. The anger I felt at their arrogance now left no room for doubt in my mind that I would fight back, that I would not submit to their savage attacks. I would, somehow, find a way to defeat them.

I took Plod for a long walk, through the beech woods to the quarry, along farm tracks and footpaths to the other side of the village, and then back along the wide grass verge of the main road. It was late by the time we got back to the forge, and we were both tired and hungry. I fed Plod, and lit a fire in the living room. I had a plan only for a first line of defence, but it was at least a start, and it appealed to my sense of humour, too, which helped to restore my balance. I scribbled down lists of stock for ordering, and I entered the work I had done in the big ledger, and then, as I chewed a thick beef sandwich, I began to draw outlines and measurements in my sketch pad.

My order book was already full, and the unfortunate Forbes, still laid low with viral influenza, had left a croaking message on his telephone answering machine to the effect that he expected to be off work for at least three weeks. Four more racing stables telephoned me, explained carefully that travelling to me was out of the question because of the risk of infection, because of the time involved, or because they quite frankly didn't want to do it, and two of them eventually agreed to try. I shuffled orders around, postponed what I could, and asked Jake to keep Lyric for another three weeks.

'No problem,' he said. 'Look, can I bring some hunters over to you? Forbes is ill.'

'If you can get them here at five in the morning, yes. I can fit two in then before Ulverton arrives, anything else I'll have to do after eight in the evening.'

'Bloody hell, Ann . . .'

'And anything difficult to shoe comes back unshod. Sorry, Jake, but I already knew Forbes was ill.'

It was an exhausting three weeks. I was up every morning at half-past four, and seldom got to bed before midnight. I worked on Sundays and late into the nights, and I lived on sandwiches and what I could empty out of tins. In some cases I even got the customers to help by sweeping up hoof shavings and used nails, and I actively encouraged the riding school children, who turned up in the evenings and at weekends, and cleaned tools and walked Plod, and treated the horses in a proprietorial manner that sometimes earned them a kick.

But in between customers, and as I chewed my sandwiches in the forge, and while I waited for horses to be unloaded and brought in, or tied up outside, I sketched, and measured, and pondered, and sometimes I smiled.

Forbes recovered, and telephoned to tell me he was back at work. I said I was glad to hear it, and he recognised the relief in my voice and laughed.

'I could sleep for a week,' I said.

'Aye. Well, I'm grateful you helped my customers.'

I noted a slight emphasis on the possessive pronoun.

'I'm sure you'd do the same for mine, if I was ill,' I replied.

The workload didn't slacken immediately. There was a backlog, not only of my customers, but also of those that Forbes couldn't deal with straight away, and it was nearly two weeks before we were both back to normal working hours. We spoke on the telephone almost daily during that time, covering urgent work for each other in whatever way would save the most time, and we built up a good understanding. We still exchange work in emergencies.

Glory came again, and this time a secretary telephoned and made an appointment. When she stepped out of her little car I accused her of showing off, and she agreed, laughing.

'She's not *my* secretary,' she said. 'I just thought you ought to know I could have one if I wanted, so you treat me with proper respect.'

'Consider yourself respected,' I said. 'What is it this time? More angels' wings?'

It was a head-dress for Oberon, and the drawings were spectacular. Bracken fronds and brambles swept high in a form suggestive of antlers, the crown of a wild and dangerous creature, nature rampant and barbaric.

'Good lord!' I exclaimed, staring at the bold black pencil lines. 'Glory, it'll weigh about fifteen pounds. And it's over two feet tall, isn't it? Who's playing this part? Will he be able to manage it?'

'He'll play it on his hands and knees if I say so,' she replied, and I realised the remark about the secretary had only been half a joke. Glory was indeed a person respected in her own field. She looked up at me and smiled.

'It's all right,' she said. 'He'll manage.'

There was a softness in her voice and in the look in her eyes that told me the head-dress was a special effort for a special man. I smiled back at her, catching a little of her happiness, feeling the hope and the exhilaration of her love.

'Well,' I said after a moment, 'I hope he's a big, strong lad, that's all. Let's see what we can do.'

It took me two days, and again it had to be sent by taxi. This time, I didn't wince; if the company could afford Glory, it could afford taxis.

I wrote to Uncle John and told him about the dead horse, and the lock on the gate, and he wrote back, anger and sympathy in equal measure in his letter. He suggested I contact a company of private detectives, and gave me the names of two of them he could recommend.

'They can carry out most of the investigations the police would do, given time, and money. They have access to forensic laboratories as well if necessary, but that can be expensive.

'Under normal circumstances, I'd recommend a client to think carefully about that offer you received. Moral victories are sometimes very expensive, and this might be a dangerous situation.'

Oberon's head-dress had given me a few more ideas for my own work, and I was sketching again when Glory telephoned.

'It's a triumph,' she said. 'The whole cast's wild about it, and Peter's agent's trying to get his contract rewritten so he can keep his costume at the end of the run.'

'Will you let him?'

She chuckled.

'Only if he's very, very good. He asked me to thank you. Oh, Ann, it's marvellous! Thank you. Thank you very much.'

I finished my drawings later that day, and telephoned an order to the mills for special spring steel. When it arrived, I set to work. In the little spare time I had I forged and hammered, and I cut and measured, and I bent iron, and shaped it, and twisted it and tempered it. I flattened iron, and curled it, and carved it, and then I welded it together, and stood back and looked at my work, and I laughed.

It was a gate, and it might have gladdened the heart of Mad King Ludwig of Bavaria. There were curlicues and cornucopias, and intertwined among them were roses, and lilies of the valley, their stems curling around each other, opened leaves and furled leaves, buds and blossoms, and the flowers hung on sprung steel, and shook and rang as the gate moved. There were no bars, no uprights, not one line in the entire design was straight, and the top of the gate was a wild tangle of flowers and leaves. Roses sprang out on either side, lilies bent their fragile-seeming bells, and the gate gleamed black, and gilt glittered on the edges of the petals and leaves.

There was nowhere on the gate that a lock could be fixed, and no single piece of steel stood straight enough or long enough, or wide enough, to offer a foothold. The gate stood two metres high, a riotous medley of foliage and flowers, a salute to exuberant bad taste.

Jake agreed to keep Lyric for another two weeks.

I tied a rope between the corner of the stable yard and the wall of the cottage, stretching it about two feet from the ground across the gravel drive and the little lawn, and I let Plod out into the paddock. I whistled to him, and he came running towards me, and then, at my command, stopped at the rope. I left him free in the paddock and the stable yard, and watched as he trotted around, and then, when he crossed under the rope I checked him, and took him back to the other side. Puzzled, he followed me, and at the paddock fence I turned and went back, and as he reached the rope I checked him again. He cocked his head at me, his tail waving. I patted him and praised him, and then took the rope down and we played together in the garden and the yards.

Mrs Laverton rode her favourite Palomino over to be shod, and gazed at the gate in the forge with awe in her eyes.

'God of the Little Fishes!' she exclaimed. 'Where on earth is that thing going?'

Plod roamed the paddock and the stable yard, and learned to stop at the boundary of the rope until I took it down in the evenings when the last customer had gone.

Never again would I have to leave him locked in the workshop.

Jane Laverton talked about the gate in the village shop, and people came to see it. Somebody asked how much it cost, and I said five hundred pounds, without seriously considering the question. Two days later a reporter and a photographer from the local paper arrived, and I carried it out into the light for them to photograph. I refused to stand beside it. It appeared two days later under the heading 'Five Hundred Pounds for Local Blacksmith's Masterpiece'.

I took the cutting torch into the paddock, and I cut down Uncle Henry's gate. The posts for my own had to be stronger. I sunk them a metre deep, and poured concrete around them, and I welded three flat springs to them, and a massive catch with a deep ratchet, and then I hung my gate, and welded plates over the hinges, and stood back to look.

There was no lock and no bolt, nothing held the gate closed against the post except a loop of rose stem and three rose leaves, with the veins and the thorns carved and gilded. There was no handle, except, on my side, a loop of twisted lily stem, backed by a plate of three leaves.

I took hold of the stem, braced my hand against the post, and pulled. The first spring flexed as the gate moved against it, and then the gate juddered against the second spring, and the lilies rang. I pulled harder, and the gate came against the third spring, and rang louder, as the leaves and the blossoms shook against each other.

I smiled, and pulled again, and the gate flexed against the last spring, caught the ratchet on the post, and stood open, the ringing and humming of the shivering flowers dying slowly away.

I tripped the ratchet and the gate flashed shut, crashing against the springs and slamming back against the post. Every flower and leaf shook wildly, chiming and reverberating, harmonics ringing in my ears, and I clapped my hands over them, laughing.

I pulled the gate open again, and slipped through to the other side. It was harder from here, with only the three lily leaves to brace my hand against as I pushed. I forced my way through against the second spring, and then turned to grip the handle with my other hand and pull the gate open again. I let it swing shut, and laughed as the flowers rang their carillon.

My crazy gate had two advantages.

Only somebody who was very strong could open it, and nobody could come through it silently.

I telephoned Jake, and asked him to bring Lyric home.

12

Lyric tried to run away with me almost as soon as I mounted her after coming through the gate, but I succeeded in holding her to a canter, and, after a lot of determined head-shaking and a half-hearted buck, she settled down and I turned her towards the Manor. Plod ran alongside us, keeping a wary eye on Lyric's skittish hooves, loping easily over the rough ground.

In the pocket of my jacket the heavy security lock, that I had cut free from Uncle Henry's gate with the oxy-acetylene torch, bumped against my hip.

I was glad to be on my horse again, glad to feel the late winter wind whipping my hair, glad to see the pale blue of the sky through the trees with grey clouds streaked across them, to feel Lyric's hooves drumming on the drying earth. I had thought about my next action, worried over it, but now that I had steeled myself to commit it there was a feeling of recklessness about the risk I was taking which sent the blood running fast and quickened my breath, and which carried its own brand of enjoyment. In the Middle Ages, I might have been carrying a battle pennon.

As we reached the crest of the hill I pulled Lyric to a halt and looked down at the house. I wanted to be sure that there were plenty of the Children of God around. I could see them in the big vegetable garden, digging and hoeing, and smoke rose from the many chimneys, telling of others inside. I'd never wondered how many there were, but having seen the work they'd done on the hedges I had finally realised it was no mere handful of unfriendly fanatics; no matter how hard, or what long hours, they had worked, it had been a task for at least twenty, and possibly many more.

I walked Lyric carefully down the path until we were only a few hundred yards from the house, and then I let her break into a canter. Plod ran alongside us, and I turned Lyric onto the hard packed earth beside the drive so that her hooves drummed, and I shouted to him.

'Who's that? Who's that, Plod?'

And he threw back his head and barked.

They came out of the garden, looking towards the drive, running onto the gravel and calling to each other, and faces appeared at the windows. Somebody shouted, and pointed towards us, and three young men ran out of a side door, calling to the people on the drive, and looking back over their shoulders.

Lyric pulled hard and tried to break into a gallop, but I held her back, keeping her to a pace that Plod could match, calling him in close, and still calling to him.

'Who's that? Who's that?'

He ran faster, barking, and I dropped my hands and Lyric bounded towards the house as I sat up straight in the saddle and waved a fist in the air.

'The blacksmith's back!' I screamed. 'The blacksmith's come back!'

Then we were racing across the gravel drive, horse and dog alongside each other, and the Children of God shouted to each other in alarm, running out of our way as I pulled the horse to a skidding halt in front of the oak front door, and called the dog to my side as Lyric circled on the gravel, snorting, her hooves scattering the stones under them.

Lyric swung away from the door, throwing up her head against the bit, her hooves clattering on the grey flagstones that lay in front of the door, and Plod circled in front of her, turning to face the Children of God, barking angrily.

I looked at them, looked into their faces, seeing surprise, amazement, anger, and, in some of them, fear. I backed Lyric up to the door, bent down, and pressed the bell. I heard it ring, and I listened for a moment, and then I swung my foot, still in the heavy hunting stirrup, against the wood, once, twice, and again, hearing it crash and seeing the wood splintering under the blows as the steel slammed against it. Lyric tried to jump away from the door, frightened by the noise, but I pulled her to face the Children of God, and then backed her up against the door, and she kicked out in alarm, her hooves hammering against the oak panels, one of them shattering under the impact. I dropped my hands and she sprang towards the angry and frightened people on the gravel, and they backed away hastily, speaking sharp words of warning to each other.

Behind me, I heard running footsteps, and the sounds of the bolt being drawn, and I turned Lyric and as the big door began to open I forced her forwards, driving my heels into her flanks so that she snorted and thrust herself against it, and it flew back against the thin man, who stumbled and fell onto the tiles.

He lay, staring up at me, his mouth open, and I rode into the hall, ducking under the lintel, and pulled the horse to a halt. I looked down at him, and he tried to climb to his feet, scrabbling away from me. I turned Lyric to face him, and she plunged, nervous, her hooves sliding and clattering on the tiles, and he threw up a hand to try to ward her off.

'No!' he said. 'No, please!'

I took the lock out of my pocket. He thought I was going to throw it at him, and he thrust out his hands, palms towards me, to try to shield his face.

'No, please!' he said again.

I slammed the lock down onto the little table where I had dropped the padlock and chain when I had first come to this house. The wood cracked under the force, white splinters showing jagged under the dark polish, and Lyric shied away from the noise, shaking her head, her eyes white-rimmed. The man squirmed away, drawing his legs close up to his body, huddled against the wall, shielding his head with his arms.

'You killed the wrong horse, you stupid little worm,' I said.

And then I rode out onto the gravel again, and called Plod to heel.

'You killed the wrong horse, you stupid bastards!' I shouted.

Some of them dropped their tools and began to run towards the house, hearing the man inside calling for help. I spoke sharply, and Plod bayed, and rushed at them, his teeth bared. I called him, and he stopped, standing steady where he was, snarling.

'It was the wrong horse!' I yelled again, and then I rode Lyric straight at the largest group of them, driving her into a racing gallop, and they fled, screaming, throwing themselves out of her path. I called Plod, and he flew after us, flat out across the gravel, silent now, intent only on reaching us, on obeying that last command.

I had no chance of stopping Lyric now, once she was galloping I could only hope to steer her and wait until she tired. But I pulled her hard to the right, and although she fought me, plunging against the reins and shaking her head, she turned and we circled back along the grass that edged the gravel drive, and I shouted again at the people who milled in bewilderment in front of the door.

'Blacksmiths have ridden this land since Henry VIII was king!' I screamed. 'You won't stop us! There'll always be blacksmiths riding on Gorsedown land! King Henry's Deed is still law on Gorsedown!'

Lyric was close to panic, foam flying back from her bit

and the sweat turning to lather on her shoulders, her ears flattened against her neck. I turned her towards the hill, and home, and let the reins slide through my hands. She put her head down and pounded up the rise, and I leaned over her neck and spoke to her, soothing her and praising her, telling her she was wonderful and I loved her. I glanced over my shoulder, and behind us Plod galloped in our tracks, his head low, following as closely as he could. I called his name, shouted that he was a good dog, a good boy, and I saw his tail lift in happy response as we cleared the crest of the hill and galloped down the track towards home.

Lyric slithered to a stop as we approached the gate, her flanks heaving. I swung out of the saddle and went to her head, stroking her and reassuring her. Her ears were flicking nervously, but the frightened white rim had gone from her eyes, and although she was sweating she didn't seem to be distressed. I looped the reins over my arm, and forced the gate open. It took nearly all the strength I had, I was tired from the ride, and from trying to control the horse, but I did manage to force it past the ratchet, although Lyric shied away from the noise, throwing up her head in alarm. I led her through, and waited for Plod, who arrived, panting, only a minute later, his head high, and proud with the knowledge of his work well done. I knelt in the mud and hugged him, patting his head and telling him he was a good dog, and Lyric bent her head and blew softly at us both.

That afternoon a woman came out from the detective

agency Uncle John had recommended. She was small, rather fat, and wore a look of enquiring disapproval. Earlier, on the telephone, she had told me her name was Mrs Hunter and that the charges were three hundred pounds a day, plus expenses. It seemed a startlingly high amount.

'We guarantee complete confidentiality up to the point at which it becomes apparent that crime is involved. Should that eventuality arise, we would inform you that confidentiality could no longer be guaranteed.'

'I don't need confidentiality,' I had replied. 'You can broadcast your findings to the nation, if you want.'

Mrs Hunter had sniffed, and said that such was not her practice. She would require a retainer, five hundred pounds would be adequate.

She refused my offer of tea, took a tape recorder out of a shopping bag, a notebook out of a handbag, and said she was ready.

She sat silently, listening intently with her eyes lowered to her notebook as I told her what had happened since the Children of God had moved into Gorsedown Manor. When I finished, she nodded briskly.

'May I ask what you hope to achieve by employing me?'

The words, if not the tone, seemed hopelessly discouraging, but she smiled as she spoke, and went on without waiting for an answer.

'If you want me to discover who killed the racehorse, and to provide you with evidence that might lead to a criminal prosecution and conviction, I should tell you now that such a course of action would be unlikely to succeed. If what you have told me is correct, that these people are secretive and disinclined to discuss their affairs with outsiders, my best option would be infiltration, which is a lengthy business, and by no means certain of success.'

'No,' I replied. I found her words curiously formal. They should have been stilted, but she spoke fluidly, without any hesitation, and I could only guess that the easy usage came from long practice. 'No, I don't hope for that. I want you to find a way to stop them harassing me. I want to ride in the park. Ideally, I suppose I'd like them to stop staring at me, but I doubt if you'll manage that.'

She smiled slightly, and ducked her head.

'Do you think you can do this?' I asked.

She lowered her eyes to her notebook again, and pursed her lips. There was a long silence, and when at last she looked up her face was quite grave.

'Miss Mayall, these people killed a horse. The police may not regard that as a particularly grave crime, but in my opinion it denotes a dangerous situation. It was an act of unusual violence, prompted, I suspect, by quite extreme determination. They intend to keep you out of the park, and are prepared to go to extraordinary lengths to achieve that objective. One has to ask oneself why. And I also have to tell you that I feel you may be in danger. Not only have they so far failed in their objective, your actions today have made it quite clear that you refuse to be intimidated. Laudably courageous, no doubt, but perhaps somewhat imprudent.'

'My horse needed exercise,' I said, and her lips twitched.

'And got it, it seems,' she said drily, 'although kicking down a front door seems a rather unusual form of physical education for a horse. I suggest you refrain from repeating it, and also from telling anybody else about it. I shall find out what I can about these Children of God, and about the charity, Reconcile. As for your objective, I shall be able to give you a better assessment of my chances once I have carried out some preliminary investigations. Please contact me immediately if there are any further developments, particularly if you are in any way molested or your property damaged. We too can take plaster casts and fingerprints should the police be disinclined to do so.'

She was packing her tape recorder into her shopping bag as she spoke, and seemed to relax once it was no longer running. Perhaps she felt she was no longer on duty.

'This is about the fourth lot who call themselves the Children of God,' she remarked. 'I like the sound of your gate. You be careful in the park, though. This lot are a nasty bunch, if half of what you tell me is true.'

'It's all true.'

'Doubly nasty, then,' she said, and smiled. 'Oh, well. Since you've declared war, up sticks and at 'em. Now, I'd like to see the stable where the horse was killed, and the paddock.'

She glanced only quickly at the stable, paid a little more attention to the paddock gate and fence, but spent several minutes at the gate to the park, looking carefully at the woods beyond it and assessing lines of sight.

'How long was it between the time you heard the horse scream and the time you got the door open and let the dog out?'

'About five seconds.'

She nodded.

'And the dog couldn't have jumped the old park gate? No. Well, whoever killed the horse can run like a greyhound, can't he? To have got back through the gate before the dog caught him.'

'Plod comes when I call him.'

'Yes. Have you noticed how clear a view someone would have of your house from that wood? Wouldn't surprise me if they're not there now, watching. You might take a look, see if there're any signs, footprints, cigarette ends, whatever, if they're not too holy to smoke. Yes, they could certainly see you going between the house and the forge. With binoculars, they could see through your windows.'

I turned and followed the line of her eyes. I could see the curtains in my bedroom window, dark blue against the pale shadow of the glass. I could see the yellow roller-blind at the top of the kitchen window. The beech woods were only another hundred yards away. They'd hardly even need binoculars. I wondered, numbly, why I hadn't thought of that.

'Make sure you draw your curtains,' she said.

Somebody brought me a billy goat that afternoon and asked me if I had five minutes to trim his feet for a club show. As it happened I had, Jane Laverton having tele-phoned to say she'd be late with the posse, but I had reason to regret it. He had a magnificent pair of horns, and was agile, intelligent, and uncooperative. Even tied up tight and wedged into a corner he managed to cost me half an hour and several bruises. I like goats, they have an attitude that appeals to me, anarchistic and inde-pendent, but that afternoon, thinking of eyes in the beech woods, binoculars trained on my windows, I was in no mood to appreciate him.

As I was making out the bill for his owner, I heard the gate, and Plod barked. I ran out through the workshop, and found him standing by the paddock fence, his head up and his tail waving.

Emily was at the gate, with somebody standing beside her.

I let them in, excused myself while I finished the bill, and then turned to them where they had followed me into the forge, and smiled.

'Long time since you came,' I said, and Emily nodded.

'We never get out. Locks on all the gates, no way out when you got no key. We ask, they say sure, tomorrow. Always tomorrow. Kathy and me, we don't like this.'

Kathy raised her eyes to my face. She was lighter-skinned than Emily, and shorter, with a pretty, rather childish face, big round eyes under arched brows.

'I see you with that horse,' she said. 'They say you smashed up their gate. I think maybe no gate, we get out. I tell Emily, and we come. We say we going for a walk.'

209

I heard hoofbeats on the road, three horses from the dude ranch.

'Can you wait?' I asked. 'Wait till I've finished my work?'

Kathy looked at Emily, a quick glance before turning back to me. There was something of despair in her eyes.

'Yes,' said Emily. 'We wait. We wait in the cottage, okay?'

She laid a hand on Kathy's shoulder and smiled at me, but her face was grave and worried.

Jane Laverton was dressed as a cowgirl, with a white stetson hat, a heavy woollen poncho thrown over her fringed leather divided skirt, and lavishly tooled boots. No matter what she wore she seemed at home in her clothes, unselfconscious and comfortable. She greeted me with a grin, tilted her hat over one eye, and spoke out of the side of her mouth.

'Howdy.'

'Good evening, Mrs Laverton,' I replied, smiling, and she pulled a face at me as she slid out of the saddle.

I had to make two new sets of shoes for those horses, and it was nearly dark before I finished and sent them on their way. The riders had stood around the forge chatting to each other as I worked, and it had seemed crowded and claustrophobic. Jane Laverton noticed that I was nervous, and asked what was wrong.

'Neighbour trouble,' I said.

'Not another dead horse?'

I shook my head, smiled at her, and put an end to the conversation by working on a shoe. Talking over the noise of the hammer is almost impossible. Thinking, however, if the work is routine, is easy, but at that time far from pleasant.

I'd never bothered to draw the curtains in the cottage. As a child I'd lain in my bed beside the window looking up at the sky, and I still did so. I'd read for a while until I felt sleepy, then turn out my light and watch the stars, or the clouds, and listen to the wind in the trees. It had never occurred to me that people might be watching. I wondered how I could have been so stupid.

Jane Laverton was speaking to me again, and I shook my head and looked up at her.

'I'm sorry, what was that?'

'Could you make me one?' she demanded, impatience touching her tone.

'One what?'

'Oh, Ann! A bloody hitching rail, weren't you listening at all?'

'Aren't they made of wood?'

'Yes, of course they are!' she snapped. 'That's why Punch has chewed half-way through it. I just told you, he's a cribber, he's worn out our hitching rail. Could you make me one of iron?'

'Yes. I'm sorry. Draw me a diagram. Sorry, Jane.'

They rode away at last, trotting briskly down the road to try to beat the darkness, and I began to tidy the forge and clean my tools. I had completely forgotten about Emily and Kathy.

Emily came out to help me, and startled me by appearing in the door. She always moved quietly. She told me she had got into the habit while doing night duty in the hospital, trying not to disturb sleeping patients.

'I sorry,' she said as I jumped. 'Can I help?'

'I've nearly finished,' I replied. 'Who's Kathy?'

'She from Togu, come here last week. Been in England two months now, Nottingham. She a nurse. Somebody come to her house one night, both arms broke, she help him. Police done that, but he got away. Then they got him again, ask him who help him. He told them. Now they looking for her. They don't want her talking about no prisoners with two broken arms.'

I hung up the last of the rasps and looked around the forge to make sure everything was tidy. Plod stood up, shook himself, and ambled over to us, his tail waving, thinking hopefully about his supper and a walk in the beech woods.

'You finish now? We can talk?'

I thought about Lyric, needing her evening feed and her box mucked out, her bed made up, her night rug. I thought about Plod's meal and his walk. I hate spoiling the routine of animals, it upsets them, it isn't fair.

'I need another hour, Emily. I'm sorry.'

'Can we help? We got to go soon, they miss us, then there's trouble. Please, Ann, we got to talk.'

I hesitated.

'I'll be as quick as I can,' I said.

I'll never forgive myself for that.

When I went into the cottage they were putting on their coats. Kathy's fingers were trembling on the buttons. Emily smiled at me, and shook her head.

'We come tomorrow?' she asked. 'We got to go now.'

'Yes, I'll have more time tomorrow. I'm sorry, it's been a bad day, I didn't think those horses would take so long. Can't you tell me anything? What's wrong, why are you so worried?'

'Oh, I not sure.' She spread out her hands in a gesture of resignation. 'They probably just sending us back.'

'No.' Kathy was emphatic. 'They not sending us back.'

'Back where?' I asked.

'London, Nottingham, Manchester, wherever.' Emily shook her head again. 'We don't know.'

'They not sending us back,' said Kathy again. 'We don't know where they going. Last month, two people gone. They say they gone home. But there's no cars, and they don't go with the Children of God, not with the groups. Where they gone? How they go home, no cars, and don't go with the groups? Last week, another one gone. And we never get out of Gorsedown, always they say sure, we can have a key, ask Peter when he gets back. Who's Peter? We don't know. We want to use the telephone, talk to a friend, sure, no problem. But the telephone's in the office, somebody always there listening. Sure we can go into town, we go tomorrow, ask Sue. We don't know any Sue. We ask if we can go with the groups, sure we can go with the groups, Hal makes up the groups, ask Hal. Where they gone, these people? Why they say we never must talk to you, you a godless evil woman? Why we here? Religious retreat, that's what we come for, that's what they say we do here, we never been to church, we never seen a priest. I go to church three times every Sunday when I at home, I love my saviour, I want to go to church. They say they fix it, but this church in Anford no good, vicar a sinful man. I don't care, I just want to be in a church with Jesus, I want to kneel in a church and pray to my saviour.'

'Kathy, we don't go now they miss us.'

'You can stay here,' I said. 'Why go back if they're keeping you prisoner there? Stay here, there's room. We'll go to the police tomorrow. Don't go back.'

Kathy looked up at Emily.

'Yeah, Emily, let's stay! Let's not go back.'

Emily hesitated, looking from one to the other of us. Then she shook her head.

'We come tomorrow,' she said. 'All our papers there. But yes, we come tomorrow, and we don't go back. Maybe two, three more of us, okay?'

Kathy nodded, her eyes bright and trusting.

The moon was rising as we walked across the paddock, a half moon covered by shreds of cloud, only a little light, they said it would be enough. I pulled the gate open for them, and they laughed at the noise, their eyes and teeth shining white in their dark faces.

'We come tomorrow,' said Emily again as they walked through, and Kathy smiled at me.

'I'll be listening for the gate,' I promised, and I let it swing shut.

'Ann?'

I turned back. Kathy was trotting away along the path to the beech woods, but Emily was looking at me through the gate, her eyes huge in the half-dark.

'Yes?'

'Ann, we're scared.'

And as I watched, trying to think of an answer, she raised her hand, smiled, and followed her friend along the path back to Gorsedown.

13

They didn't come.

I left Plod running free in the paddock and the stable yard, with the rope stretched across the drive to hold him there, and I listened all day for the sound of the gate. Three times, when there were no customers, I walked through the paddock and stood, watching and waiting, listening. I looked at the mud, saw footprints where they had trodden on their way back, but nothing overlaid those prints.

I waited until late in the afternoon, and then I telephoned to ask two customers to postpone their appointments. I saddled Lyric, and I rode up to the beech trees, from where Mrs Hunter had said people might be watching. Plod put up a rabbit and set off in pursuit, but I whistled him back. He came reluctantly, looking at me reproachfully as the rabbit sped off towards the hedge, but he stayed close when I called him in.

The Children of God had made no effort to cover their tracks. There was quite a well worn path, and clear prints where the ground was soft. The path led through the trees and up a steep bank to a stand of three big trees right on the edge of the wood. At least two people had been there, standing behind the trees.

I dismounted, and stood where they had been.

I could see everything. I could see, faintly, the colours of the curtains in my windows, I could see the stables and the corner of the forge behind them, the smoke rising in a thin haze from the chimney. I could see the drive between the cottage and the forge, I could even make out the rope.

With binoculars, I would have been able to see much more.

There was a mark rubbed on the bark of the biggest tree, shiny and brown against the thin green mildew. Binoculars, or perhaps even a telescope. Mrs Hunter had been right.

I mounted again, and I rode to Gorsedown, the second time in two days.

There was no need for the melodramatic charge down the hill that I had planned and executed the day before. We rode slowly along the track beside the drive, and although Plod growled and his hackles rose he remained quiet beside me, watchful and alert.

I dismounted at the door, and I rang the bell. The marks of the stirrups were still clear, dented scars on the wood, but the panel Lyric's hooves had smashed had already been replaced, the black oak carefully fitted into place. I had to look closely to see that it did not quite match.

I rang the bell again, and listened for footsteps, but there was silence. I slipped Lyric's reins over her head and looped them over my arm, led her back away from the door and stood looking up at the windows.

'Hallo!' I called. 'Is anybody there?'

Somebody came to an upstairs window, and stood looking down at me, a black man. He made as if to open the window, but then turned his head as if called, and a moment later he went away.

'I'm looking for Emily Peters!' I shouted. 'Emily Peters, and Kathy from Togu. Where are they?'

In the distance I could hear some people calling to each other in the woods, but from the house there came no sound. I led Lyric along the drive around the corner of the house and down the side of it, to the vegetable garden, and stood looking at it.

It was beautiful. The soil was dark and loamy, crumbled to a rich tilth, without a weed in sight. Winter vegetables grew in long, straight rows, sprouting broccoli, cabbages, leeks and spinach, all huge with shining leaves spreading wing-like over the earth. There were drills of early potatoes with the first sprouts showing at their sides, and trenches had been dug for the beans and peas, lined with compost. At the back of the garden, tied back to the brick walls, espaliered fruit trees, neatly pruned, showed the first green of spring.

They must love that garden, I thought. Nearly three acres, and only last summer it had been a desolation of bramble and nettle and tussocky grass, the skeleton of a shattered greenhouse shedding the last panes of mildewed glass onto the sour soil, the sheltering walls broken, the fruit trees dead, or choked with ivy. But now the red clay was cleared, and not only cleared, but rich and black and fertile, with magnificent vegetables, and the promise of a fine summer harvest.

I could only marvel at their work.

Plod growled beside me, and I hushed him, and turned my head as two men came round the corner. They were carrying hoes, and were dressed in heavy winter clothes and rubber boots.

'It's wonderful!' I exclaimed. 'Your garden, it's wonderful.'

They said nothing. They stood, staring at me, silent, the same hostile expression on their faces, waiting for me to go. They did not even look at the garden.

'I haven't seen it this year,' I said. 'It seems like a miracle, how did you do it?'

Still they said nothing. As I turned towards them they stood aside, one on each side of the path, and the older of the two gestured to me that I should leave the garden.

'I've come for Emily Peters,' I said. 'And for Kathy, Kathy from Togu, I don't know her last name. Where are they, please?'

Still they stared at me, wordless and antagonistic, and the older man repeated his gesture.

'I'm not going until I've seen them,' I said. 'You can stand there all day if you like, waving your hand around, I'll go when I've seen Emily and Kathy, and not before.'

I turned away from them, and looked back at the garden. Out of the corner of my eye I could see them, watching me, and then they looked at each other, and the older man jerked his head. They turned, and went back along the side of the house.

After a few minutes I led Lyric to the front of the house, and we stood on the gravel, Plod at my side, and waited. I tried to appear unconcerned, but I was very nervous. I looked up at the windows. There were people at a few of them, looking down at me.

'Emily Peters, and Kathy from Togu!' I called. 'Where are they? I want to see them.'

A young woman in a window on the first floor shook her head, and flapped a hand at me, gesturing at me to go away. I looked back at her.

'I'm not going until I've seen them. Where are they? Emily and Kathy, where are they?'

She shook her head again, angrily, and went away. I looked up at the other faces. They were all blank and hostile. Nobody tried to open a window.

I walked to the door, and rang the bell. I could hear it, shrill, echoing far back in the house. I waited a moment, and then pressed it again, and again. Then I stepped back from the door and looked up at the windows again.

'You know I can smash that door!' I shouted. 'Where are Emily and Kathy?'

I rang the bell again, and then held my hand on the bell push, hearing the sound high and trembling, and I waited.

It was the same thin-faced man who came at last, but

as he drew the bolt I heard the clink of a chain, and the door stopped short, only a few inches open.

'Emily and Kathy,' I said. 'I'd like to see them, please.'

'You are trespassing,' he replied. 'You have no right to be here.'

'Emily and Kathy,' I repeated.

'Go away. You are not welcome here.'

The door began to close, and I thrust my shoulder against it.

'I'll smash this thing to matchwood if you close it,' I spat. 'And I can, don't doubt it. Where are Emily and Kathy?'

For a moment he pushed against the door, and then he gave up.

'They have left. They spoke to you, against our rules. We asked them to leave.'

'Where have they gone? When did they go?'

He glared at me, his face pale, a tiny muscle twitching at the corner of his eye.

'Where have they gone?' I insisted. 'If you answer my questions I'll go. If you don't, I'll break your door down, silly little chain and all.'

'London,' he said at last. 'On the early train from Gloucester. We gave them money and called a taxi for them. They broke our rules.'

'Their address,' I said. 'I want their address.'

'No address. We do not know their address. We have no interest in them. We gave them money and called a taxi. That is all. We have no address for them. Now go.'

I stepped back from the door, and he slammed it shut and shot the bolt. I did not believe him, but I could not search the house, could not insist on seeing people he said were no longer there. I could call him a liar, even carry out my threat to smash the door, but there was nothing to be gained from that.

I mounted Lyric, and we rode away. Once off the gravel I let her run, and within a few paces she was galloping, her head low and her shoulders moving powerfully and rhythmically as she pounded up the hill. Worried though I was, I found time to marvel at her lovely strength, carrying my weight uphill at such effortless speed. I turned my head to check that Plod was following, and saw him running on our tracks, head and tail low, his coat rippling in the wind.

I telephoned Mrs Hunter's office when we got back, and left a message asking her to call me urgently, no matter how late, as soon as she could. Then I telephoned the police, and asked to speak to Royce or Irons. Royce came to the phone, and I told him what had happened.

'I see,' he said when I finished. 'And these two ladies, what makes you think they haven't gone to London, as the man said?'

'They'd have come to me instead.'

'If you say so, Miss Mayall. But I can hardly start getting search warrants on those grounds, your opinion that they'd rather come and see you than go up to London. Anyway, if it was early perhaps they didn't want to disturb you. The early train goes at about six, not the normal time for social calls, is it?'

'What about the three other people they said had disappeared?'

'Well, now, Miss Mayall, this word "disappeared", just what does it mean in this case? They didn't tell your friends they were leaving? I can think of a few reasons they might not have done that. It doesn't amount to much, does it? Just what do you expect me to do?'

Nothing, I thought hopelessly. I could expect nothing. How could I explain to Royce that my friend had had fear in her eyes when she left? How could I express Kathy's insistence that the three people had not gone, how to explain that they were prisoners?

'Sergeant Royce, would you come and look at these hedges?' I asked. 'And the gates? Please, would you?'

'Look at hedges and gates, Miss Mayall? Why?'

'Because they're designed to keep people in, not out, that's why. You look at these hedges, they're mostly beech, with a lot of other bushes, just like normal hedges. But when you look again, on the inside they're all blackthorn. And the gates, why these security locks? They're like prison gates.'

'You've got a key,' he pointed out. 'I'm sure everybody who needs one's got a key. Sorry, Miss Mayall, but I don't think there's anything I can do. I expect your friends will be in touch. Might even be trying to ring you now, getting the engaged tone while you're talking to me.'

I telephoned all the taxi services listed in the Yellow Pages. None of them had a record of a call to Gorsedown. I telephoned Gloucester station, but the early morning staff were not on duty. Somebody suggested I call back early the next day.

I telephoned the police again, to try to persuade Royce to find out what had happened to Emily and Kathy, to tell him no taxi had been to Gorsedown. I was put through to the CID offices, and I heard his voice in the background, but somebody told me he was out, and asked if I could leave a message.

'No taxi called at Gorsedown this morning,' I said. 'I've telephoned them all. Would you tell him? It was a lie, I've called all the taxi services in the book.'

'I'll tell him.' The voice sounded bored. 'But they're not all listed, or it could be a private arrangement, just somebody with a car earning a bit on the side.'

I hung up, wondering frantically what to do next. It was getting dark outside. I went across to the forge, and carried out some routine tasks, raking out the clinkers, cleaning the anvil, tidying already tidy tool-racks. I telephoned Mrs Hunter again, but was told she had not yet returned or called in.

'Please ask her to phone me as soon as she does,' I begged. 'I think something's happened.'

The girl promised to do as I asked. Perhaps she was too accustomed to distressed clients on the telephone to take much notice of just one more.

After that, I didn't dare use the telephone again, in case she should try to contact me, and give up on getting the engaged tone. Not for one moment did I believe that Emily or Kathy would be trying to call me. Again and again I saw the despair in Kathy's face as I asked them to wait while I finished my work in the forge, saw her hands shaking as she did up the buttons on her coat. I saw fear in Emily's huge eyes, and heard her voice.

'Ann, we're scared. Ann, we're scared. Ann, we're scared.'

Emily, Doctor Emily Peters, who had escaped gunmen in Liberia, who had made her way to England, calm, educated, sensible Emily, who walked quietly by habit, so as not to disturb sleeping patients at night, who had asked for my help, and had been put off because I had my animals to feed.

'Ann, we're scared.'

Why had I let them go? Kathy had told me three people had disappeared, and I had seen the Children of God, seen the menace of those five young men with the slashers in their hands standing across my path, knew they had cut the throat of the horse, believed Mrs Hunter's warning when she told me I was in danger. Emily had said they would come back early in the morning, had wanted to collect her papers. Papers are important to a refugee. Had they been seen coming to the forge? Had somebody been watching from the three beech trees, and seen them at the gate?

What had happened to them?

Plod barked sharply, and then bayed, an angry yell in his voice, and I heard the gate. I ran to the paddock, vaulted over the fence, and sprinted as fast as I could along the path.

'Emily? Kathy? Is that you?'

I was out of breath, and it was almost dark. There was

no reply, and Plod, running ahead of me, was barking, jumping up at the gate, his hackles up and his teeth gleaming.

There was a woman at the gate, standing a few yards back from it, watching Plod warily.

'What is it?' I asked. 'Who are you?'

'I've come about your friends.'

'Well?'

'They're being taken to the north gate now. I came as quickly as I could. They're crying.'

She turned away and began to run back along the path. I called after her to stop, but she ignored me and ran on. I thought of chasing her, but she was running faster than I could, so I turned and went back to the forge, forcing myself to think and to plan.

It had to be a trap, but I did not see how I could avoid it.

I telephoned the police again, and asked for Royce. I was told he was no longer on duty. Irons, too, was unavailable.

'Please,' I said. 'I think this is serious. It really is urgent, please give me somebody who can help.'

'I'll put you on to Detective Constable Shepherd.'

I told Shepherd about the message from the girl at the gate. He knew nothing of the Children of God, or the dead horse, or my earlier calls to Royce. I drew a deep breath, and told him what I had told Royce.

'I'll ask somebody to keep an eye on the north gate of the park, then,' he said.

'Can't you do any more than that?'

'Well, it doesn't seem like a crime's been committed, Miss Mayall. But if you're worried about this message, don't go. If you don't think it's genuine.'

'Please,' I said. 'Please, think about it. Either they've disappeared, and this message is a trap, or the man was lying yesterday, and they're being held prisoner. Please, can't you see?'

'I'll see what I can do, Miss Mayall. Thank you for calling.'

'Just a minute, please don't hang up. I'm going into the park. Please, could you get a car to come here, in an hour? If I'm not back, something's happened. Please, could you do that?'

'I'll see what I can do,' he said again, and rang off.

I telephoned Mrs Hunter and got an answering machine. I tried to explain what had happened, but the tape ran out before I finished. I telephoned again.

'It's half-past seven,' I said. 'I'm going into the park just in case it's true, but I think it's a trap. Please come, I should be back in an hour.'

I had never ridden in the dark before. I could only trust to the animals' senses to keep us out of trouble, my own vision was frighteningly limited. We trotted along the track, Lyric with her head high and ears pricked, Plod a few yards away, his dark coat almost invisible, just the panting of his breath and the gleam of his teeth telling me where he was. Every so often we stopped, and I strained my ears for any sound of the Children of God. I could hear nothing, except for the distant hum of traffic on the main road, and the creaking of the trees in

227

the small night wind. If they were near, Plod would hear or scent them.

From the hill I looked down at the manor, saw lights in a few of the windows, and listened intently. There was nothing to be heard. We turned eastward, along the broad grass ride down the slope, and I let Lyric break into a fast canter, hoping there was nothing over which she would stumble, trying to balance my anxiety and the need for speed with caution over the darkness, and the danger of the unseen terrain. At the bottom of the slope I reined her in, and we waited for Plod, and listened again.

To the north, I heard somebody call, and a faint answer.

We went on, trotting fast across the grass towards the pine woods and the voices, heading for the wide track that led to the north gate. I dared not risk riding through the pine trees in the dark. The wood was full of fallen firs, with broken branches standing out from the trunks like spears. The only safe approach to the north gate was the track, with the dark sheltering trees on either side of it.

I stopped when we reached it, listening, straining my eyes to see along it. Lyric sidled uneasily, sensing my fear, and Plod circled away from her. The wind was behind us, blowing from the south; he could scent nothing ahead of us.

A voice called again, and then came a scream, high and shrill.

I jumped, startled, and Plod barked.

228

'Quiet,' I said, and he whimpered softly. If this was a trap, and I was almost certain it was, the scream was part of it.

I began to ride along the track, as close to the centre of it as I could. It was only a few yards wide, and the trees were thick and dark, crowding in on either side, black fir, creaking in the wind, pine needles thick on the ground, muffling the sound of hooves, or of footsteps.

Plod had time for only one warning bark, and the lights blazed out from the trees beside us, and behind them a cymbal clashed and voices rose in a yelling chorus as the Children of God ran out from the trees, blinding torches searing through the dark into our eyes, the cymbal clashing again and again, and Lyric snorted in terror, threw up her head, and bolted along the track.

I yelled at Plod to follow, but had no chance to see if he obeyed. I was frantically trying to pull Lyric back to a manageable speed, but she was panic stricken, terrified of the lights and the noise, blindly fleeing the danger behind her, oblivious to what might lie ahead.

I saw it only yards in front of her flying hooves, a thin gleam across the dark earth. I made one last effort to drag her round, then I kicked my feet free of the stirrups and threw myself clear as the wire caught her squarely just below the knees and brought her down, squealing, her legs thrashing in the air as she somersaulted across the track to land on her back, the ground shaking under the impact of her heavy body.

There was a searing pain in my shoulder and blood running down my face. I could see lights, flashing and whirling, I did not know whether they were real, or inside my head. I stumbled to my feet, staggered, and fell again, crawled forward, and found the wire, broken. Lyric was lying on the track, her ribs heaving, I could hear her gasping, and I climbed to my feet again. I felt sick, waves of nausea and giddiness, I wanted to fall down again, to wait for the kind darkness to take the spinning lights away, to drown the shouting voices, but Lyric raised her head, and her legs were flailing as she tried to roll onto her belly, to raise herself and escape again, and I stumbled towards her, tried to crawl again, and screamed from the pain as my shoulder collapsed under my weight. I fell forward and rolled away from the agony, and felt leather under my face, a thin strap dragging. I reached out, caught it, and wound my hand around it as Lyric grunted, her hooves inches away, and heaved herself to her feet, blood running down her forelegs onto my outstretched hand.

The lights whirled, and faded, and blazed again, and the voices were yelling, somebody screamed. I closed my eyes, tasted vomit in the back of my throat, and tried to roll over. Lyric was dragging on the reins, her hooves stamping by my head, and then there was another scream, and Plod was baying and snarling close beside me. I tried to tell him to be quiet, the noise hurt, but I could not speak. The lights flickered and spun in my head, hooves stamped, people shouted, another angry yell and Plod was barking again, his paws beside my face scratching. Something wet on my cheek, and I turned away, and my shoulder burned with pain, Lyric stamping and snorting and dragging at the rein, it was cutting into my hand, the buckle was sharp and hard against the side of my finger, it hurt.

I opened my eyes, and Plod licked my face again, and then jumped forward, growling. The lights were there, blazing into my eyes, they hurt, the noise hurt, and my hand, and Lyric was pulling, she must not get away, my hand hurt, and my shoulder, Plod was baying again, there were people shouting, the noise hurt.

I had to get up. They were there, behind the lights, the Children of God, I could hear them, the lights were moving, they were trying to get behind us, Plod was going berserk, what was the matter? Why was there all the noise? I had to get up, the lights were spinning again, Lyric, she must not run away, she was frightened and pulling at the rein, it cut my hand, it hurt. Get up. My knee hurt, my ankle. Bend it, get onto my knee, it hurt. Get up onto my knee, don't let Lyric get away, somebody screamed, Plod snarling and baying, get up, get up, the lights, they hurt, all round us now, behind us, get up, Lyric, don't bolt, please Lyric, stand still. Get up, off my knees, get up onto my feet, my ankle hurts, my knee. Get up, hold onto the rein, Lyric, please stand, stand still. Lights everywhere, Plod turning fast, baying and snarling. Saddle, hold onto the saddle, grab the stirrup leather, hold on. Please, Lyric, stand. Please, stand. Feel so sick, noise, lights, it hurts. Hold on. Reins over her head, don't throw up your head, darling Lyric, please stand. Get up into the saddle. Plod, please be quiet. Please stop baying.

Hammers. Behind the lights, they've got hammers, big sledge-hammers. Get into the saddle, quickly. Get up, foot into the stirrup. It hurts. Quickly. Plod, good dog, good dog. Hammers, quickly, careful, Plod! Be careful. Lyric, stand, stand still, girl. Foot in stirrup, get up. Get up, pull yourself up, pull yourself *together*, quickly! Good dog, Plod, keep them off, good boy. So sick. The lights, spinning. Go on, Plod. Good dog, get them, Plod! Yelling again, hammers, come on, forward. Lyric, go on, damn you! Now, forwards, get through them. Go on, Plod! Have at them, good dog!

Thudding, hooves, Lyric moving forward, frightened, Plod barking again, lights, hoofbeats again, and Plod barking, and a yelp, someone shouting, hammers, they've got hammers! Plod, get away from there! Oh, God! No, please, my good dog, yelping, the shouting, Plod! Come here, Plod, get away from there! Lights, and shouting, my dog, please, Plod, come away!

So sick, the lights, hoofbeats, please, Lyric, stop. Stop, Lyric, go back. Reins, where are the reins? I can't find them, please stop, hoofbeats drumming, faster and faster, going home, Plod, my good dog, my poor dog.

14

I couldn't open the gate. My left arm was useless, hanging slackly from my shoulder, I couldn't move it. My right knee and ankle hurt so much when I put any weight on them I nearly blacked out again. I clung to the steel flowers, hearing them ring, hearing in the echoes of their ringing the cries of my dying dog, feeling the tears scalding in my eyes, cold on my cheeks.

Lyric stood beside me, quiet now, sweat and lather drying on her shoulders and flanks. I knew she shouldn't stand like that, getting cold after running so fast, she'd catch a chill, she should be in her stable. I tried to think what to do, but all that would come into my mind was that my lovely dog was dead, and my horse should be in her stable, warm and dry, with the sweat cleaned out of her coat, and her thick night rug buckled on as she ate her evening feed.

I had vomited several times on the way back, leaning over Lyric's shoulder, clinging desperately to the pommel, giddy and sick. After a mile she had slackened her headlong gallop, dropped to a canter, and at last a tired, dragging walk. She was lame, favouring her near hind leg, and blood was still running down her shins from the cuts the wire had made. I should have dismounted, I should have walked her home, but I could only cling to the saddle and hope that the pain in my shoulder would subside before I passed out. Every time I opened my eyes blackness swam in front of them, waves of black and red, and the giddiness made me reel in the saddle. At last I leant forward, resting my head on Lyric's mane, wrapping my hand in the thick, strong hairs, and trusted her to take us home. She stumbled on the dragging rein several times, and at last I heard it break close up to the bit, and she shook her head. She was tired, and I couldn't help her, I could only leave it to her to bring us back safely.

She stopped in front of the gate, her head drooping with weariness, and waited for me to let her in. Slowly, I straightened up in the saddle, slid my right foot out of the stirrup, and tried to dismount. My leg crumpled under me as it took my weight, and I fell hard, my injured shoulder sending sheets of agony across my body as I jarred it. I blacked out again.

I don't know how long I was unconscious. Lyric was still standing, tired and patient, her nose almost touching the gate, when I came round. I began to cry, tears of grief and weakness running down my face. Slowly and painfully, I stood up, leaning against her shoulder. I hobbled forward to the gate, and pushed against the steel lilies.

It hardly moved.

I needed both arms, and my left arm was hanging useless, a burning weight, only pain, nothing more, no strength, nothing. I leaned against the gate, pushing with my right shoulder, bracing against it, forcing it away from the frame, my left foot digging hard into the earth, and it swung back, and hit the second spring, and stopped, the steel flowers ringing. I held it there for a moment, waiting for the nausea to die away, wondering if I could do more, and then I pushed again, and felt the powerful resistance of the steel plate, and I gritted my teeth and forced myself against it. Slowly, the gap between the frame and the edge of the gate widened, and I pushed harder, and then it hit the third spring, and I could do no more.

Sobbing with rage and weakness I fell back, and the gate sprang against the frame, the clanging of the steel startling Lyric so she half-reared away, her head high and her eyes rolling. I sank down onto the earth, sick and giddy, and heard her hoofbeats slowly dying away. I knew I should go after her, catch her, bring her back. I knew, too, we were in danger. This was the only way out of the park for us, and the Children of God might well be following.

I lay on the ground, my face against the cool, damp earth, and waited for them. They'd killed my lovely, brave dog, they'd killed a horse, they were going to kill me. Had it not been for Plod, I would already have been dead, under the blazing lights, and the hammers, and the shouting voices. Perhaps if Lyric wasn't here when they killed me they'd let her go. When the lights came.

And the lights were coming, I could see them, but there were hoofbeats too, Lyric was coming back, slow, and tired, and lame, limping home again, standing over me, her head drooping, waiting for me to open the gate for her, but there were lights flashing, and coming nearer, and flickering, a blue light, flickering.

And the voices, I could hear the voices now, and with the lights and the voices would come the hammers, and death. I lay on my face on the cool earth, crying with weakness and grief for my dog, and I waited for the Children of God, and my own death.

The gate, the gate was shaking and ringing, and somebody was swearing, and a woman's voice.

'There she is!'

I sighed, and hoped they would leave Lyric alone.

'Get this damned gate open, what's the matter with you?'

'It's stiff, Madam, I can't move it.'

'Yes, she told me you had to be strong. You'd better get the other constable, perhaps both of you can manage. For God's sake hurry, she's hurt.'

I raised my head, and looked towards the gate. Light shone into my eyes, and I turned away again, laying my cheek back onto the cool earth.

'Miss Mayall? Ann? Come on, wake up. It's Julia Hunter and the police, now get up.'

It was so comfortable on the soft earth, waiting for the end, I was so tired. I wanted to rest, to stay there and not move, not move my arm, no more pain.

'Get up! Can't you hear me? Damn you, Ann, get up! You've got to get up, we can't get this bloody gate open. *Ann*! We can't get the gate open.'

I gritted my teeth, and dragged my good knee up alongside me. It was too much. I couldn't do it.

'Get up! Your horse is hurt, get up and help him. Or her, whatever. Come on! You going to leave her bleeding there, you bitch? Get on your feet! Get up, get to this gate, you bloody slut!'

I looked back at the light, hating her.

'Get up! On your feet, stop wallowing around there.'

The gate was shaking and ringing again, and I could hear men speaking and swearing. Lyric was bleeding, I looked at her forelegs, two wicked deep cuts with the dark blood black on her poor shins and her hooves.

'Ann! Come on, show us how this fucking gate opens, get up and do something, that horse is hurt.'

I couldn't do it. It was too much. But Lyric was bleeding, hurt, she'd brought me home. I crawled to the gate, crying again with the pain in my shoulder, my arm dragging in the mud, and I pulled myself up and leaned my head against the frame.

'Come on, Ann, you slut, you whore, get this gate open! You want that horse to bleed to death, is that all you care about her?'

I leaned against the gate, my right hand on the lily leaves, and dug my foot into the earth. I felt so ill, so giddy, and if the gate swung closed again Lyric would run away, and the Children of God might find her and kill her. I heard voices, the men, and Mrs Hunter, and I pushed, digging into the ground with my foot, and I felt the gate shiver and swing against the spring. There were hands in front of my face, gripping the gate, gripping the loop of the rose stem, and voices again, and Mrs Hunter telling me to open the fucking gate, calling me a useless slut, saying Lyric was dying because I, a whore, wouldn't save her, and I pushed again, falling against the gate, and a man was beside me as I fell, his hand over mine on the lily leaves, pushing, and the gate swung against the third spring, but they held it, and forced it back, cursing it, and I heard the ratchet catch and Mrs Hunter was kneeling beside me telling me I was fine, I was wonderful, I'd saved my horse, everything was all right, they were here now, she and the police, we were safe.

I didn't care. I wanted her to leave me alone, I'd done what she told me, now I could lie on the cool earth. Somebody was leading Lyric past me, and I saw her poor bleeding legs and heard the uneven beat of her hooves as she limped past, one of the policemen at her head. They were talking, but I didn't care what they were saying, I didn't want to hear about ambulances and doctors. I wanted somebody to look after Lyric for me. I wanted them to stop talking, I wanted to tell Mrs Hunter about Lyric, and then I wanted to sleep on the earth, with nobody there, quiet and alone.

'Jake Brewer,' I said, as loudly as I could, and Mrs Hunter was kneeling at my head.

'Jake Brewer?' she said. 'Yes, dear, what about him? Who's Jake Brewer?'

But the waves of blackness were back in my head, and there was roaring, and my mind was swimming in the darkness, and the only peace and the only comfort was the earth under my cheek, cool, and damp, and still.

I woke up when the ambulance came, rocking over the grass in the paddock, the lights flashing, and I screamed when they tried to lift me, because I opened my eyes and saw the lights with a shadow behind them, I thought the Children of God were back, and I could face that, but not the hammers on my shoulder.

'Sorry, love. Sorry, didn't know. Shoulder, is it? Right, let's just get up nice and easy, that's right, soon have you fixed up.'

'She keeps passing out,' Mrs Hunter said.

'Jake Brewer,' I said.

'Yes, dear, Jake Brewer. I'll telephone him when you're in the ambulance, no doubt he'll know what it's about, is that right?'

I wanted to answer, but I was vomiting again, doubled over somebody's arm, somebody else was holding my head, and telling me not to worry, I'd be all right soon.

'Bloody great swelling behind her ear. Probably concussion, it's that shoulder that's the nasty one.'

I tried to straighten up, but my knees began to buckle, and somebody caught me around the waist, but he couldn't hold me, and I was sitting on the ground and leaning against the wing of the ambulance, looking up at Mrs Hunter.

'He'll look after Lyric,' I said.

'Look, love, let's get you in the ambulance, you're

more important than the horse.' One of the policemen. I pushed him away, Lyric was very important. Mrs Hunter was beside me again, telling him to let me explain.

'Tell him to come and get Lyric. Before they come. They killed Plod.'

'*Who*? Who did she say they'd killed?'

'Her dog.'

'Christ! I thought she meant . . .'

I was crying again, thinking of Plod, wondering what he had felt as I rode away on Lyric, leaving him under the hammers, hoping he knew I hadn't wanted to go, hoping he hadn't thought I was abandoning him.

'I'll stay with Lyric until Jake Brewer comes.' She was smiling down at me. 'Can you stand up? Yes, just try. I'll telephone him and ask him to come straight away. That's it, lean on the ambulance. I won't leave the horse alone, I'll stay with her, don't worry. Now, just walk slowly, lean on the ambulance, just a bit further. Jake Brewer, yes, I know. He'll take her, will he? Good. Just a bit further, can you manage those steps?'

They strapped my arm to my side to hold it still until we reached the hospital, and I lay on the bunk in the ambulance, trying to stop crying. One of the men asked if I wanted a pain-killer, said it would be better if I could wait until the doctor had seen me, but it wasn't the pain. I said I could wait. One of the policemen was in the ambulance too, asking me what had happened. I couldn't face telling him everything.

'How much do you know?' I asked.

He hardly knew anything, only that they'd been sent to the forge and told to meet Mrs Hunter there, she was insisting I'd been abducted and that they had to get into the park. They'd found me by the gate.

It was too late anyway. Emily and Kathy were dead, I was sure of that, and my dog, and I had loved my dog more than any of them. I closed my eyes, and heard somebody say I'd passed out again.

There was a doctor, pulling at my eyelids and shining a torch into my eyes, and nurses, and too much bright light, until one of the nurses laid a cool cloth over my forehead, and it felt so good. I was on a trolley, and somebody was cutting off my boots, and my jacket, and then there was the great rolling pain again and I wanted to be sick. There were X-rays, with people asking me to move, and turning my leg, trying not to hurt my shoulder, putting cold grey slabs under my head, and a thing like a bomb over my face, whirring and clicking. And at last a needle in my arm, and a voice telling me to count, and when I reached three everything went away and I was in the cool darkness and all the pain and the misery was somewhere else.

15

There were ice packs around my knee and my foot, and tight bandages, and a strap that lifted my leg, suspending it from a harness on a track over the bed. Badly sprained, a smiling black nurse had said. And my shoulder had been dislocated, but it was back in place now. It felt sore, but the flaring agony was gone.

'Would you like to see your face?' he asked. 'Not recommend it. You are no advertisement for Elizabeth Arden this morning. Tea?'

'Gin,' I replied, and she laughed.

'Concussion and gin, not a nice cocktail. You drink your nice tea, there's a handsome policeman coming to see you.'

It was Royce. He asked how I was, and sat on one of the hard chairs by the side of the bed without waiting for an answer, taking a notebook and a ballpoint pen out of his pocket.

'It's a bit late for that,' I said. 'If you'd listened to me yesterday I wouldn't be here, and my dog wouldn't be dead.'

He ignored me, looked at his watch, and wrote something in his notebook.

'There's a record of a call from you at seven-thirty yesterday evening. DC Shepherd. He says he advised you not to go into the park. You ignored his advice.'

'What do you suppose happened to them?' I asked. 'Emily Peters, and Kathy, and the three other people they said had disappeared?'

'Do you often go riding in the dark?'

'Never.'

'Only on desperate rescue missions, is that it? Would you care to tell me what happened?'

I told him. I described the track to the north gate, with the fir trees close on either side, and the sudden lights and the cymbal, Lyric bolting in fright, and the wire. I told him about Plod, and the hammers, and my eyes were dry and hot, and my throat was tight with rage. I couldn't remember how I'd managed to mount Lyric, with a dislocated shoulder and concussion. I told him about getting back to the gate, and Mrs Hunter coming with the policemen.

He wrote it all down.

'How's my horse?'

'I've no idea.'

His voice was indifferent. He turned a page, wrote a few more lines, and then closed his notebook and stood up, slipping it into his pocket.

'I may be back,' he said. 'If I have any more questions.'

My head was aching, and I felt sick and hot and thirsty. I fell asleep before he'd even left the room.

A doctor came in and woke me. He held fingers in front of my eyes and asked me to count them. I misheard him, and counted from one to fifteen before he stopped me, laughing. He asked me my name, my age, my mother's maiden name, and told me I would be all right, and I could go back to sleep.

Mrs Hunter was beside my bed when I woke again.

'Lyric's going to be all right,' she said as soon as I opened my eyes. 'Do you know what extensor tendons are?'

'Yes.'

'Well, Mr Brewer said I should tell you they're not permanently damaged, he said you'd want to know. Everything else is cuts and bruises and a sprained hock.'

I drew a deep breath, and felt the weak tears starting to my eyes again. She patted my hand, and said she'd be back tomorrow, she'd wanted to make sure I knew about Lyric. In case I forgot, concussion being concussion, the nurses knew about Lyric, too.

There were pills for my headache, and people kept asking me to count their fingers. I wanted to sleep. I was thirsty, but drinking made me feel sick. That evening a nurse fixed a drip, the needle in the back of my hand. After a while the thirst died away. The bandage on my head felt tight, and I asked somebody to take it off. Tomorrow, they said. After Dr King's seen it. Did I know my horse was all right? Good, somebody had telephoned and said the vet had seen her.

Dr King said the big bandage on my head could come off, but the dressing on the wound behind my ear would

244

have to stay, eight stitches needed protecting. As for the rest of my head, fresh air would help. He warned me about my shoulder. The dislocation had been a bad one, some of the ligaments had been torn, it would need care.

When Mrs Hunter came back she brought a manila folder with her, and opened it as she sat by my bed.

'How's your head?' she asked.

'Better. I'm not sure about my memory. Did I hear you calling me names when I was behind the gate?'

'Yes. It's a good idea, that gate, only a handhold for one person, we couldn't get through, you see. You were the only one on the other side, I had to wake you up.'

She settled herself more comfortably in the chair, and looked down at the folder.

'Reconcile is a registered charity,' she read, adopting her official voice. 'It's been running for just over four years, and its constitution is founded on the idea of arranging reconciliations between asylum seekers and refugees and the governments or other organisations from whom they have fled. The original founder, a Mrs Janine Alderan, is the Chairman, and there are twelve other trustees. There is an office in Tottenham which deals with the day-to-day running of the Charity. Mr Clive Alderan, Mrs Alderan's son, is in charge of the office, with two women who handle the financial and administrative affairs. There were two large bequests, one from Mrs Alderan's deceased husband, and most of the funds derive from them. Some four million pounds is invested in gilt-edged stock.'

'*How* much?' I asked.

'Just over four million pounds. The constitution of the charity states that all refugees or asylum seekers may apply for help, regardless of race, colour, religion, or sex. It also allows for its work to be delegated to other organisations, with funds granted to those organisations, in order to further its aims. There are no restrictions on the sums that may be granted, nor on how the funds may be spent, apart from the general aim of reconciliation. In addition, the term "other organisations" is the only description. There is no requirement for them to be registered charities or recognised religious orders.'

'The Children of God,' I said.

'Quite. There is no registered charity by that name, and I was given to understand that an application using that name would probably be refused. The registered owner of Gorsedown Manor is Stephenson Holdings Limited, a private limited company with four shareholders, all of whom give their official address as a lawyer's office in Leeds. Gorsedown Manor was bought for £750,000, the cheque for the full amount being drawn on the Stephenson Holdings account at Lloyds Bank, a branch in Mill Hill. There have been no applications for a change of use at the planning office, nor for any building work or alterations to the existing building. It is still a private residence, according to the records in the council offices.'

'Who are the shareholders?'

'Jonathan Stephenson, his wife Angela, Samantha Grafton, and Anthony Clinton-Smith.'

Mrs Hunter looked at me, and smiled.

'Those are the facts,' she said. 'Now. Clive Alderan is a fool, and he and Reconcile's money are soon parted. He knows little or nothing of the Children of God, only that they are, in his words, wonderful people who do great good. They have arranged for the safe return to their homelands of lots of refugees. He does not know how they achieve this, they have explained to him that they have to use secret contacts, and quite often, unfortunately, bribery is involved. However, so long as these poor people can be happily reunited with their families, that doesn't matter. Reconcile will continue to support them in their wonderful work.'

I stared at her.

'Without,' she continued serenely, 'any check on the funds, as naturally no receipts are given for illegal bribes. Refugees stay at Gorsedown Manor so that they are readily to hand to take part in the negotiations that are carried out on their behalf. Reconcile pays for their keep while they are there. It makes a delightful holiday for these poor souls, with people who genuinely care about them.'

'It's unbelievable.'

'Unfortunately it's not uncommon. Woolly-minded people can set up charities with laudable aims, and unscrupulous crooks can milk those charities of every penny they possess.'

I was puzzled by what she said.

'Is there a need for this charity?' I asked. 'If they're refugees, why do they want to go back? I don't understand.'

She raised her hands, and let them fall back into her lap.

'Oh, my dear, so many of these people are just innocent bystanders. It's dreadful. There's a taxi driver, he took a fare to the airport, but the fare was a politician on the run, and the army were looking for the taxi driver as an accomplice. He's in Birmingham now. A lorry driver gave a hitch-hiker a lift over the border, and it's the same story. People who went to demonstrations, just for the fun of it really, their photographs are on police files and they daren't go home. Oh, I'm afraid there's plenty of work for Reconcile.

'As for the Children of God, there's nothing so far. I'm afraid I've come to a dead end with all the enquiries I've pursued, but there are still a few lines to go. Apart from the four shareholders of Stephenson Holdings, I have no names, I don't know where they come from. The people who handled the sale dealt only with the Stephensons themselves.'

'What about Emily Peters?'

'Reconcile recommended a firm of lawyers in Brixton, and they confirm that they are acting for her, but will divulge no further information. I told them her story, as you gave it to me, and they said they were not in a position to confirm or refute it. In effect, what the quite pleasant young man said was yes, it was true. So far as they know, Dr Peters still lives in Wandsworth. They know nothing of Gorsedown Manor or the Children of God. It was Reconcile who put Dr Peters in touch with the Children of God, by the way, they thought she would like a little holiday there, but they say they have no record of any refugees from Togu. Mr Alderan said that the Children of God often find refugees themselves, and then apply to Reconcile for funds to help them. These funds are never refused. In my opinion, Reconcile has nothing to do with your problems. Mr Alderan said he had never visited Gorsedown Manor, but had been told it is a lovely old house set in a peaceful park.'

'Peaceful,' I said bitterly. 'Yes, I see.'

'Are you all right?'

'Yes. You've found out a lot.'

'Four people from Gorsedown Manor are helping the police with their enquiries into a possible attempted murder.'

I closed my eyes, and sighed.

'I have to say I would be very surprised if the police can make it stick. I'm sorry, but I really doubt if they'll get far.'

'Why not? What about my poor dog? What about the wire?'

'Ann, there won't be any wire. There'll be a group of concerned citizens coming upon the scene of a riding accident, trying to help the victim, being attacked by her dog. The victim was concussed, and confused. Very sad about the dog, but they had to defend themselves. They won't know how the accident happened.'

'Did Royce tell you this?'

'Royce? No. He wouldn't tell me the time. I'm afraid the information about the four people cost fifty pounds, but I'll get the names for that. We might get a bit further with those. It's also possible the police will dig into the Children of God, even if they can't make this charge stick. There was the dead horse, too. Royce is nobody's sweetheart, but he's not a fool either. And Jake Brewer's vet says Lyric's legs were, without a shadow of doubt, cut by wire, nothing else causes that sort of injury. If it came to court, though, the defence lawyers would certainly produce two vets to say it could have been done by broken branches. Unless somebody cracks under questioning it's a no-hoper.'

I spent two more days in hospital, restless and bored, and then I discharged myself. Dr King had said that all my injuries needed was rest, and I insisted I could rest just as well at home, if not better, since there wouldn't be people waking me up every few hours. I found it impossible to think, somebody else had been brought into my room, an old woman who was to have an operation on her hip. She wanted to talk all the time, if not about her nephew then about her knitting, and she complained, sharply, that I didn't have much to say for myself.

As soon as I limped into the cottage, I smelt soap, a tang of carbolic, faint but quite clear. I stopped on the threshold, sniffing, my hand dropping by habit to my side, fingers snapping softly to summon a friend who would never be there again. Soap, a strong soap that I never used, faint and dispersing but still just there, just enough. I stood still, listening, scanning the room for any sign. There was nothing to see, nothing to hear, just that light trail in the air, all that was left of the stranger who had been in my home.

I went through the cottage, slowly and carefully. It had been searched. Everything had been left tidy, nothing had been stolen, but things had been moved, clothes that had been folded in drawers had been replaced differently, papers moved from one side of the table to the other, books that had been taken off the shelves had not been put back in the same order. Whoever had searched the cottage had made no effort to hide his activities, had not cared that I would know he had been there.

There were no broken windows, no smashed locks, but the key to the kitchen door lay on the table. The door was unlocked.

I've never been security conscious. There are always windows open in the cottage, unless I'm going to be away for a while. I had little worth stealing, the radio and the television were both old, and I keep money locked up safely in the forge.

There were marks on the door to the workshop, scratches on the lock, but I knew the door was bolted from the inside, big steel bolts slotting into mortices that were set deep into the oak frame. It could be forced, but it would take sledge-hammers.

They had sledge-hammers.

The padlocks were in place on the forge door, but there were scratches on them, too. Somebody might have been in the forge.

I went back to the cottage, and telephoned the police, asking, as always, for Royce. This time, he came to the telephone.

'Somebody's been in the cottage,' I said. 'It's been

searched. They may have been in the forge, too. I think somebody tried to pick the padlocks, I don't know if they succeeded.'

'What's missing?' he asked.

'Nothing, so far as I can see. I haven't been into the forge yet. I thought maybe you should know first, in case you wanted to take fingerprints.'

Three men came that afternoon, and they sprayed a sort of pink dust onto all the surfaces, and then took photographs of the resulting smudges with a special camera. They said a lot of the surfaces had been wiped, and asked when I'd last dusted. They took my prints, and asked who else came into the cottage. Nobody, I told them. Sometimes customers in the living room, nobody went upstairs.

'There's glove prints on the bedside table,' said the youngest of the three. 'Wear gloves in bed, do you? Thought not. Well, that's it, then. They've been careful, cleaned up after them and worn gloves. Might as well pack up.'

Nobody had been in the forge. The padlocks were old, but they had been the best when Uncle Henry had bought them, and it would have taken an expert to have picked them. I could find no sign of any search there, and the pink dust showed no suspicious smears, only dozens of clear prints, my own, and those of my customers.

'You've been lucky,' said the youngest man. 'Nothing nicked, nothing smashed.'

They said goodbye, and left. I telephoned Mrs Hunter,

and left a message. The girl promised to pass it on when she called in.

That evening Constable Harris drove up to the cottage and climbed out of his car, looking around him. I limped to the door, and wished him good evening. He nodded at me.

'I've been asked to keep an eye on this place,' he said. 'As if I hadn't got enough to do.'

I didn't reply. There was a bandage on my head, my arm was in a sling, and I was using a walking stick. Somebody had been in my house. I wondered, briefly, what Harris thought a village policeman was for.

'No more burglars, then?' he asked sarcastically. 'No arsonists in the hayloft, no rapists under the bed? Right, I'll get back to work then. I'd have thought you could have taken care of yourself, big girl like you.'

I took Plod's blankets and I threw them in the dustbin, along with his food bowl and the big plastic washing-up bowl in which he had had his water. I wondered what the Children of God had done with his body.

I had never felt so lonely.

That evening I drew the curtains as soon as it grew dark and I locked and bolted both the doors and closed all the windows. I lay in the dark with my face turned, not to the windy skies, but to the heavy blue wool that shut them out, and with them the eyes that might be watching from the beech woods. I'd been given pills in the hospital, pain-killers for the headaches, but I didn't take them. I thought about Plod, and tried to reconcile myself to his death, but there was only a steady anger in my mind.

Once again, the Children of God had stopped on the brink. They had invaded my home, but they had stolen nothing, had done no damage. The police had more pressing business, better ways of spending their limited time and resources, there would be one more note in the file, and nothing would be done.

Had they succeeded in killing me it would, in the end, have been an accident, a riding accident.

The Children of God did not know about Julia Hunter, and had not known I had contacted the police about Emily and Kathy. Now, with Royce asking about them, that had changed, but I wondered if that would stop them. They had tried to kill me. It would not be possible to prove that, Mrs Hunter had been right, their defence was very strong, but I knew the truth. I had been concussed, and there had been blood in my eyes, but I had seen that wire before I hit my head, heard the shouts and the cymbals, seen the lights that had driven my horse into her headlong blind flight. I thought of Lyric hitting the wire, the way she had turned in the air, the ground-shaking force with which she had landed on her back. Had I not seen the wire, had I not thrown myself out of the saddle, I could have been under her. That would have been enough. But in case I had fallen clear, they had followed. They had not been running to help an accident victim, they had been carrying hammers. Concussed, and with blood in my eyes, yet I had seen those hammers in the blinding lights, only shapes and shadows, but I knew what they were.

Would they try again? If I went into the park again,

would there be traps? It would be easy now, there was no dog to give warning of their presence. And even if I stayed away, would that be enough, now that I knew of Emily and Kathy?

I lay in the darkness, wondering, and listening, and waiting, and grieving for my dog.

16

I was in the forge early the next morning, measuring off lengths of steel to make horseshoes, one of the few tasks of which I was capable. I should have been resting my left arm in the sling, but could no longer bear the inactivity. In a fit of irritation I had thrown the sling into the corner, and was just beginning to regret it. The dislocation hadn't been as bad as a fracture, but the ligaments needed time to heal.

When farriers cut mild steel, the usual practice is for an assistant to hold the cold set, a big, sharp-edged steel wedge held in a metal grip or mounted on a handle, onto the bar of steel, and for the farrier to hit the set with a sledge-hammer. I like to work alone. I use a sledge-hammer with a shortened handle, and the grip I've made for the cold set lets me hold it closer to the bar than usual. Most farriers adapt their tools, those of them that they don't make for themselves. No doubt two people can cut bars of mild steel more quickly than one, but I've had plenty of practice now, and I manage. With the weight I can put behind a hammer I don't need to take as much of a swing at it as most.

I heard footsteps on the gravel, but I wasn't alarmed. Visitors were not uncommon at the forge.

As the four shadows fell across the forge floor and the anvil I looked up. I'd been thinking about Plod, and I was already angry. At the sight of the men, standing so arrogantly in the sunlit doorway watching me working, that anger boiled immediately into rage, and I straightened up, raising the hammer and stepping forward.

They looked surprised for a moment, and the smallest of the four backed away. I smiled.

'Haven't you brought yours?' I asked. 'Am I the only one with a hammer today?'

I didn't wait for an answer. I turned back to the anvil, laid the cold set on the bar, and hit it, hard, with the hammer. The bar fell in two pieces. From where they were standing they couldn't see the cold set, and I dropped it behind the anvil as the steel was still ringing on the stone floor. I picked up one of the bars and turned to them, the hammer in my right hand, the bar in my left. There were four of them, and my shoulder was not only painful, but weak.

'And what can you do?' I demanded of the tall blond man who stood slightly in front of the others. 'Handy with the crochet hook, are you? Where did you bury my dog?'

'We sacrificed the dog,' he said. He had a thin, high voice. 'We took him back and sacrificed him. He was a good dog. He was an acceptable offering.'

257

'Where did you bury him?' I had to keep control of this situation, and I could only do that by forcing the conversation in the direction I dictated. The two men who stood closest to him were young and fit, one of them short but burly, with wide shoulders and long arms, and the other, a taller man with a shaven head, looked as if body-building might be his hobby. The smallest man, who had stepped back, was sidling up alongside his companions again. Just in case it came to a fight, I marked him down as the weak link, but I had very few hopes of winning any sort of physical contest with them.

The blond man's eyes were wandering around the forge, looking at the tools, at the high shelves in the dark corners, at the drawers of tools under the work-bench.

'We've come for the key.'

There was a faint smell of carbolic soap.

'It never was in the cottage,' I said. 'What sort of gloves did you wear? You forgot to wipe the bedside table. Perhaps you'd better *sacrifice* the gloves, glove prints are quite incriminating. Where did you bury my dog, Blondie?'

He was indifferent.

'Where is the key?'

'Do you think I'll let you search for it here? You're wrong. You'd have to break in, and those padlocks aren't so easy, are they? It'll take more than four of God's Toddlers to get past me here, with this hammer in my hand.'

'You won't be riding in the park again,' he said. 'You won't need the key.'

He turned his head and nodded to the three men and they moved into the forge, the broad-shouldered one reaching for the tool drawers under the work-bench, the man with the shaven head making for the shelves.

I caught the smallest man as he tried to pass me. He squealed in surprise, clutching at my arm, and I quickly shifted the hammer to my weakened left hand and forced him to his knees beside the anvil, my right hand grasping his collar, knuckles digging hard against his neck. He was quite strong, but none of them had expected resistance, not from one woman alone in the forge. The blond man stepped forward, and for the first time there was anger in his face. I raised the hammer.

'You saw me break a steel bar with this,' I said. 'What do you think I could do to a skull?'

'You wouldn't dare!'

'They haven't proved attempted murder last week, but that doesn't mean they don't believe it happened, Blondie. What would you do? You came here to terrorise me, four of you. I'm about as scared as this anvil, but the police won't know that. If you rush me, he's dead, and I'll be glad of it. I loved that dog. You made a big mistake, killing him.'

I could feel myself beginning to shake, my hands trembling. To hide it, I let the man's collar go and instead grabbed his hair, forcing his face down towards the beak of the anvil. He hissed with the pain, but said nothing. Behind me, I could feel the other two waiting for orders. Of the four only the blond man had spoken.

I was listening as I spoke, listening for the sound of

steel on wood, to hear if they picked up any of the tools. A blacksmith's tools make deadly weapons. For the moment I had the advantage, but it wouldn't last.

'Where did you bury my dog?' I demanded again, and then I heard the scrape of metal on the work-bench.

I threw the hammer, and I was lucky. I can't aim with my left hand, and I was turning, but it spun in the air as I hurled it, and caught him squarely in the chest. He staggered back against the work-bench, more surprised than hurt, but he dropped the hoof-knife, which clattered on the stone floor. He recovered his balance immediately, but he looked at the blond man, and the expression on his face was apologetic, and a little nervous.

The blond man hardly spared him a glance. He stepped towards me, raising his hand, his lip curling scornfully. I slammed the kneeling man's face against the beak of the anvil, and jumped towards the forge.

The kneeling man screamed in pain and fright, clasping his face in his hands. Blood seeped between his fingers. The blond man stopped, staring down at him, shocked, and by the time he raised his eyes to me again I was standing in front of the forge with a shovel full of hot coals in one hand and a six-foot steel bar in the other.

I looked quickly at the shaven-headed man. He was standing still, watching the blond man, calm and relaxed. It was he I feared most, and I couldn't watch him and his leader at the same time.

The kneeling man whimpered, and looked up at the blond man. He sniffed, took his hand away from his face, and stared down at the blood on his palm. He looked up again, shocked, and made as if to speak, but the blond man motioned him to keep silent. He whimpered again, touching the cut on his eyebrow with tentative, dabbing fingers.

I laughed.

I had never felt less like laughing. They were on three sides of me, and I could not watch them all at the same time. I feared the shaven-headed man most, but the one at whom I had thrown the hammer was powerfully built, and had not been hurt by the blow. There were still three of them fit for a fight, and the weight of the steel bar was sending sharp warning flashes of pain to my shoulder.

'Perhaps I'd better find the dog myself,' I said. 'Shall I do that, Blondie? Shall I bring a pack of bloodhounds into the park? What will they find if I do?'

He backed away from me, watching the shovel as the coals died from red to a smoking black. The man kneeling by the anvil was sniffing quietly, his head bent over his hands, blood dripping slowly from his face. I turned my head to look quickly at the man behind me. He was watching the blond man, and standing still, but now he was tense, his hands clenched into fists. The burly one at the work-bench was rubbing his chest where the hammer had hit it, and there was a look of uncertainty on his face.

For the first time, the blond man looked nervous. He had not expected resistance, let alone defiance; he had anticipated dominating the situation from the moment he faced me, and he had miscalculated, although he could not know how close he had come.

The pain in my shoulder blazed suddenly, and I dropped the bar onto the anvil, trying to disguise the grimace of pain with a look of disgust. I threw the coals back into the forge and leaned the shovel against the wall.

'Oh, get out,' I said. 'Go on, pick up your lackey and go home.'

It was a bluff, and it didn't work.

He gave the briefest of glances to the shaven-headed man behind me and nodded to the man at the work-bench. I heard a foot slide on the floor, and I was already turning, so the fist aimed at my kidneys scraped instead across my back. He had been ready for that, and he followed it with a left cross aimed up at my face. I stepped backwards, jerking my head out of the way, and most of the force of the blow was lost, but the backs of his knuckles hit my chin.

I've never learned to fight, never studied any of the martial arts, never even learned self-defence. I'm hardly a likely target for a rapist. The man who had hit me knew what he was doing, and was not in the least put out by his first two punches having missed, or only grazed, their targets. His head was held low, his chin tucked in, and he danced back out of my reach, eyes calculating, preparing for another attack.

The man kneeling at the anvil was climbing to his feet, the one at the work-bench was stooping, looking for the knife that he had dropped. The blond man was standing in the doorway, watching, a smile on his face, waiting for the inevitable outcome.

I turned my back on the shaven-headed man and jumped towards the work-bench, reaching for a hammer. A knife might have made a more threatening weapon, but I have been working with hammers since I was five years old, and they are like an extension of my arm, I can use them without thinking. And I didn't think as I swung it, not at the shaven-headed man who was coming after me, whose fists were already shaped for another blow, but at the shorter one who was straightening up with the hoof-knife in his hand. I watched the head of the hammer arcing down towards him, a slow and easy strike such as I have made hundreds of times every day for years, aiming not at his head, but at his shoulder, past and behind his rising arm, three pounds of tempered steel on a hickory handle, and at the last moment I turned my wrist so the edge of the head struck, and I felt the blow through the wood, not the humming ring of iron, but the dead crunch of bone.

The man shrieked with pain and fell to his knees, clutching at his shoulder and gasping. His eyes rolled up to stare at me, shocked disbelief in his face as the blood drained from it.

A fist thudded into my ribs, a short, hard punch with a lot of weight behind it. I turned towards the shaven-headed man and aimed a wild swing at his head with the hammer. He ducked it easily, and threw another punch towards my head, a curving right hook, deceptively slow. I raised my left arm to ward it off, and his fist caught me high on the upper arm, directly under the damaged joint.

For a moment it made me wild with rage. I went straight for his face with the hammer, chopping at his head and ignoring his fists. Once I caught him on the forearm as I tried to smash through his guard, and I saw him grimace with surprise and pain, but he danced back out of my reach, moving lightly and easily, a trained boxer with no doubt of his ability to defeat me, shaking his bruised arm to get rid of the pain, and then raising it again as he clenched his fists and moved towards me.

The next blow caught me in the stomach, and it stopped me. I had seen it coming and tried to dodge, but he was much too fast. I drew in my breath sharply, and the edge of his hand cracked down onto my wrist, numbing it.

I dropped the hammer.

His hand flicked out again towards my face. I turned away, not fast enough, and felt his palm slap hard against my cheek. Not a punch, an open-handed blow. As I turned to face him again I saw him smile.

This wasn't to be a fight, then. This was to be a beating, a punishment.

There was no point in trying to outwit him, he was a fighter and I was not. He was as strong as I was, and against his speed I was helpless. He was certainly going to win. In the end, I would be beaten and punished. But I was not going to make the victory cheap.

Once again I turned my back on him, and this time I attacked the smallest of the four, who was standing with his back to the forge, his hand against his injured face, watching. I took two long strides and jumped onto the anvil, using the momentum to launch as powerful a kick as I could at his chest. He tried to fend it off with his hands, and I felt my foot land solidly against his elbow.

In common with most farriers, I wear steel toe-capped boots.

His eyes widened with shock, his face turning white, and the blond man shouted something, angry, and perhaps even frightened.

From the anvil I threw myself at him, aiming wild punches at his head, and he backed away, fending off my fists with his hands. I was nearly six inches taller than him, and far heavier, and when one of my punches broke through his hands and landed on his forehead his head snapped back under the force of the blow, and he cried out.

Then the shaven-headed man attacked again, not with his fists, but with the steel bar I had dropped. I heard it whistling through the air as he swung it, but I had no chance to do more than try to drop to the floor, and I wasn't fast enough. It caught me squarely across the back, just below the shoulder blades, and threw me forward against the blond man, who pushed me away.

I dropped to my knees, my arms hanging helplessly at my sides. I couldn't breathe. I could hardly move. If that blow had landed where I think he had aimed it, low across my back, over my kidneys, it would probably have killed me.

It was very quiet. The blond man looked down at me,

his hooded eyes unblinking, his lips thin, faintly smiling. I heard the scrape of metal on the flagstones as the man whose elbow I had kicked picked up the shovel. I heard shuffling as the man with the broken shoulder climbed slowly to his feet.

The blond man drew a knife from a sheath at his belt.

This time, I thought, they would kill me.

I struggled to breathe, tried to force air into my lungs, wondered if I was truly paralysed, if perhaps my back had been broken. I closed my eyes, and swayed forward, and then at last I could breathe and I drew in a great whooping lungful of air. I was on my hands and knees in front of the blond man, staring down at the flagstones, looking at the worn golden sandstone, wondering how many thousands of horses had trodden those broad blocks since they were laid, thinking of the pack ponies, the war horses, the great draft animals who had stood here, thinking of anything other than the searing pain across my back and the air dragging into my lungs, and the man with the knife in front of me, and the other man with the steel bar behind me.

I could feel the blood throbbing in my head, beating fast in my ears, the body's reaction to oxygen starvation, just beginning to slow now, but still fast and irregular, a thudding, drumming sound, blocking out the voice of the blond man who was speaking again in his high, thin voice, blood drumming and thudding in my ears, like hooves, like little pony hooves over a high, thin voice.

'Where is the key?'

I rocked back onto my heels and looked up at him. He

was holding the knife in both hands, up above my head, the blade pointing down towards me.

The knife was gold. There were tiny dents in it, all along the sides of the glittering blade, hand-beaten gold. I stared up at it, and slowly he lowered the blade, looking down into my face, his lips curling in disgust, and then slid it back into the leather sheath.

'That was the knife that killed your dog,' he said. 'It is a sacred knife. We will not defile it on such as you. You are worthless. Where is the key?'

'Lost,' I sighed.

The blond man looked over my head, and nodded, and I heard swift footsteps on the flagstone.

I held up my hand, a gesture of resignation, and they stopped.

'A moment,' I said. 'Just a moment.'

I had to stand up. I wondered if I could do it. Breathing was so painful, I was so weak, but I had to get to my feet. I looked down at the flagstones again, drawing deep breaths, trying to remember, and then I climbed slowly to my feet and stood bent, with my hands on my knees, waiting and hoping for my strength to come back. I felt drained, dazed with pain, weary, and very frightened.

But under it all, I was raging. I kept my eyes lowered so the blond man would not see the fury and the hatred I felt sure I could not disguise. This place was mine. Unknowingly, I had been working for it since I was five years old, and I had won it, earned it, I deserved it. It was mine, and they had invaded it. I loathed them for it, and I wanted to kill them.

I straightened up, but I did not raise my head. My shoulders were slumped and my knees bent, the old posture of apology for my size, the signs of defeat that I had never before used here. I swung my head slowly from side to side, and saw on the stones the faint shadow of the shaven-headed man, cast by the glow from the forge. He was standing, waiting, the bar still raised ready for another blow.

'The key. Where is the key?'

I sighed, and moved to the doorway of the forge. I laid my hands on the massive oak doors, and then I reached up. Nine feet high, those doors. And a thick slab of oak above them, a ledge, a place where anybody might believe a key could be kept.

I felt along the ledge, my fingers brushing through the dust, through some old nails, and then they touched some cold little metal cylinders that rolled under my touch. Three of them. I felt further along, trying to remember, a little further, and there it was, cold and dusty, where I had put it two years before. A revolver.

I couldn't have moved quickly even if I had tried. I covered the gun as best I could as I brought it down, and I flicked the chamber open and tried to load it. My left arm was throbbing where the punch had landed on the already torn ligaments, and I dropped two of the cartridges.

The shaven-headed man saw them roll on the flagstones at my feet, and he leaped forward, raising the bar for a killing blow, but I had turned and was pointing the gun straight at the blond man's face. There was only one cartridge in the chamber.

'No!' he shouted. He was backing away, his eyes wide with shock and fear, his hands stretched out in front of him, the palms towards me, as though he could stop the bullet.

'Stand still,' I said. 'If you move, I will kill you, and I very much want to kill you.'

He stopped, and stood where he was, staring at the gun, his mouth slightly open.

'You with the bar,' I said. 'Put it down. Now.'

The shaven-headed man looked at me, calculating the distance between us, his eyes narrowed. He gripped the bar tightly at one end with both hands. Six feet of steel bar, as steady as stone, not a quiver in the entire length of it. He was not only strong, he was completely unafraid.

'Put it down, or I'll shoot your friend. Not you, him. I'll get you with the second shot.'

He didn't move. He was waiting for me, waiting for my resolve to falter, and if it did that bar would come swinging round from behind his shoulder with all the speed and weight he could put into it, and that would be the end.

The blond man's hands had dropped to his side. He was watching again, and his chin began to lift, his eyes no longer wide and scared but hooded, arrogant.

I squeezed the trigger.

I meant to kill him. I wanted the bullet to plough into his face, to destroy him. But I missed.

It was very close. He screamed, and clapped his hand to his ear. The sound of the bullet passing alongside it must have almost deafened him, and with the fear that had come back to his face was pain.

'Tell your friend to put down the bar,' I said. 'The next one will be between your eyes.'

He couldn't hear me. The noise had stunned him. And now the gun was unloaded, and although the shaven-headed man had jumped back half a pace at the shot I was still within his reach; if anything, I was in even more danger from the longer swing he would make with the bar.

'Tell him to put down the bar,' I said again, slowly and loudly, but the blond man stared back at me, stupefied, his hand still held to his ear. Behind the shaven-headed man I could see the small one with the injured elbow begin to shuffle towards the door, and I felt his frightened eyes fixed on me, and on the gun. The shaven-headed man heard him too, and I saw him glance swiftly at the blond man and then turn his calculating stare back to me. If the little man got between me and the blond man, he would swing that bar. And the burly man at the tool-bench was also on his feet, his hand clasped to his broken shoulder, but watching, and ready.

I raised the gun, and gripped my right wrist with my left hand. Slowly, I sighted down the short barrel, aiming it directly at the blond man's face. I moved my hand on the grip, curling my fingers around it, and I began to squeeze the trigger.

'No!' he screamed. 'No, don't shoot!'

I didn't move my hands. I stared down the barrel at him, and it was, mercifully, steady.

'Tell him to put down the bar.'

'Put it down,' he said. 'Put it down.'

The shaven-headed man glanced at him, and then unhesitatingly bent and laid the bar on the flagstones. He stood up, his arms at his sides, watching me, listening to the blond man, relaxed and unafraid.

'Now get out,' I said. 'Take your flunkies and go. If you come back, I will shoot you. Don't doubt it, I really want to kill you. Don't give me an excuse.'

He jerked his head at the three men.

'Come,' he said, and then he looked back at me.

'We shall change the lock on the north gate.'

'I must remember to take my cutting torch when I next want to use it,' I replied. 'I have the right to ride on Gorsedown. You have no rights on the forge. If you come back, I'll kill you.'

17

I knew the number of the police station by heart, and I dialled it and demanded Royce. Some of my anger was directed at him.

'If the best you can do is send that futile little wood-entop Harris over here, then don't bother,' I said. 'I've had visitors again, four of them, what I believe are known as "heavies", throwing their weight around; one of them attacked me with a steel bar. Aren't our police-men wonderful? Just what the hell are you doing?'

'What did they want?'

'The key to the north gate.'

'Did you give it to them?' His voice was sharp.

'No, I didn't. Are you doing anything about these bas-tards? Or am I just to put up with all this, attempted murder, my horse bloody nearly crippled, my dog smashed to death with sledge-hammers, my friends dis-appearing, thugs threatening me in my home? What are you doing about it, *Detective Sergeant* Royce?'

'Where is the key?'

'You go to hell. You sound just like Blondie.'

I hung up on him, and telephoned Mrs Hunter. She was, for once, at her desk, and she told me, apologetically, that she needed more money. She'd been to Scotland and Lancashire, and it had been a successful journey, but quite expensive.

'How much?' I asked, and I probably sounded anxious. It would be at least ten days before I could work again, and there would be a heavy bill from the vet for Lyric, and the livery fees, on top of my usual expenses.

'Another five hundred, I'm afraid.'

'Would three hundred do for now? My accident insurance doesn't cover private detective's fees.'

There was a smile in her voice as she said she could manage with that, but she became serious immediately after.

'I did tell you about confidentiality only being possible up to the point where I find evidence of crime? We're quite close to that now, I think.'

'There's nothing you need keep confidential so far as I'm concerned,' I said. 'What sort of crime?'

'Murder,' she replied. 'Stay out of that park for now, my dear. This is very nasty.'

It was only after she had hung up that I realised I hadn't told her about the four men.

I stared out of the forge window, and thought about the Children of God, and murder. The blond man had said they had sacrificed my dog. He had been an acceptable offering. I didn't believe Plod had survived the hammers, but I wondered, unhappily, if he might have done, if he had died in some other place, under that gold knife. Sacrifice was a word that made me feel cold, that spoke of savagery and cruelty, of gods who took no joy in life.

Murder, Mrs Hunter had said, and this is very nasty. Her words. I thought of them, of the quiet way she had spoken. They would have killed me, those men. With the hoof-knife, or the iron bar, they would have killed me.

I pushed the thoughts aside and dialled her number again, but she had gone. I left a message for her to telephone me.

I was making horseshoes when Royce arrived with two other policemen, and a very slow process it was, as I was trying to do much of the work with the shoes clamped into the vice rather than held in the tongs. My back felt as if somebody was holding a hot branding iron against it, and breathing hurt; I wondered if any of my ribs were actually broken. My shoulder was aching. I had wanted to go to see Lyric, but a four mile walk was more than my ankle and knee could stand. Almost everything I needed or wanted to do was either impossible, or exceedingly difficult. I was also worried about money.

'I've had to hire a private detective to find out about these Children of God people,' I yelled at him as he came to the door. 'Do you know what that costs?'

'We need to borrow the key to the north gate,' he said, as if I hadn't spoken. 'Where is it, please?'

'I'm not lending it to you, and I'm not telling you

where it is, either. Why the hell should I help you? You've been as much use as a sick headache so far.'

One of the other policemen looked startled, and held up his hand to stop Royce speaking again.

'Miss Mayall, I'm Detective Inspector Stone. Could we discuss this? Quietly, I mean?'

'Discuss what, Inspector Stone? What exactly would you like to discuss, quietly? A racehorse was killed here, his throat was cut, whoever did that ran off into Gorsedown Park, would you like to start there? Five people have disappeared from Gorsedown Park, is that what you'd like to discuss, quietly? A trap was set for me, *in Gorsedown Park*, it was only thanks to my dog I wasn't killed, but *he was*, and if we're going to discuss anything, we're going to discuss *that*. Do you know what wire can do to a horse's legs, Inspector Stone? Would you like to discuss that, quietly? I'm going to be off work for another two weeks, do you know what that's going to cost me? Shall we discuss that? And the four men who came here this morning, *from Gorsedown Park*, they wanted that bloody key too, they were quite prepared to kill me in order to get it, and you've got something in common with them. They're not going to get it, and neither are you.'

He was looking at me gravely as I yelled at him, and he made no attempt to interrupt me or stop me. When I'd finished, he nodded.

'I can't say I'm surprised you're angry,' he said. 'I can only say I understand. I can't even tell you what we're doing. I'm sorry. There's very little I can offer, and I have to ask for your help. No doubt there are other ways of achieving what we need, but they'd take time, and I've got to act quickly. Please let us have that key.'

He had a pleasant voice, quite low, with a slight north country accent, and he spoke slowly, as if he had thought about what he was saying.

I turned the tommy bar on the vice, and the horseshoe fell at my feet. I looked at it in disgust. It had been heated and cooled so often the colour was mottled, and I hadn't even been able to hit it straight. It was the third one I'd attempted, and I'd broken the first two. It was a disgrace.

'Are you in charge now?' I asked Stone.

He nodded.

'And just what are you investigating?'

This time he hesitated, and his eyes narrowed, but he did answer.

'Attempted murder.'

'And you need to get into the park without them knowing. I suppose you have looked at those hedges, have you? I did suggest you should. I want two things from you, Inspector Stone, one easy, one probably not. I want to know if my dog was killed by those sledge-hammers. One of those men said he'd been sacrificed.'

Royce muttered something, but Stone gestured at him, and he fell silent.

'What exactly did the man say?'

'He said he was a good dog. He was an acceptable offering.'

'But he used the word sacrifice? Try to remember, Miss Mayall.'

'"We sacrificed the dog. We took him back and sacrificed him. He was a good dog. He was an acceptable offering." I think those were the words. He certainly said "sacrifice".'

The other man, the one I hadn't seen before, was writing in a notebook, and he read it back to me. I nodded, and looked back at Stone.

'Can you find out about the dog?' I asked.

'I think so. I can ask for the body. If I can get the body, then I can find out, or rather a forensic pathologist can, and I will try to get the body.'

It was the most I could expect. I nodded again, and reached for my jacket.

'The key's clipped to my saddle, and the saddle's with Jake Brewer. We can get it now, and I want to talk to Jake about my horse. I'll need about half an hour. That's the second thing.'

I refused to answer any of his questions until he'd done as I asked. I said we could talk on the way, and at last he agreed, reluctantly, but with a slight smile. Royce drove us, and the third man, young, dark haired and pale faced, sat in the front seat screwed round to face us, and took notes. Stone asked me to describe the men, and then asked what had happened. I thought about it.

'They barged in and started to search the place,' I said. 'The blond one demanded the key, he said I wouldn't be riding in the park any more. When I asked him where he'd buried my dog he said they'd sacrificed him. He kept asking for the key, and when I refused to give it to him he nodded at the other three and they started to search the forge.'

'What happened when they couldn't find it?'

I was not going to tell him about the gun. Since I'd put it on the shelf two years earlier I'd forgotten about it until fear and desperation had brought it back into my mind, but owning a gun without a licence, let alone firing it at someone, even in self-defence, could have put me in prison. Also, Stone would have taken it, and I was by no means sure I wouldn't need it again. I'd rather be in jail than dead.

'I caught one of them and threatened him with a hammer,' I said. 'There was a lot of bluster, and one of them threatened me with a steel bar, and for a few minutes there was some pushing and shoving. Then the one with the shaven head, he attacked me, and I did hit one of them with the hammer, on the shoulder. I think I broke it. There was a fight, and I got hit across the back with the bar, but I think they were worried about the man with the broken shoulder, and the little one, I'd kicked his elbow, so he couldn't fight either. Luckily, they gave up. I'd managed to grab a sledge-hammer.'

Stone was watching me out of the corner of his eye, silent and cynical. I stared back at him.

'Do you know who they were?' I asked, and after a few moments he answered.

'The blond man, the one who spoke, that was probably Anthony Clinton-Smith. He seems to be their spokesman. I can't be sure about the others, there's one with a shaved head called Mlnarski and it might have

been him. Ukranian father, Dutch mother, he was a mer-
cenary until a few months ago. You know we probably
couldn't prove this attack? There's no real evidence, and
it's your word against theirs again. They'll say they were
collecting for charity. I'd be prepared to guess they
called at other houses with their collecting tin. They
won't take the man with the injured shoulder to hospital,
either. Do you want us to investigate it? I mean, sepa-
rately?'

I thought about the gun, and shook my head.

'No. Not if you're doing something else about them,
anyway. They seem to be getting reckless. Don't they
care if they're caught? I couldn't believe it, after all this,
coming to the forge and threatening me. Are they crazy,
or something?'

He didn't answer my question, but he did give me a
warning.

'Don't go into the park, Miss Mayall.'

It was the second time within an hour somebody had
said that, and Stone's voice was grave. He had a way of
staring at me as we spoke, eyes very straight under dark,
level brows, as though he were calculating the words
and looking for other meanings behind them.

'Get another dog,' said Royce, and I looked at him
with hatred.

Lyric's forelegs were bandaged, the white dressings a
sharp contrast against her dark coat. She came to the
door of her box and nuzzled at my cheek, an affectionate
greeting that brought tears to my eyes. I hugged her,
and buried my face in her mane.

'She was lucky,' Jake had said. 'When I saw those legs I really thought she was done for. Wicked, that was. Wicked.'

'What about her hock?'

'Oh, that's not much, that's nearly better. She must have come down a hell of a crack, though. She was sore all over, poor old girl. And your new saddle, that needs repairing. The pommel's broken.'

I stripped the rug off her, and ran my hands all over her body, looking for bruises. She flinched once, a sore spot on her shoulder, but she was moving quite easily around the box. As Jake said, she was lucky. I borrowed a body brush and gave her a quick grooming, more from affection than need; her coat was smooth and clean. Jake was taking good care of her. I left the bandages alone.

'I'll turn her out for a little potter in the paddock if it's fine tomorrow,' he said, rubbing her forehead as I rugged her up again. 'Don't worry, she's on the mend.'

Stone had collected the key, and then he and Royce had hung around the yard, looking at their watches and staring at me with increasing exasperation. I'd refused to be hurried; half an hour was what we'd agreed, and I took it. They drove me back to the forge fast, breaking speed limits, and as I climbed out of the car Stone said he'd return the key in due course. I nodded absently, knowing I wouldn't be needing it for a while, and anxious to get away from them. There was a skewbald mare tethered under the tree, with a foal lipping at the long grass, and I wanted to see about them. Stone watched me for a moment, and then shrugged.

'Stay out of the park,' he said again. 'No matter what happens, stay out. As you said, they're reckless.'

'Yes,' I replied. 'Yes, all right.'

Gypsy horses, I thought, looking at the tether. The only customer who hadn't been able to read the notice on the gate. Where was she? Maggie didn't like strangers, the three men in the car would have alarmed her.

'I'll have to be off now,' said Stone. 'Miss Mayall, do you have to stay here?'

The skewbald mare was looking at us, ears pricked.

'Yes, I must,' I said. 'It's all right, I won't go into the park.'

'I can't spare anybody to stay with you. I don't like you being here alone.'

I turned to him, impatient and a little exasperated.

'For a man in a hurry you seem to have a lot of time to spend dithering,' I said. 'I've nowhere else to go.'

The radio in the car crackled and the third man answered it. Royce leaned across the car and called out.

'We're late, sir.'

Stone nodded to him, and smiled at me.

'I'll find out about your dog,' he said. 'Stay out of that park.'

I watched the car until it turned the bend in the road, and then I turned back to the forge, and called out.

'Maggie? Maggie Ripley? They've gone, you can come out now.'

She was behind the forge, watching from the shadow of the big rainwater butt, very still until I called, and then there was the sudden flurry of a long skirt as she came out, grinning at me. I hadn't seen her until she moved.

'Hallo, Maggie,' I said. 'I can't work. I've hurt my shoulder.'

'We'll wait, lady.'

Maggie never explains what needs doing. She just brings the horse, and smiles, and waits, and does whatever I ask her.

'Well, let's see,' I said. 'Walk her up the path, would you?'

Maggie untied the rope from the mare's head-collar. My clothes line, I was amused to note.

The mare walked straight, her broad, chipped hooves clopping on the concrete, no sign of a limp. Maggie's horses are never shod. The mare was sound. The foal, then.

'Is the foal halter-broken?' I asked, and Maggie shook her head, her grin widening.

'Maggie, I've hurt my shoulder. It's been dislocated, the tendons are damaged, do you understand? The ligaments? They're damaged, I can't wrestle with a foal.'

'We'll wait, lady. Me and Daisy, we'll wait.'

Foals must be the most appealing of all young animals, but they aren't often a farrier's favourite customers. They can be playful, and this is lovely to watch in a field, as they scamper around on the grass, bucking and jumping, but it isn't so pleasant if you're trying to handle them. I have a scar on my forehead where a young colt reared up and caught me squarely between the eyes as I was trying to check his forelegs.

'Oh, damn it, Maggie, what am I going to do with you? I can't use my left arm, have you ever seen a one-armed farrier? No, I'm bloody sure you haven't.'

I talk more to Maggie than I do to any of my other customers. I don't know how much she understands, she just smiles, and nods, never gives an opinion of her own, but she does as I ask with the horses. That's why I talk to her.

'We'll have to get a halter on her, Maggie. And you'll have to hold her, I can't. Can you do that? There's a foal slip on the peg at the back of the forge. Tie the mare to the ring, then we'll try to halter the foal, God help us.'

She grinned, and nodded, and tied the mare to the ring, a quick and expert twist of the rope, a highwayman's hitch, the knot for a quick getaway. I wondered about old habits.

'We'll manage, lady,' she said, and laughed.

She caught the foal quickly, driving it into a corner and then dodging in front of it as it turned, the soft leather slip sliding over the broad head, and then she kept the foal turning, its head towards her, so that it couldn't brace itself and pull away. I watched in admiration; Maggie was ragged and dirty, and far from normal, but she was a past master at handling young stock.

I found the problem quite quickly, but there was nothing I could do. The foal had contracted tendons in her forelegs, and Maggie had rasped the hooves down at the heels. With the heels cut low and the fronts of the hooves, the toes, left long the weight of the horse is pushed to the back of the foot, which stretches the tendons and helps to correct the problem. Maggie had done a good, neat job on the foal's feet, but the long toes were beginning to crack. The foal needed shoeing, and I couldn't do it.

'Maggie, I can't shoe her,' I said. 'That's why you've come, isn't it? She needs shoes, I know. But I can't make shoes, and I can't shoe her, I've hurt my shoulder.'

'We'll wait, lady.'

I looked at her, helplessly. She'd only been to see me twice before, both times for grass cracks, and although on her second visit she'd had to wait all day I'd done the work for her in the end. There's something implacable about Maggie's friendly patience. I had no doubt she'd do exactly as she said.

The vet, Travis, told me she'd once waited for him for two days when he'd been flat on his back with bronchitis, leading her mare to the grass verge by the road to graze, but coming back to his door every hour until he'd finally given in and staggered down to treat the horse. She always paid immediately, with crumpled banknotes pulled out of the pockets of her ragged skirts.

I went into the forge to telephone Neil Forbes. He was already shoeing several of my customers' horses anyway, and complaining happily about overwork, but he owed me a favour. I dialled his number, and eventually his father answered. The old man had been a farrier himself, and couldn't be persuaded to stay away from the new forge, even though his son bought the business from him and tore down the old buildings to set up a thoroughly modern workshop in their place. Neil Forbes refers to his father, fondly, as 'the old pest', and quite often shouts at him, but he won't put him in a home, or try very hard to keep him out of the forge.

I told Mr Forbes I wanted to complain about some work his son had done, and the old man said he'd go and look for him. The lie would save a long argument about what a woman could know about shoeing horses. I could hear voices in the background, somebody arguing, Neil's voice raised in exasperation. I let my eyes stray around the forge, thinking vaguely of the fight I'd had there only that morning. My back began to ache again at the memory, and I rubbed gingerly at my bruised ribs. I was beginning to feel stiff.

I looked down at the answering machine. There was no red lamp burning, no messages since I'd last listened to the tape. Neil was still arguing, and then there was a clatter as he threw something down, and footsteps approaching. I was still looking at the machine, wondering why I thought there was something wrong.

'Hallo?' His voice was wary.

'It's Ann Mayall, no complaints.'

'You crafty old mare! What do you want?'

I told him about Maggie, and he laughed. No, he said, he could not come and shoe the foal, he had two hackney horses to do and he was running late. He'd send one of his apprentices over to measure her feet, and maybe the old pest could still swing a hammer and make up the shoes, might even nail them on if wound up and pointed in the right direction and given a push.

'But he won't do it until tomorrow,' he warned. 'He's got his Bingo tonight, he won't miss that for a gypsy pony. You can have Our Dave this afternoon, and you're bloody welcome and all.'

Our Dave arrived half an hour later on a motor cycle, roaring onto the gravel and sending the foal into a frenzy of fright. Maggie shouted at him, calling him an evil young bastard, and then for the rest of the time he was there said not another word, but watched him out of angry eyes. In answer to my question he admitted he'd been an apprentice for eight months, but that didn't stop him telling Maggie she'd rasped the foal's feet unevenly, or from pointing out to me, in a parody of patient explanation, that the hooves were splitting and needed to be rasped down. When he left, pushing his motor cycle to the road in response to a threat from me to report him, Maggie and I looked at each other.

'He'll do no good,' she said. 'He'll do no good with horses. Evil young bastard.'

'You're so right,' I agreed. 'Listen, Maggie, old Mr Forbes is going to make up the shoes, okay? And he'll come tomorrow to fit them. Tomorrow, Maggie, understand?'

She shook her head, vehemently.

'You fit the shoes, lady. You.'

'I've done in my shoulder, Maggie. I can't shoe the foal, I'd make a mess of it, frighten her, lame her, I don't know, but I can't shoe her, I can't hold her foot until my shoulder's better.'

'We'll wait.'

I stood up, and beckoned her to follow me into the forge. She came in uneasily, rubbing her hands on her skirts and looking up at the ceiling as if afraid it might fall on her. I realised that Maggie hardly ever ventured under a roof; her caravan was the closest she ever came to it, and she was rarely in that. Except in the wildest of weather Maggie was outside, crouched by her fire, watching her horses, whittling wood to make clothes-pegs, or binding up little posies of dried wild flowers with tiny silver horseshoes or wedding bells to sell as good luck charms.

I stripped off my smock, and pointed to my shoulder. The bruises from the fall were beginning to fade, but they were still a dark grey, with angry yellow streaks running down the back of my arm, and the dull crimson mark of a fist high up below the joint.

'Technicolour,' I said, pointing to it. 'Look, Maggie, I can't.'

She walked round behind me, looking at my shoulder, and running her grimy brown fingers over the bruises. I felt her hand on the other shoulder, and I laughed.

'You're checking me out, aren't you?' I demanded. 'Just like a horse, right? Do you want me to trot up that concrete path for you?'

Maggie cackled at me, but her hands ran down my back and touched the angry patch where the bar had landed. I winced.

'That's no fall, lady,' she said. 'Somebody done that, oh yes. Maggie knows. Somebody been cruel, lady. That shoulder, that's a bad fall, yes. Maggie knows.'

'If I were a horse, Maggie, you'd turn me out to grass for two weeks. I'm a farrier, I'm out to grass. No work for two weeks. Old Mr Forbes, he'll do the foal tomorrow.'

I was standing up and pulling my smock over my head as I spoke, and Maggie grinned at me.

'Maggie's going home now,' she said. 'Daisy and the baby stay here, Maggie'll be back soon. Maggie's got something for that shoulder. Maggie'll be back.'

We turned the mare and foal out into the paddock, and Maggie left. I watched her setting off down the drive, the fast, swinging walk of the gypsy woman, her bright ragged skirts flapping around her strong legs, and I smiled.

I went back into the forge. I knew what was wrong with the answering machine. I'd rewound it only the night before, but it had wound on again since I'd last played the messages, although the red warning lamp was not glowing. The bulb behind the red cover must have failed; I'd have to replace it. In the meantime, I'd listen to whatever had been recorded.

There were four messages on the tape, the first two from a steel supplier about my last order and a customer about a shetland pony with laminitis, and the last from a double glazing salesman who promised to call back later.

The third message was from Glory.

'Ann, it's Glory, and I'm coming down, it's a celebration, so you kill the fatted frozen chicken, I'll bring the bubbly, it's marvellous news! Darling Ann, I'm too excited to talk, I'll be with you at about eight tonight unless the traffic's utterly poisonous, if you haven't got a fatted frozen chicken pizza will do. Bye!'

I smiled with pleasure, but then I hesitated. With the Children of God attacking me, and becoming so reckless and dangerous, I wasn't at all sure I wanted Glory at the forge. I was scared enough on my own behalf, and I didn't think I could protect my lovely sister.

I sighed, reached for the telephone, and dialled her number. It rang three times, and then her own answering machine came onto the line.

'Glory?' I called. 'Glory, if you're there, please answer!'

But the message wound to an end, and the tone chimed.

'It's Ann. Please telephone before you come, it's urgent.'

Then I went into the cottage, and looked in the freezer for something special in case I didn't manage to reach her. I keep a few oddments there for celebrations, mostly meals that can be boiled up in a tough polythene bag. I'm no cook.

The telephone rang while I was in the kitchen, and I went into the living room and picked up the extension in case it was Glory. I heard my own voice on the taped message from the answering machine in the forge, and a man's voice muttered, 'Shit!' I said nothing, and listened.

As the message came to an end, the salesman's bright voice began.

'It's Mark Jansen from Fleckets Double Glazing. Sorry

to have missed you again! I'll try later. We've got some really exciting offers in the new Stay Warm range, I'll tell you about them when I call back. Goodbye!'

Coq au vin, I thought, hunting through the jumbled bags in the freezer. Glory is very weight conscious, not too many carbohydrates, not too much fat. French beans with black pepper and slivers of smoked bacon. Baked potatoes with soured cream and chives, she might make a little exception and eat them. Then black cherries in brandy, and that was about as far as my culinary imagination could stretch.

I pulled the bags out of the freezer and threw them into the washing up bowl to thaw out in cold water.

My lovely sister, I wondered what we were celebrating, and what I could give her for a present. I thought about booking a room for her with Mrs Pagham, she'd be safe there, safer than here with me. I tried to telephone her again, but there was only the answering machine.

I went back into the forge to damp down the fire and make everything tidy, and then I stopped in the door, staring at the work-bench.

The little red lamp was glowing on my answering machine. The bulb had not failed.

Somebody had listened to my messages. The Children of God knew my sister was coming.

18

I tried three more times to reach Glory, but with no success. I grew sick of the sound of her voice on her answerphone. I telephoned Mrs Pagham and booked a room for her; no matter how much she protested I would not let Glory stay here.

The revolver was loaded with the last two remaining cartridges, and jammed into my belt, where it rubbed uncomfortably every time I moved. I was nervously aware that I had no knowledge or experience of hand-guns, and was quite likely to shoot myself in the leg if I'd misunderstood the safety catch, or if it wasn't working properly.

It wasn't a very good revolver anyway, and it was old and slightly rusty. Most of the moving parts were slack, and it rattled when I shook it. I doubted if it would fire straight, but it was the only hand-gun I had.

Feeling slightly foolish, I'd taken Uncle John's shotgun out of the gun cabinet, and cleaned and oiled it. I kept reminding myself of the expression on the shaven-headed man's face as he'd stood in front of me with the steel bar. He'd intended to kill me if he could, but although I knew it, I couldn't believe it. Death, with guns and bars and hammers, on a late March afternoon in England.

I could not believe it.

Nevertheless, I oiled the shotgun, and I carried the revolver jammed into my belt.

I massaged my knee and my ankle, and then rubbed the lotion the doctor had prescribed into them. The swelling had almost completely subsided, but after I'd been standing on them for a while they still ached. I tried not to think about my shoulder, still less about the savage weal across my back. I wondered if Maggie would come back.

The mare and foal were grazing quietly in the paddock, and I went to the fence to watch them, leaning on the top bar and propping one foot on the lower rail. The foal must have been born late in the summer, unusual for Maggie's horses, she preferred spring foals. I thought I knew the reason.

If anyone asked Maggie about the breeding of her horses she'd laugh. She'd tell you the mares were called Blossom and Daisy and Old Mary, but the foals were always called Baby. And she'd never tell you the name of the sire.

'Can't race them, lady,' she'd say. 'Don't need names, can't race them.'

Blossom and Daisy were skewbald, big brown patches

on white, and Old Mary was black, but most of the foals were chestnut. Only a mile away from Maggie's caravan was an old Suffolk Punch stallion, long retired and turned out to enjoy his last few years in a pleasant little paddock. Last spring he'd had a cough, and the farmer who owned him had brought him in during the wet weather, and left him in the big covered barn.

I doubted if Maggie believed in stud fees. She'd had to wait.

I watched the foal as she moved slowly across the paddock, cropping at the early spring grass. She was rocking back onto her heels as she walked, just as Maggie had intended. With luck, Maggie's work on her hooves would be enough to stretch the tendons. If that didn't work, there'd be a heavy vet's bill for surgery.

I raised my head and looked at the beech trees, wondering if anybody was watching me. Five days ago, I thought, only five days ago, Emily and Kathy had come through the gate to ask for my help. Four days ago I had ridden Lyric to Gorsedown Manor to search for them, and on that same night the trap had been laid to try to kill me. Only four days.

I climbed over the fence and walked through the paddock, slowly, so as not to alarm the horses. Daisy raised her head as I passed, munching a mouthful of grass, placid and content with her foal. There was a patch of nettles beside the path, and I noted it, thinking of bringing a fork to dig it out. Lyric never touched nettles. She was a fussy eater, I had to keep the paddock clear of weeds, a constant task, but not an unpleasant one. With luck, if my shoulder healed quickly, I could have her back in a week or so, although I'd no idea how long it would take for her injured tendons to heal. I might not be riding her again before the autumn.

My gate glittered in the late afternoon sunshine, black and gold against the new green of the beech hedge. If the Children of God were stopped, I could take out the second and third springs of the gate. One would be enough to hold it against the post. I walked over to it to see how easy it would be to do that.

Hard up against the gate, three of them planted so close that they leaned against it, were five blackthorn saplings.

I was still looking at them when Maggie came back. She saw me from the drive, and came across the paddock, her bright skirts swinging, a red headscarf knotted over her dark hair, a grin on her face. The mare followed her, ears pricked eagerly, and Maggie turned and said something to her, something friendly, and reached out to pull her brown ears.

'Hallo, Maggie,' I said. 'Look what they've done, those Children of God people. Planted blackthorn across my gate. I never did them any harm, you know that, Maggie? Nothing, I've done nothing to them. They've killed my dog, and they've tried to kill me. Twice, now. This fall, the one that hurt my shoulder, do you know what they did? They set a trip-wire. Wire, right across the track, my poor horse. I still don't know why it didn't cripple her. Poor Lyric, a damned trip-wire.'

I looked down at Maggie. She wasn't grinning any

more. There was a wildness in her eyes I'd never seen before, and it made me uneasy.

'Wire?' Her voice was hoarse with anger. 'Maggie knows wire, oh yes. Hedges, it used to be, dog roses and honeysuckle, now it's wire, and that bob wire too, that bob wire, that can hurt, that can. Hedges, they was shelter, they was shelter for us, oh yes. And for the beasts, but wire, that's no shelter. Maggie knows wire, oh yes. That's evil, that wire, bastard bob wire, Maggie knows.'

Bob wire. Barbed wire, that was her name for barbed wire, and not the first time I'd heard it. Barbed wire had killed Maggie's father, in front of her eyes, the horse with his feet tangled in barbed wire in the river, her father drowning underneath him, and Maggie, ten years old and alone, had tried to drag the horse away, and had failed. Oh, yes, Maggie knew barbed wire. Barbed wire, and electric fences, where once there'd been dog rose and honeysuckle, bramble and ash and beech, nesting sites and shelter and food. Hedges needed trimming and layering, and not many people know how to do that. Maggie would know, and the gypsies used to do that work, for money, and a place to stay for a while, and a blind eye turned to ferrets and lurchers on the rabbit warrens. Cheaper to put up barbed wire fences, and turn the gypsies away, salve the conscience with talk of social services and council housing.

'The Children of God use hedges, Maggie. Twelve miles of blackthorn, what do you think of that? Would you layer my hedge for me? It's only a four acre paddock. Would you do that?'

But Maggie wasn't listening. She was spitting on the ground and rubbing the spit into the earth with her foot, stamping her sandalled foot on the drying mud and muttering angrily. Her fists were clenched at her sides, rigid, and when she looked up there were tears in her eyes.

'You've done a good job on the baby's feet,' I said, trying to get her attention again. 'She's rocking back on her heels. It might work, Maggie. A good job. That's the trouble with a summer foal, isn't it? Too much good food, they grow too fast, outgrow their tendons, don't they, Maggie? Did you overfeed the mare in the winter, then? Keep her condition too good? You did well to leave her a few months. Good thing that stallion didn't get another cough this last winter. Don't like summer foals, do you, Maggie?'

She'd stopped spitting and stamping, and was looking up at me, her head on one side.

'You wouldn't have put a coughing horse in the barn, would you, Maggie? Worst thing for a horse with a cough, I'd have thought.'

'Bruises and splinters,' she said. 'You get a fall on a hedge, that's what you get, bruises and splinters. But that bob wire, that's cruel, that tears, that does. Maggie knows, oh yes.'

'What do you get if you fall on a blackthorn hedge, Maggie?'

But the mare nudged her from behind, and Maggie turned and laughed.

'Hallo, my lovely, my Daisy, hallo, my pet!'

We walked back to the forge together, with Daisy following only a few paces behind The foal ignored us both, cropping at the tops of the tussocks of grass, flicking her short, woolly tail at the early flies and lifting her long legs high as she moved.

Maggie had a jar in the pocket of her skirt, an old Marmite jar with rust showing through the yellow screw top. She gestured at me to pull off my smock, so I went into the forge and did so, and she followed, still looking uneasily at the roof as though expecting it to collapse on her.

'It's stood for a thousand years, Maggie,' I said, but she wasn't listening. She was digging her fingers into her jar and sniffing at them. I sat on the anvil, and watched her.

'What is that, Maggie?'

She walked behind me, moving quietly and slowly, and laid a hand on the side of my neck.

'All right, my pet,' she crooned. 'Stand still now, my pet. Maggie'll make it better.'

She smeared the ointment onto my shoulder, and I sniffed.

'That's horse liniment, isn't it?' I asked.

She cocked her head at me, confused for a moment, not used to her patients asking questions, and then dug her fingers into the Marmite jar again.

'Maggie'll make it better,' she said again. 'Maggie knows, oh yes.'

She was still rubbing the ointment into my arm and shoulder when Mrs Hunter arrived. I'd reached for my smock as I heard a car turn into the drive, and Maggie had immediately wound her fingers into my hair and held it tight.

'Stand still, my pet,' she said. 'Maggie's nearly done now, stand still.'

'I've got a visitor, Maggie, I've got to put my smock on!'

But Mrs Hunter was standing in the doorway staring at us in astonishment before I could make Maggie understand, and it was becoming urgent. Maggie's ointment was meant for horses, and horses have thick hides. My skin was beginning to burn quite fiercely, and I wanted to get into the cottage and wash the ointment off as quickly as possible. Maggie's method with restless patients was to grasp them firmly by the mane and hold them still. She had very strong hands.

'Please let me go, Maggie,' I said. 'Please! You've rubbed it in everywhere now, please let me go!'

Just when it began to seem I would have to fight her off she let go of my hair and stood back, wiping her hand down her skirt and screwing the lid onto her jar.

I ran for the door, pulling my smock over my head as I went and muttering a brief excuse to Mrs Hunter. Oil, I thought frantically as I burst through the kitchen door, something to dilute whatever it was in that old Marmite jar, then soap and water.

My shoulder looked as if it had been sunburnt. It was a fiery, angry red over the bruises, a big red patch spreading down my neck and arm. I poured olive oil into the palm of my hand and rubbed it carefully into my stinging skin, muttering curses on gypsy medicine as I did so.

I came out about twenty minutes later, my hair damp from the shower, my skin still hot and red but at least with the savage burning sensation abated. Maggie was curled up at the foot of the chestnut tree, apparently asleep, and Mrs Hunter came out of the forge at the sound of my footsteps on the path. She glanced at Maggie, and smiled.

'Somebody been cruel?' she asked. 'Your friend didn't tell me much apart from that. That's a wicked bruise on your back. The Children of God this morning, I assume.'

I stopped and looked at her.

'Yes,' she said. 'Inspector Stone told me. Four of them?'

'That's right. Just before I phoned you. They tried to kill me in the end.'

I wondered if saying it would make it more believable, but I was standing on the path between the cottage and the forge, facing a plain middle-aged woman who was looking at me with a faintly enquiring smile on her face, and there was a mare and foal in the paddock at my back and a slightly crazy gypsy woman asleep under the tree. It all seemed a long way from death.

But the revolver was still rubbing at my hip, and it was, as Mrs Hunter said, a wicked bruise.

She didn't seem surprised. She nodded.

'I've a lot to tell you,' she said. 'Where can we talk?'

I took her into the cottage. It was getting dark, so I switched on the lights, and we went into the living room and sat at the table by the window, facing each other across the dark polished wood. She leaned on it, clasping her hands and bowing her head. Her hands were shaking, and she gripped them together tightly to control them.

'I've already given everything I found out to the police,' she said. 'They're raiding Gorsedown Manor, they're probably there now, and they've got warrants for the arrest of several people. Not everybody, they don't know exactly who's there, although they might find enough to round them all up, but all the ringleaders, they're named on the warrants. I think we can say it'll be the end of the Children of God.

'This is the third house they've had. The first one was in Yorkshire, on the edge of the dales. They were taking in young drug addicts there. Then in Scotland, quite near Edinburgh, a recovery centre for alcoholics. The house in Lothian was quite big, there were more of them by then, the one in Yorkshire was smaller, but it was very private, no footpaths or rights of way. They were in Yorkshire for three years and in Lothian for four. They were financed at least partly by local authorities and by charities.

'There were only four of them at first, the shareholders in Stephenson Holdings. But they've gradually built up a following. There are clubs in some of the big cities, quite discreetly advertised, some people came from them, and word of mouth, that's something else. And films, you can hire films, videos, that sort of thing, people who hire them out get to know. People who run those sort of clubs, they can recommend other places, other contacts.'

'What sort of clubs?' I asked.

'Different sorts of sexual appetites.' For a moment she looked quite distressed. 'All sorts of things, most of them harmless, sad. Old men who can't attract women any more, they start with prostitutes. Some of the prostitutes offer special services, of course. Most of the time it's nothing but acting, silly things sometimes. If the men, or, I'm afraid, the women, want things the prostitutes won't do for them, then they'll often ask for addresses, clubs, other contacts.'

She clenched her fists on the table, opened them again, and looked at me.

'Do you know what a "snuff" film is?'

'Pornography, isn't it? Sadistic pornography?'

'Yes, but it goes right to the end. The victim's killed. Most of those films are just acting, but there are some of them that aren't. In some of them, the victims really do die, and their deaths are filmed, and those films are sold, for very, very high prices.'

'The Children of God make snuff films?' I thought of Emily and Kathy, and I felt sick, and my eyes filled with tears.

Mrs Hunter nodded, and reached out to pat my hand.

'Yes, my dear, I'm afraid so. They do a rather specialist line, human sacrifice films, pagan worship, fertility things. It's revolting and rotten, it's nothing to do with any real religion, of course, just an excuse for what passes for a story line.'

I couldn't speak. I thought of Kathy, wanting to go to a church to pray, trotting away from the gate after promising to come back the next day. I remembered Emily's wide eyes in her intelligent face, both of them going back to a disgusting death in front of the cameras, for the entertainment of perverts, and for the money the films would earn. I wanted to protest, to deny what Mrs Hunter was saying had happened, but there were no words, just a dry, hard feeling in my throat, and a dreadful sorrow.

I stood up.

'Fresh air,' I said, and my voice was tight and hoarse.

Mrs Hunter nodded, and picked up her bag. I led the way out of the house, fighting the tears away, and I stopped in the doorway, looking at Maggie, before walking on towards the paddock.

In the distance, a police siren wailed.

'Not too far from a telephone, my dear,' said Mrs Hunter behind me.

'Oh, God. Emily.'

We stopped at the paddock gate, and I turned my back to it and leaned against it, my head bowed. There were tears running down my cheeks, and I tried to scrub them away. Tortured to death. Emily and Kathy.

Mrs Hunter was standing beside me. She fumbled in her bag, and handed me a packet of paper handkerchiefs.

'Shall I go on?'

I nodded, wiping my eyes, my cheeks.

'They'd have got away with it for a lot longer if it hadn't been for Anthony Clinton-Smith.' She was speaking of unimportant things now, to give me time to get myself under control. 'He seems to have started to believe in it. Blood for the soil, or something, he made himself into a sort of high priest, got some silly young women as a group of acolytes, all bowing and scraping, and digging his gardens, and no doubt cavorting around in his bed. If they'd kept it to the four of them, and moved on every few years, they might never have been discovered.'

Another siren, over the sound of the first, from behind us, from Gorsedown, and two cars driving fast along the road. I looked up watching them, and Mrs Hunter waited for a moment until they had gone.

'It was when they went up to Lothian it began to get out of control. When I asked the police there they were by no means unfamiliar with the names, even though they weren't too communicative. However, they've been in touch with Detective Inspector Stone, and there's quite a big operation planned for tomorrow. Shovels and spades, I'm afraid. More people started turning up at the house, you see. Through these clubs, they'd got the names, and the films weren't enough. They wanted to take part. Clinton-Smith began to see himself as a religious leader, not just a nasty avaricious pornographer. He called himself Lord, everybody had to obey him immediately, without question, nobody was to speak in his presence. Sooner or later somebody was bound to talk, and he started getting reckless, he seemed to think he was invulnerable. Arrogant, power of life and death, maybe he started to believe in it all. In Scotland the laws about trespass are different, they couldn't keep everybody off their land. There were some quite ugly rumours. But then they closed down the house and vanished. Nobody had actually made any complaints. Homeless alcoholics do disappear, quite often. But a lot of people were going there to look at the gardens.'

'The garden at Gorsedown's marvellous,' I whispered. Once again I wiped at the tears running down my cheeks.

'They'll start searching it tomorrow,' she said. 'I'm afraid they'll find your friends. Once the Lothian police contacted them they had to move very fast. They can, you know, when it's something like this. That's why they wanted the key, those gates are very strong, it would have taken time to break in, and it would have made a lot of noise. With the key they just might be lucky, they might surprise them. Not give them enough time to destroy the films. With luck, they'll get them. The films, I mean. And the four shareholders, and the real murder gang. They've brought men in from other forces.'

'Did you find all this out?' I asked. 'I mean, you, rather than the police?'

'Oh, no. That's a very flattering question, but no. I had a start, you see, because I believed you when you said your friends had disappeared, and because I was very worried about those fools at Reconcile once I started digging. So many refugees going back to their own countries, with no questions being asked, and no proper documentation. But the Lothian police were asking about some young people who'd disappeared from the house up there, even though they hadn't turned it into a murder enquiry then. Once I told them about the trouble here, and gave them those names, they put it all together. And Yorkshire, there too. No, a lot of what I'm telling you I got from them. All this about the films, and there had been visitors at the house in Lothian, and in Yorkshire. A few people who thought it was a new religion, they were curious. Some of them talked about it. Not about the murders, I doubt if they realised about that. Clinton-Smith wasn't so reckless then. Now, he just doesn't seem to care. And then, the Children of God tried to kill you. Stone was in no doubt about that, he knew quite well it was attempted murder, and with several of them involved he was asking why.'

It was very quiet. The sirens had stopped, there was only the wind in the trees.

'You're going to be a very important witness. A surviving victim. Stone said I should come here and wait with you. Somebody may be along later. Perhaps you'd better give me that revolver, I don't suppose you've got a licence for it. He said you'd been "unbelievably lucky" this morning. When he uses that word, he means he doesn't believe your story. Did you actually shoot anybody?'

'No, I missed.'

'Well, thank God for that. Give me the gun, Ann. It's over now, you won't need it. They won't search me, but if one of those men says you shot at them with a revolver they'll look for it here, and they're very good at finding things. Stone isn't just being kind about this, you shooting at them with a revolver would be a worrying line if the defence took it up. It might weaken the police case.'

I took the gun out of my belt and handed it to her. She unloaded it, and dropped it and the cartridges into her bag.

'Are there any bullets embedded in walls? Anything we should dig out?'

'No,' I said, dully. 'No, I think the bullet went out over the park. I only fired once, I dropped the other cartridges while I was trying to load it. The cartridge case, that's in the rubbish bin.'

'Yes, well, I'll go and get it now. You stay here, my dear. I won't be long.'

Efficient and kind Mrs Hunter, protecting her client's interests. I watched her walking away past the stable, down the concrete path to the forge. Maggie was still asleep under the chestnut tree, probably planning to stay there all night if what the vet had told me was true. I'd find her a blanket, I thought, and something to eat. She'd never come into the house, but it didn't look like rain.

I rubbed my shoulder, and rotated it slowly, feeling for the pain. It moved more easily now, and the sudden flares from the damaged ligaments had subsided into aching twinges.

I didn't want to think about the Children of God. I wanted to turn my mind away from what they had done, and so I thought about Maggie and the foal, and whether old Mr Forbes would come tomorrow, as Neil had said he might, and whether Maggie would let him nail on the shoes, or whether she'd insist that I do it. I moved my shoulder again, shrugging it and stretching out my arm, and thought that perhaps I could manage it after all.

I thought about Glory coming, on her way by now, and wondered what we were to celebrate, and whether I could pretend, at least until tomorrow, that nothing was wrong, so we could have our evening with the champagne. But then I thought how hurt she'd be at my pretence. I'd have to tell her what had happened.

Two police cars drove down the road, no blue lights, no sirens. Perhaps it was over.

I pushed myself away from the gate and walked back to the cottage to find a blanket for Maggie.

Oh, Emily. Kathy.

A cheese sandwich for Maggie, I thought as I went into the cottage. She'll be hungry. And the blanket.

The telephone rang, and I jumped, jerked back to the present, and reached for it.

It was Detective Inspector Stone.

'I'm at Gorsedown,' he said. 'Miss Mayall, can you please get out of there? Can you go to the police station?'

'No, my sister's coming.'

'*Damn* it!' he exploded. 'This is not some blasted burglary, it is serious. What is this, some sort of social occasion? Put her off.'

'I can't, I've tried. I can't get hold of her.'

I felt very weary. I wondered if I should explain, but it was just too much trouble.

'Listen to me,' he ordered. 'There are some women

out begging or whatever they do, we haven't been able to find them, and I can't spare anybody to hang around the forge. Leave a note for your sister and get out of there.'

'No,' I said. 'Somebody listened to my answering machine, they know she's coming. They know who she is.'

He swore again, and told me to hold on. I waited, hearing voices and banging noises, somebody shouting about a lorry.

Emily. Poor Emily.

'Listen!'

I jumped, and dragged my attention back to the telephone.

'I'm sending somebody, but it's going to be about half an hour. You stay in that cottage, and you lock the doors and don't answer if anybody knocks, unless it's your sister. You be careful, Miss Mayall. Do you understand?'

'Yes.'

'Is Mrs Hunter there?'

I told him to hold on, and I reached across the table and opened the window, calling out to her. When she appeared at the door I told her who it was, and said she should pick up the extension in the forge. She nodded, and turned back through the doors. When I heard her voice, I hung up.

He'd promised to find out about Plod, if he could. I hoped he hadn't forgotten, dead people being so much more important to him than a dead dog. Emily Peters, tall, dark and slim, dying horribly for the cameras. Emily laughing in the rain and the mud, Emily clinging to Lyric's stirrup as we walked back to the forge through the winter evening talking about Liberia, Emily grieving for her family, her voice a high, thin whine. Sitting in front of my fire, drinking spicy beef broth, thinking about the hospital, where she had learned to move quietly so as not to disturb sleeping patients. Emily, clever and lovely, dying to pamper the greed and vanity of Anthony Clinton-Smith and his friends.

Mrs Hunter was walking back to the cottage, and I went to meet her at the door.

I glanced at my watch. Half-past seven, Glory would be here soon, I'd have to start heating up the food. Ridiculous, to think of such mundane affairs in the middle of mass murder.

'Would you like a drink?' I asked. 'I think there's some whisky in the cupboard. I'm going to have one.'

'I'd love one.' She was very white and her hands were gripping her bag tightly. I realised, and was surprised at the realisation, that she was suffering from shock. I took two glasses out of the cupboard and poured the whisky, thinking of the young policemen who would start tomorrow, digging up the wonderful garden. Shocked young faces, shaking hands gripping spades and shovels. Here, and in Yorkshire, and in Scotland, young men finding dreadful evidence, people only slightly prepared by their training, only slightly shielded by their uniforms, from the horrors they would uncover.

I began to cry again, and there were tears running down Mrs Hunter's face, so we clung to each other, hugging, looking for comfort and finding a little. Mrs Hunter pushed herself away after a moment, smiling shakily through her tears and groping in her bag for a handkerchief.

'I'm sorry,' she said. 'So silly. But I've never . . .' She sniffed. 'Never, anything like this.'

I rubbed the tears away from my own face with the back of my hand, and gave her her whisky. She sniffed, and smiled again, and drank the whisky quickly, handing back her glass. I filled it again.

'There'll be an identity parade, probably on Thursday. Stone asked me to tell you, the four men who attacked you, if you could.'

'Yes,' I said. 'Yes. Whatever they want.'

She laid down her glass and wiped her eyes again.

'I'm to stay until the police come,' she said. 'He said they'd be as quick as they can. About half an hour.'

'You don't have to.'

She shook her head, and touched my arm.

'My dear, it's over. Remember that, it helps. They're finished, no more deaths, it's over.'

I smiled down at her, efficient and kindly Mrs Hunter who'd achieved what I'd asked of her, and uncovered mass murder as she did so.

'Maggie,' I said. 'I'll get her a blanket, make her something to eat.'

'You're supposed to stay in here. Can't she come in?'

'No,' I said. I thought of explaining about Maggie's fear of roofs, but it was too much trouble. If Mrs Hunter thought I wouldn't let Maggie into the house because she was a gypsy, or dirty, then so be it.

I fetched a blanket for Maggie, and made her a thick cheese sandwich. She woke as I approached, and sat up, supple and easy, comfortable on her sleeping place under the tree.

'I thank you, lady,' she said as I gave her the sandwich. She ate it hungrily, and I sat beside her on the grass, silent, thinking, listening for the sound of Glory's little red sports car, wondering what to tell her. I couldn't cook our celebration meal. We'd open her champagne, she'd tell me her news, and for a little while I could pretend to be happy and excited with her, for a few minutes, perhaps. Then I'd have to tell her, who the Children of God were, what they'd done.

Maggie finished her sandwich, wiped her hands on her skirt, and looked at the sky, to the south, from where the wind was blowing.

'The water from the tap by the forge,' I said. 'It's clean, Maggie. You can drink it.'

'Forge water,' she answered eagerly. 'Where the hot iron's been. Oh, yes, that's good water. Maggie knows.'

Many people like to drink the water from the cooling trough, they say it's good against rheumatism, that it's full of minerals. There's a tin mug hanging from a hook in the forge for anybody who wants it.

'Help yourself,' I said. 'Will you be warm enough out here? You could sleep in the loose box, if you like.'

She was on her feet, looking towards the forge, nervous. She turned and bent down to touch my shoulder.

'Get it for me, lady?' she whined. 'Bring the water for Maggie?'

I climbed to my feet, and went with her to the door of the forge. There was only a faint glow from the dying coals, but I didn't need light to find my way around. I dipped the tin mug into the cooling trough, and carried it out to Maggie. She took it from me, and drank eagerly.

It was a late March evening, windy and cold. I shivered. I couldn't have slept out under a tree that night, but Maggie seemed quite content.

The telephone rang. I turned away from Maggie, and went back into the forge to pick it up.

'Ann?'

It was Glory. She was half laughing, and I could hear voices behind her, somebody singing.

'Hello, Glory.'

'Look, Ann, I'm at the . . .' She apparently turned away from the telephone, and spoke to somebody. Then she came back. 'Sorry, I'm not sure where I am. They're giving a party for you, they want you to come.'

'Who are?' I asked. 'What are you talking about?'

But I was suddenly cold, and Glory's laughter didn't disguise her own apprehension.

'Your neighbours, they say.' She laughed again. 'Ann, they're awfully insistent that you should come. Just a minute, one of them . . .'

There was a scuffling noise, and I heard her voice raised in sharp protest, and then somebody else spoke.

'Hallo, blacksmith.' It was a woman's voice, very high-pitched, and she giggled as she spoke. 'You're coming to our party. Down by the quarry, and you come alone.'

'Let my sister go.'

'You know about our parties, don't you? You nearly gatecrashed one once.' She giggled again. 'In ten minutes, blacksmith, or we'll start without you. Your sister wouldn't like that.'

'I can't get there in ten minutes,' I said. 'Last week your bloody trap injured my leg, I can't run.'

'Then you crawl. That bitch with the car, she stays there, she stays by the car, where we can see her. You come alone, we're watching you every inch of the way. We've been doing that for a long time. You know that, don't you? We're watching. You set off right now, blacksmith, alone, or we'll start the party without you. Not at the quarry. And everybody you bring will miss the best bit.'

19

She didn't hang up. The line went dead. I ran to the door of the forge, and saw, silhouetted against the darkening sky, a figure climbing down the telegraph pole by the road.

I stood in the doorway, trying to think. The figure jumped down the last few feet, and waved, an almost friendly gesture, before vanishing into the woods. A torch flashed skywards, twice, a bright stabbing beam. A signal.

No telephone. No time.

I screamed towards the woods.

'I'm coming! Wait for me!'

Maggie backed away from me, dropping the mug onto the concrete, her eyes wide with startled alarm.

'Maggie? Maggie, I need help.'

'Yes, lady?'

'Maggie, lend me Daisy. Please.'

Mrs Hunter was running from the cottage.

'What is it?' she called. 'What's the matter?'

'They've got Glory,' I said. 'Oh, God. They're watching. You're to stay here, beside the car, where they can see you. They're signalling with torches. I've got to go to the quarry.'

'No. They'll kill you. Call the police.'

'They've cut the line.'

I turned back to Maggie, reaching for her arm.

'Maggie, lend me Daisy! Please lend me Daisy!'

But she had heard Mrs Hunter.

'Police!' She spat on the ground, and rubbed the spit on the flagstones with her foot. 'Police, they turn us off our camps. Bastard, police. Turn us off our camps.'

'Oh, God. Maggie, please, these are the people who set the wire for my horse, they've got my sister.'

'Bastard!' She spat on the ground again. 'Bastard!'

Ten minutes. Nine, now. I'd never reach the quarry, not on an unbroken gypsy pony, not over those rutted tracks.

'Maggie!' I implored. 'Help me!'

Her fists were clenched again, arms rigid by her sides. She was intent on her own angry world, crazed and lost.

Mrs Hunter seized my arm, pulling me round to face her.

'Listen to me!' she demanded. 'They'll kill you, it's no good trying to get there. I'll drive to the village. I'll call for help from there. Please stay here.'

'No!'

I wrenched my arm away from her, and turned back to Maggie. Eight minutes, maybe only seven. What would they do to her, to my lovely sister? How could I get there in time?

'Maggie, can I have Daisy? Please, can I take Daisy? I have to help my sister, *please*, Maggie, let me have Daisy.'

Her eyes flicked towards me. Crazy eyes, flicking, but awareness coming back.

'Can I take Daisy, Maggie? Damn you, Maggie, I have to have that horse, do you hear me?'

She was looking at me, her head tilted, her own brand of intelligence in her dark eyes.

'Daisy ain't broke for riding.'

'It'll be faster than running. I've got to have her.'

I was crying with fear and anger and frustration, and Maggie reached up and touched the tears on my face, wondering.

'You take her, lady. You take my Daisy, there's tears enough, my lovely, my lady.'

'But take the *car*!' Mrs Hunter was despairing. 'Take my car!'

'It won't get down the track,' I said. 'There are ruts a foot high. Wait here and tell the police when they come. Please, tell them to hurry.'

I left her standing in the yard beside her car as I ran into the forge. I had only head-collars, no bridles. I took the best of the three from the peg, and followed Maggie towards the paddock. She was running for the gate, whistling, a shrill warbling sound, and I heard hoof-beats on grass. The mare was trotting across the paddock towards her. By the time I reached them

Maggie had the gate open, one hand wrapped in Daisy's forelock.

I slipped the head-collar over Daisy's white blazed face, and Maggie was stooping, her hands cupped to make a stirrup for me. Daisy shied as she felt my weight on her back, sidling away, jerking her head against the rope. Maggie was thumping at my leg, thrusting something up at me, a little bottle.

'Drink it, lady! That's good, that'll do good. Maggie knows.'

She still had one hand on the mare's mane, so I seized the bottle and she stepped back. Daisy turned once on the gravel, her eyes rolling, pulling against the rope, shying away from Mrs Hunter and the car, but I managed to turn her head towards the road, and I thumped her flanks with my heels. She jumped forward, her back humping, swishing her tail, but as I kicked her again she broke into a canter, a short and bumpy stride. I gripped as tightly as I could, trying to ignore the sharp twinge of pain in my knee, hearing Mrs Hunter calling after me, a last plea to stop, to come with her in the car to the village.

Hardly realising I was doing it, I twisted the cap off the little bottle Maggie had given me, and swallowed the liquid that poured out, gagging at the sharp taste.

Daisy tried to break into a gallop on the road, but I pulled her head in almost to her chest, and she slowed to a hard, short trot, almost shaking me off her back. She was already sweating, nervous and bewildered, dragging at the rope, her ears flicking back towards me. Her unshod hooves thudded on the road, an uneven beat as she tried to adjust to the weight over her shoulders, and at every few strides she jerked her head downward, pulling me forward, and shying away from the shadows in the trees. I was sliding helplessly on her broad back, clinging to her mane and trying to grip, determined to stay on despite her rough stride. There seemed to be no strength at all in my knee, no way I could grip her sides, I could rely only on balance and on one hand wrapped in the coarse white hairs of her mane.

We reached the cart track, and I pulled her head round to face her into it. She resisted fiercely, shaking her head furiously and sidling crabways along the road, swishing her tail, until I kicked her again, and then she bucked, and I fell forward, helplessly, to slide over her shoulder.

Luckily, I landed on my feet, and I led her onto the track, heading her down it and pushing her face away from me as I laid my hands on her back and sprang up onto her shoulders. She tried to buck again, but I pulled her head in and kicked her hard. She jumped forward, pulling against the rope, snorting in fright, and I let her have her head and leaned forward against her neck, talking to her, trying to soothe her, trying to urge her into a gallop.

Even an unbroken gypsy horse had to get me to the quarry faster than my own two legs.

She broke into a canter, holding her head high and slightly to the side, a frightened eye rolling back in my direction. Not fast enough, we could have only four minutes left at the most, perhaps less, even if the Children of

God held to their word and gave me ten to reach them.

I kicked her again, and shouted at her.

'Come on, Daisy! Get on now!'

I slapped her down the shoulder with the end of the rope, and she jumped in surprise and shied away from it.

'Run, you bitch! Get on, run!'

I slammed my heels into her flanks, and she grunted and tried to buck again, but I was ready for her this time, jerking hard on the rope and kicking her again, whipping at her shoulder with the rope and screaming at her. If I could, I was going to make her bolt down the track, at the end it was only a couple of hundred yards from the quarry. I might stop her by dragging her into the wood, if not I'd throw myself off her.

It was a stumbling gallop, hard and rough over the rutted track, and she was tired already from the unaccustomed weight, and frightened by my shouting and my flailing heels. I was crazy with fear for Glory, and with rage at the women who held her, who threatened her, who would torture and kill her if I didn't stop them.

I was going to stop them. I was going to kill them instead, and I screamed at the horse and at the woods and at the murderers it sheltered, I swung the end of the rope, slashing at the mare's shoulders and screaming, and she snorted, and stumbled again, righting herself, and galloping on, bewildered and frightened and tired, her unshod hooves thudding on the hard packed earth and the sharp flints.

There were two of them in front of us on the track, two

women running, looking back at us, so I screamed again, my voice rising in a wild shriek of fury and hatred, and I kicked Daisy to drive her into a faster pace, faster than they could run, so we could reach them, and I could ride them down, trample them under her hooves, batter them into the hard earth, kill them, destroy them.

They cried out as we reached them, one of them turning and waving her arms frantically in Daisy's face, so she shied in fear, crashing into the bushes by the side of the track, and I couldn't reach them to kill them, though I shrieked my loathing at them and tried to pull back to get at them, but we were past them, stumbling back onto the track, the mare's neck and shoulders lathered, foam flying back, her eyes wild with terror but I had no time for pity, no mercy for a horse with Glory at the mercy of the women who would kill her.

But I would destroy them, I would scatter their dirty bodies on the earth, trample and ruin them.

We were at the end of the track, a gate into a ploughed field standing half open, and Daisy plunged past it into the deep, clinging earth, staggered and stumbled, and I fell beside her, and stood again, and dragged her after me, her head stretched out, stiff, ribs heaving, eyes rolling with exhaustion and fear, and I shouted at her and heaved at the rope, so she scrambled to her feet, and lunged after me as I crashed through the bushes into the woods, down the steep, crumbling earth towards the quarry, I was screaming my hatred and my rage, hauling the mare behind me, I felt as though I were burning with anger, my skin flaming and sweating, my rage driving me plunging down the steep slope, the mare back on her haunches, her hooves ploughing into the earth, her breath in great groaning gasps, and she gained her feet again and shied past me, shaking her head to try to free herself of the rope, but I caught her, and jumped, and was on her back again, forcing her forward towards the lights I could see through the trees, to the voices, the singing, and the mare was too exhausted to resist me, she plunged up a bank, stumbled, down on one knee, but I yelled at her and drove my heels into her flanks.

They were there, there was a fire, and lights, and they were naked and dancing by the fire, black, silhouetted by the flames, and singing, and we broke through the trees as I screamed at them, I was howling and wailing, and the horse's frantic head was high as she fought for air through her scarlet nostrils, flames shining in her maddened eyes, and the singing was changing, it was higher, there was fear, they were running, and squealing, and there were little knives in their hands.

Glory hung naked from a tree, hung by a knee and a wrist, her hair draggled in the earth, and there was blood, blood in black streams across her breasts, blood scarlet and crimson between her thighs, her head hanging down.

The mare was blinded by the lights and the flames and she reared up, her hooves flailing, a face in front of her, fear in the face, and a striking hoof, and blood spurting, and she fell, her big body crashing against dead wood, there was screaming, she rolled, her white belly huge in the firelight, somebody under her, somebody screaming, and I was running to the fire, one of them ahead of me, turning, a little knife flashing, flashing up my arm, blood on my arm but my hand in her hair, and wrenching, and twisting, and something like a rotten branch breaking, a dead weight, I was holding a dead weight, dead.

They were flying, running for the lights, screaming, and I flew after them, flaming with hatred and rage, another in front of me, dodging away under the tree, frightened face turned back to me, frightened face under my hand, down, down onto the earth, grinding into the earth, writhing under my hand, teeth in my hands, biting, and breaking under my hand, another knife, another, into my back, two of them on my back, knives flashing, but another running in front. I ran after her, and one of them fell off my back, the other stabbing, blood on my neck, burning, and I caught the knife, and the arm, and the knife fell and the arm broke, and the one in front had gone, so I stopped, and turned, and looked for the one who had fled, who had escaped me.

There were more lights, and voices, shouting voices, and screaming, but the one who had escaped had gone, and I roared with rage, and ran back towards the flames.

Someone in front of me, big, arms outstretched, dark, not one of them, I pushed past, a hand grasping my shoulder, and I stumbled. I was burning, my skin was burning, and Glory was hanging from the tree, people there, beside her, cutting her down, somebody holding her, and there was blood on my neck, on my shoulders, everything was dark, I couldn't see, it was getting dark, but the horse was there, moving stiffly against the dark woods behind the flames, and more people, there were arms around me, and the rage was dying, but I was burning, and sick, and weak now, and frightened.

I put out my hands to touch the earth, and the arms around me slipped away so that I could lie down, and I saw the blood running down my arms. I could see more clearly, there was the fire and the headlights, several cars, more coming up the gravel road, and blue lamps flickering behind. I could hear the voices, I could understand what they were saying, and footsteps on the earth, so I raised my head and looked up.

'All right, love, lie still. Doctor's coming.'

'Glory?' I asked, but he didn't understand, and I was too weak to ask again, the blood was pumping out over my shoulder, and somebody else knelt on the ground beside me, a hand on my wrist, and then he swore, and somebody was pulling at my smock, cutting it away, and he shouted.

'Stretcher over here! And bring those clips, hurry, man!'

It would have been peaceful, lying there, but I was worried about Glory, I remembered they'd cut her down from the tree.

'Glory?'

They carried her past me, two men half running, she was on a stretcher, wrapped in a blanket, her face turned towards me, and she was white and still, my lovely sister.

'Burning,' I said. 'I'm burning.'

There was a hand on my forehead, and somebody muttered, and there were more footsteps and a question.

'Of course they're drugged, amphetamines I should think. They'll be all right. It's her, God knows what she's taken, I don't like this fever, not with the blood she's lost.'

I tried to sit up, but a hand pressed down on my shoulder, and the voice spoke again.

'Lie still. Don't move. What have you taken?'

Something stung against my neck, and I tried to move away from it.

'Lie still! What have you taken?'

The horse. The mare, Daisy, somebody had caught her. He was leading her towards the cars. She was stiff, I could see her, her head hanging low, stiff legs, reluctant to move. Poor Daisy, poor exhausted Daisy, so frightened, so brave.

I struggled against the restraining hands, forced myself up to my knees, and pointed at her.

'Look after her!' I shouted.

The doctor was kneeling in front of me, his hands cupping my face. I tried to push him away, to see what they were doing with Daisy.

'Listen to me!' he commanded. 'She's going back with the police horses. There'll be a vet at the stable if she needs one. Do you understand? What have you taken?'

I looked at him. He was a stranger, he was dark, black hair curling on his forehead, young.

'What have you taken?' he asked again, insistent.

'That'll do good,' I said. 'Maggie knows.'

I wanted to lie down again, and I pushed him away and sank back onto the earth. He swore, but I closed my eyes and put my hands over my ears. My neck was stinging, somebody was doing something to it, I couldn't stop them. I was burning, I was so tired, and burning, and they were rolling me, I was too weak to fight them off. A stretcher, somebody looking down at me, blankets. But I was hot, too hot, I tried to push the blankets away, to get away from the stifling heat and the people, but hands held me down, and I began to cry from weakness.

'Can't you give her something?'

'I don't know what she's already had. I daren't.'

His face again, looming down over me.

'Lie still! Can you understand me? What have you taken? I've got to know what you've taken.'

'Maggie knows,' I mumbled.

'Maggie? Who the hell's Maggie?' His voice was fading away, but I heard somebody laugh.

'Gypsy woman, she was at the forge when we got there.'

They were so far away, and somebody lifted the stretcher, but I was still burning, and crying, and very weak, and there were flames, men beside the fire, further and further away, the dark flames and the shouting, too far away to hear the shouting, the flames darker and darker, and then gone away.

20

I lay semiconscious through the night, burning with fever, weak from loss of blood, only half aware of doctors and nurses around me, of policemen and women standing uneasily in the casualty ward, of bright lights.

'Glory?' I asked, but nobody heard me. 'Glory?'

Glory was in an operating theatre where a team fought for her life, and nearly lost. Her heart stopped twice.

I can't remember much about that night now, except a quietly desperate need to know what had happened to Glory, and nobody hearing, or understanding, the only question I could form.

'Glory?'

A cold, grey dawn, and I grew aware of needles, and tubes, and bottles of blood, and sweat soaking the white pillow beside me, and a nurse checking my pulse.

'Glory?'

'You're not ready for glory, my dear, you're still alive.'

'Glory, my sister. Where's my sister?'

Holding her own, they told me. She's young and strong, she's got a good chance. Critically ill, but stable.

Stone came to see me that afternoon. His face was grey with strain and anger, and he sat beside my bed, his fists on the blankets clenched so tight the knuckles were white.

'How they *dared*!' he said. 'How the hell they dared.'

'What went wrong?' I whispered.

'We thought they were in Gloucester. We were watching the buses from Gloucester. They were on the telephone to Gorsedown as we were breaking down the door, talking to Clinton-Smith. I heard him say it, but I didn't connect it. "One last service for your Lord," he said, and then he put down the phone and smiled at us. They came by taxi, by the back roads.'

'You didn't cut their telephone lines, then,' I said, and he raised his eyes to my face, shaking his head in misery.

'And you'd told me your sister was coming, and that they knew it. While we were searching the Manor they were on the Anford road, flagging down every car until they got her. Standing in the middle of the road, the cars had to stop. The drivers thought there'd been an accident. We were checking the buses for them, and they were already in Anford.'

The police found her car, in the car park behind the Black Bull, the village pub. When she'd stopped and wound down the window they'd asked her if she was the blacksmith's sister, and said they were all having a party, I'd said we were to meet there. One of them had got into the car and taken the keys. She'd protested, but they'd been laughing at her, pulling her along to the telephone box, saying she'd be late for the party, she should hurry. They'd already been high on amphetamines by then. They'd used torches to signal to each other, as I'd seen, and two women had been waiting by the telegraph pole, waiting with wire cutters. Clinton-Smith had said Glory was to be sacrificed, and they'd taken her in obedience to him, a last service for their fallen Lord. The woman who'd cut the wire, one of the two I'd tried to ride down on the track to the quarry, was telling the police about it, claiming she'd been forced to take part, forced at knife-point.

Uncle John came that afternoon, calm and quiet, asking if we'd made statements, and then telling Stone that neither of us would do so until after the inquests on the women who had died at the quarry.

'Do you know what they did to Glory?' I whispered. 'Do you know?'

I felt no remorse about the woman I'd killed. I remembered it quite clearly, her knife in my arm, my hand in her hair, the feeling of rotten wood cracking, the dead weight. I told myself, a human life, I had taken a human life. It meant nothing.

Uncle John told me two people had died at the quarry, the first from a crushed skull when Daisy had reared in panic and struck out with her front hooves, and the second had been found lying with a broken neck, a knife with my blood on it still in her hand.

Stone came back to the hospital, asking anxiously about Glory. They'd found seven bodies buried under

the vegetable garden at Gorsedown, including Emily
and Kathy.

And Plod. A hammer blow to his head, he told me,
inflicted at the same time as the other injuries, quite
quick. No knife wounds.

Glory was on the critical list for three days, nurses
telling me she was holding her own. A gynaecologist
came in to see me, a kind man, to tell me he thought
she'd make it. A better chance with every passing day,
he said.

I went home, my arm in a sling, stitches in my neck, in
my back. Mrs Hunter had left flowers in vases in the cottage. Dear Mrs Hunter, who had driven to the village as
soon as I had ridden out of the gates, had got the police
on their way, and called the ambulance, had told them
the track was impossible for cars, that they would have
to approach from the quarry road, had thought of everything, and had then gone back to the forge to wait with
Maggie, to see she wasn't harassed.

It was a potion of her father's Maggie had given me,
something he used to give horses before races. Maggie
knew nothing of dosages. More a matter for the Jockey
Club than the Drug Squad, a doctor told me, smiling.
Just as well you've got a strong heart. They'd found the
bottle I'd dropped by the gate, and the laboratory had
analysed the dregs that were left, as far as they could. A
tricksy sort of cocktail, he said, looking slightly aghast as
he read the report. She'd brought it back with her to give
me the next day, because she'd wanted me to shoe the
foal.

329

I went to the police station and identified the three men who had come with Clinton-Smith to the forge. Clinton-Smith himself was in Broadmoor by then, talking to psychiatrists. He's still there, unlikely to come out. Mlnarski stared at me impassively, relaxed and unmoved. Almost as tall as me, just as strong, and a trained fighter. A murderer, Stone told me, wickedly dangerous even before he met the Children of God. I stared back at him, remembering him standing in front of me with six feet of steel bar in his hands, waiting only for the small man to move into the line of fire, or for a word from his leader. I tried not to shiver.

Then a line of men all with their arms in slings, and I pointed to the one whose shoulder I had smashed with the hammer, and he spat at me. And the smallest of the three, who screamed that I had shot at them, and called me a monster, a pig, a slut, until a sergeant shouted him down and two constables dragged him away, still screaming abuse and beginning to cry.

'What a little petal,' said the sergeant. 'Come on, love. Cup of tea.'

Glory, unconscious for days, sedated, lying on her back, still and pale, her beautiful hair brushed neatly, blue shadows around her eyes, monitor screens glowing in the half dark over her bed. The gynaecologist, kind and reassuring. A plastic surgeon.

A psychiatrist.

Dr King told me I'd damaged my shoulder again, badly this time, ligaments torn, although I couldn't say how I'd done it. It must have happened as I dragged poor Daisy down through the steep woods to the quarry. He insisted I couldn't have done so much damage without knowing it, but I truly had no memory of pain, even though I could recall the knives in my arm, my back, my neck. Two months in a cast, six before I could work again.

Uncle John stayed in the spare room at the cottage because he knew, although I had said nothing, that just for the moment I did not want to be alone. He drove me in every day to see Glory, checked my accident insurance, made a short statement for the press that told the lingering reporters nothing, but that sent them away. He had an apparently endless supply of big white handkerchiefs for the many times that I sat at the table and cried, from shock, from fear, from distress over Glory, from grief for my friends.

Glory conscious, unable to speak, just holding my hand, tears sliding out from under her eyelids. No longer critical, a nurse told me, but still dangerously ill. Not strong enough for another operation yet.

Lucille came to the hospital, brought in a Rolls Royce by an old man who walked with two sticks. She looked beautiful, but as soon as she saw Uncle John she screamed at him, saying it was his fault for encouraging me, if I hadn't been a blacksmith it would never have happened. A doctor came running into the ward to take her out, and Uncle John stood between her and Glory, silent. She looked at me, but could find nothing to say to me. Glory lay still, her eyes closed, twisting the sheet in her fingers. Lucille moaned as the doctor led her away, and the old man followed slowly on his two sticks, shaking his head.

The inquests on the two women who had died in the quarry were adjourned at the request of the police.

Glory lay in a private room in the hospital, still not speaking, but listening, to me, to Uncle John, to the doctors. Stronger now, but still thin and pale, and distressed by strangers. Crying uncontrollably, and shaking her head frenziedly when a nurse told her a smashing young man called Peter Clements had come to see her.

'I was Oberon,' he said, shaking my hand and smiling bravely when I went down to see him to try to explain. 'Not quite enough magic, it seems. Thank you for the work you did on that head-dress, it was grand. Will you please let me know if she ever wants to see me? Please?'

Ill-met by moonlight, fair Gloriana, I thought. Oh, Glory, he's so nice, and he loves you.

Glory spoke at last, but only to me, a hoarse whisper that hurt her throat, just a few words at a time, painful, fighting back tears.

'Take me home with you.'

'As soon as you're well enough.'

'Now. Please. No more. No more . . .' And then the tears, and she was gasping, and gripping my hand, her eyes pleading.

And I understood.

I talked to the kind gynaecologist, I told him she couldn't bear people looking at her body, touching her. Nobody, not even him, not the nurses, nobody. She felt she'd been defiled. She was ashamed.

He listened to me, looking down at his desk, tapping his pen on the notes that lay open in front of him.

One more operation, he said. If she wasn't to be in constant pain for the rest of her life, there must be one more, but there would be only him, and the anaesthetist, and the two nurses she knew best, he would promise that. No students, no colleagues, just the four of them. One more operation wasn't really enough, but he would try to make it do. And when she was better, mentally, I should remember they could do more for her. With another operation, perhaps two.

She agreed, but her eyes were desperate.

Ten bodies were found at the house in Lothian, and three in Yorkshire. And they found films, and film-making equipment, quite sophisticated. Some of the Children of God were experts, cameramen and editors. There was even a marketing network, clubs in Europe, South America, one in Australia.

Uncle John went back to London, and Glory came to the forge, walking slowly, trying to smile at me, inching her way up the stairs, painfully, trying to control her tears, until I picked her up and carried her to her room, she was so light, I only needed one arm, she curled up like a child, her face pressed into my shoulder, hugging me.

The psychiatrist told me anything that reminded her of herself as she was before she was mutilated caused her distress, and she wasn't yet strong enough to stand it. The forge, with me, was the best place for her, where she felt safe, because she trusted me, and because it was familiar, although there was nothing of her past life there except me.

'Will she ever work again?' I asked.

'Oh, yes, I expect so. Not for a little while, not design-ing anyway. Perhaps she could paint? Let her take it all at her own pace.'

It was a dreadful time for Glory, she was in pain, and could never be left alone, and hated to be seen by strangers. She told me it felt as if they knew what had been done to her just by looking at her, as though they could see the scars through her clothes.

I made her a drawing table. I fitted bolts to her door and her windows, and hung dark green curtains. She could stand behind them and look out without anybody seeing her. Somebody brought her paintbox and her easel down from Birmingham, and I bought her some art board, and two canvases. She fixed one of the boards to the easel, and looked at it.

It was a time when I found I had friends. Jane Laverton rode over leading a Palomino gelding that could be ridden one-handed, neck-reining on a hack-amore. One of her favourite horses.

'He eats like a pig,' she said, giving his rump a friendly slap as he trotted through the gate into the paddock. 'Glad somebody else can pay his feed bills. You get well soon, I'm sticking shoes onto hooves with gum arabic.'

And Clive Ulverton and Jake Brewer with a crazy scheme to form a syndicate and put Lyric back in train-ing that autumn, the three of us sharing the expenses. I said they were daft.

Summer came, long, warm days, and Glory came out, cautiously, when I had closed and locked the gates, and sat in a chair on the little patch of lawn behind the cottage, turning her face to the sun. I sat with her, my arm free of the plaster cast, doing the exercises the physiotherapist had taught me.

Glory could be left alone for a little while at a time, a little longer every week.

A date was set for the inquest, and Stone told me the police would not apply for an adjournment. This time, I would have to give evidence. And I had killed the girl.

I told Glory about it. She could talk to me by then without it hurting her throat, and she could talk to Uncle John a little, but her voice was dry and tight with anybody except me, and with strangers she couldn't speak at all. She tried, when Stone wanted to interview her, but the words would not come, all she could manage were little gasping noises, and at last she turned to me with a look of such pleading misery that I carried her back to her room.

'No,' I said when Stone said he would come back the next day. 'No, no more.'

I sat on Glory's bed with the summons to the inquest in my hand, and I told her how I hated people looking at me, how I dreaded standing in the witness box with everybody staring. How, away from the forge, I felt a freak, a giantess, how I felt people were laughing at me.

Glory listened, and when I had finished she asked me for a drawing block and some pencils. I brought them for her, and she asked me to leave her alone.

I found her two hours later, drawing furiously, crying and gasping, sheets of paper all over the floor, almost hysterical, but when I tried to stop her she pushed me away, trying to smile at me, shaking her head.

'It's all right,' she said through the tears. 'Nearly done. Nearly done.'

She gave me a package of drawings in a big envelope to post to an address in Birmingham.

'I hope it was worth it,' I said doubtfully, and she nodded.

Two weeks later boxes arrived. Clothes for me, beautiful clothes, dark warm browns and golds, flowing lines, comfortable and flattering. Clothes I could wear in a witness box, and perhaps not look a freak. Clothes my lovely sister had designed for me, designed in spite of the pain and the tears.

Lyric was out in a paddock, trotting to the gate when I called her, her dark, eager head high, ugly scars under her knees, but fading, Jake said, fading slowly. He spoke again of the idea of putting her in training.

'She's too much of a puller for you to manage for a while,' he said. 'You'd damage your shoulder again. Have her back in the spring, and let Clive train her this winter. It'd be fun. With these bloody trials and things coming up, you're going to need some fun, Ann.'

'All right,' I said at last. 'But nothing too hard. I couldn't bear it if she were injured.'

Uncle John was at the inquest, tense and alert. He told me to watch for a signal from him, if I saw it I was not to answer a question but to wait for him to speak.

I had killed the girl.

I still felt no remorse. I knew I would kill again if the circumstances were the same, if somebody tried to kill me, or somebody I loved, I would kill again. I sat in the witness box, I listened to the questions from the coroner, from two solicitors who sat beside Uncle John representing the two girls' families. I watched Uncle John, watched the pen in his hand to see if he tapped it sharply on the table in front of him, my signal to remain silent.

No, I replied to a question, I had already dismounted from the mare when she reared and her hoof struck the girl in the face. No, I did not know the girl had been killed, not at that time, I was only told later. I was running towards my sister when it happened. Yes, I had been drugged, I wasn't sure what the drugs were. I knew the mare had fallen, and that somebody was underneath her, I could hear screams.

I pulled back my sleeve and showed the scar that ran up my forearm to the coroner, and then to the jury. There were police photographs of the wounds in my neck and my back. Yes, the wound in my arm had been made by the knife that one of the girls had been holding. She had attacked me with it.

Had I meant to kill her?

Uncle John's pen rapped sharply on the table, and he stood up. Miss Mayall had been drugged at the time, he said, a quite extraordinary situation that had already been explained. Nobody had been able to assess what effect those drugs had had on her mind. Intention was quite impossible to prove or disprove, even allowing for the circumstances under which this death had occurred.

Quite, the coroner agreed smoothly, but perhaps Miss Mayall could remember what she had been thinking at the time.

Uncle John threw me a sharp, warning glance.

I remembered. I remembered I had wanted them dead, I remembered chasing the one who had run from me, to kill her.

'I was trying to reach my sister,' I said. 'They were between me and her, with knives.'

'And the girl, Janice Green, the one who died?'

My hand in her hair, twisting, the rage and the hatred I had felt, rotten wood breaking, and a dead weight.

I shook my head.

'I don't remember which one she was,' I said.

I felt no remorse, no pity, except a little for the woman who leapt to her feet and screamed that I was a bloody murderess when the jury brought in a verdict of lawful homicide. Janice Green's mother, grieving for her daughter, but enjoying her moment in the limelight.

She was led from the court, sobbing, and when she had gone the coroner said I had been trying to save my sister, I had done nothing with which to reproach myself, and I should try to put the matter behind me.

I looked at him, and nodded gravely. I wondered if my lack of regret for the girl's death meant I truly was a murderess. A human life, I told myself again, I had taken a human life. But I would have killed her if I could have saved my dog by doing so, and still have felt nothing for her.

Accidental death for the first girl, her skull crushed by the mare's striking hoof. Lawful homicide for Janice Green.

I went to the police station to make a statement. Uncle John was with me, listening carefully. Coroner's verdicts can be overturned, he warned me. Be careful.

Glory won the Equity Design Award. It was her nomination that we were to have celebrated, when she came down that night. She wasn't there to receive the award, but they sent her champagne and huge bouquets of roses, and cards. Dozens of cards, from the casts of *The Merchant of Venice*, *A Midsummer Night's Dream*, even the play about the angels, wishing her well, saying they missed her and wanted her back. Cards from the stage-hands that made her laugh, or cry. From dressers and make-up girls, lighting technicians, scene shifters; dozens of cards, generous and kind and loving, typical, she said, of the theatre.

The first of the three trials. Anthony Clinton-Smith was in Broadmoor, unfit to plead, but there were three trials for the Children of God, fifty-seven murder charges for the twenty-one victims. There were films the juries had to watch, that sickened them. Four men and two women sat in the jury box after they had seen the films, crying with rage and disgust, and the others stared ahead, or at the judge, with frozen faces.

I refused to look at the films. I would not see my friends tortured to death, I told the Clerk of the Court. I would rather be sent to prison. So they showed me stills from the films, and I agreed that yes, that was Emily

Peters, and this was the girl I had known as Kathy from Togu, and that they had told me they were prisoners, and frightened, and that others had disappeared from Gorsedown.

Jake and Clive took me to Chepstow, to a friendly little meeting where Lyric was to run in her first hurdle race, to see how she liked it. She came seventh, jumping carefully, looking at the fences. Intelligent, said Clive, quite promising.

The trial of the girls who had mutilated Glory. There were six of them in the dock, young, ordinary women, plain and sullen, their lives ruined by an infatuation with a greedy mass murderer.

Glory was not fit to give evidence. Roland Mantsch said, flatly, that to come to court would cause serious, and very possibly permanent, psychological damage.

I stood in the witness box, and told the jury what I had seen, and agreed with the defence barristers that I had been drugged and had told the coroner I couldn't even remember which of the women I had killed. I showed the scar on my arm again.

That case lasted a week. Two of the women were acquitted, a verdict that enraged, but did not surprise, Stone. Bloody juries, he said. Bloody stupid juries.

Clever lawyers, said Uncle John wryly.

Winter was coming, and another trial, the one at which Mlnarski and seven other men were to face eight charges of murder. I would not be needed, but I was having nightmares about that man, and as the trial approached I began to have panic attacks. Roland

Mantsch prescribed me tranquillisers and said I should come and talk to him every week until I felt better.

Newbury, another hurdle race, Jake insisting it would take my mind off things, and Clive saying Lyric was improving. Glory said she would be all right for the day, so I went, and we stood in the pouring rain, and watched Lyric trying, hating the weather, but doing her best and coming fourth.

Stone came to see me the day the trial came to an end. I had started to work again by then, not shoeing horses, but forging metal, back to the early days of mending gates and farm implements, garden tools.

'Guilty on every count,' he said, standing in the doorway of the forge and smiling at me. 'He's in for a long time.'

But I had another nightmare that night.

Glory started coming downstairs more often, she began to do a little housework, dusting, and tidying. If she heard anybody coming she'd go upstairs again, but while it was quiet, and there was nobody there, she'd come down by herself.

Gorsedown Manor was put on the market again, difficult to sell with the horrors in its recent history. Uncle John's one of a number of lawyers trying to get the assets of Stephenson Holdings seized to pay compensation to the families of the victims, those of them that can be traced. And to Glory. This is a case that may last for years.

Christmas, and he came down to spend it with us, and stayed on for the New Year, because Clive telephoned to say that he'd entered Lyric in a two-mile handicap at Wolverhampton and he'd heard the favourite wasn't running too well on the gallops. Lyric just might be worth a little each-way flutter, if we felt like it, she seemed to like fences better than hurdles. If the rain held off.

So Jake and I drove up, and shivered in the frosty air, and we watched Lyric canter down to the start, pulling hard, and Clive came to stand beside us, chewing his nails, and grinning, and I felt sick with worry that she might fall and injure herself. Clive and Jake watched the race through binoculars, and I heard Clive muttering, 'Steady, steady,' but my eyes were closed and I was praying for most of the race, just praying she'd come home safely. Then Jake said, 'By God, she just might!' but they were over the second fence from home before I could look, and my beautiful horse was in front, and still pulling, reaching for the ground with that lovely, slashing stride that had carried me for so many miles, and Clive began to yell, 'Come on! Come on, my darling!' and Jake was jumping up and down beside me.

There was a little chestnut coming up behind her, trying hard, with his ears back and his jockey driving him forward, but Lyric came into the last fence with her ears pricked, and rose over it curling up her legs like a show jumper, and the chestnut made up nearly half a length by flying at it low and hard, and they were neck and neck coming up the straight, but Lyric put her head down and flattened her ears, and gave not an inch on that long run in, and Clive and Jake were screaming themselves hoarse, but I was just laughing with relief that she was safe, and she came into the winners' enclosure dancing with pride and excitement, and Tony Ridger jumped off her back with a broad grin on his face saying by God, she was a trier.

Driving home that night with Jake was the first time for nearly a year that I'd felt really happy, but I told Jake I wanted Lyric home soon, and he smiled, and said of course, but it had been fun, hadn't it?

It's a year now since that dreadful night in the quarry, and Glory comes into the forge sometimes, when I'm there alone. I leave the door between it and the workshop open, and if visitors arrive she slips in there and bolts the door, and sometimes she closes the shutters. She stays there until they leave.

She doesn't do a lot. I bought a few chickens, and she feeds them and collects the eggs. She's quite strong again.

Now the evenings are warmer, we sometimes go for walks together, through the paddock where Lyric grazes, through my gate, into Gorsedown Park. I dug the blackthorn saplings out just before Christmas, when I could open the gate again. I left the springs in place. Glory likes security, locks, shutters, things like that. She likes the gate, it makes her smile. Anything that makes Glory smile is good.

Gorsedown Park holds no memories for her.

She's getting better now. She's painting. Dark flowers floating on bloody water, but still, she is painting.

There's a script for a new play on her bedside table.

She looks at it sometimes. They want her to design the costumes. She's worked with the director before. I don't think she'll do this one, but she might perhaps manage the next. Or the one after it.

She is getting better, my beautiful sister. I love her very much.

Warner Books now offers an exciting range of quality titles by both established and new authors. All of the books in this series are available from:

Little, Brown and Company (UK),
P.O. Box 11,
Falmouth,
Cornwall TR10 9EN.

Alternatively you may fax your order to the above address.
Fax No: 01326 317444
Telephone No: 01326 317200
E-mail: books@barni.avel.co.uk

Payments can be made as follows: cheque, postal order (payable to Little, Brown and Company) or by credit cards, Visa/Access. Do not send cash or currency. UK customers and B.F.P.O. please allow £1.00 for postage and packing for the first book, plus 50p for the second book, plus 30p for each additional book up to a maximum charge of £3.00 (7 books plus).

Overseas customers including Ireland, please allow £2.00 for the first book plus £1.00 for the second book, plus 50p for each additional book.

NAME (Block Letters) ....

....

ADDRESS ....

....

....

☐ I enclose my remittance for ....
☐ I wish to pay by Access/Visa Card

Number ☐☐☐☐☐☐☐☐☐☐☐☐☐☐☐☐

Card Expiry Date ☐☐☐☐